THE SECRETS OF STRANGERS

JESS KITCHING

SIMON & SCHUSTER

New York · Amsterdam/Antwerp · London · Toronto · Sydney/Melbourne · New Delhi

THE SECRETS OF STRANGERS
First published in Australia in 2026 by
Simon & Schuster (Australia) Pty Limited
Level 4, 32 York St, Sydney NSW 2000

10 9 8 7 6 5 4 3 2 1

New York Amsterdam/Antwerp London Toronto Sydney/Melbourne New Delhi
Visit our website at www.simonandschuster.com.au

This book is a work of fiction. Any references to historical events, real people, or real places are used fictitiously. Other names, characters, places, and events are products of the author's imagination, and any resemblance to actual events or places or persons, living or dead, is entirely coincidental.

A catalogue record for this book is available from the National Library of Australia

ISBN: 9781761633218

Cover design: Abby Guy
Typesetting: Midland Typesetters, Australia
Printed and bound in Australia by Griffin Press

The paper this book is printed on is certified against the Forest Stewardship Council® Standards. Griffin Press holds chain of custody certification SCS-COC-001185. FSC® promotes environmentally responsible, socially beneficial and economically viable management of the world's forests.

'A terrific writer with a smart, keep-on-guessing, plot-twisting story that will keep you turning the pages until you reach the final one . . . then you'll finally be able to take a breath.' **Chris Carter, author of *The Crucifix Killer***

'From the first page, *The Secrets of Strangers* grips you with its quiet menace and emotional intensity. Jess Kitching pulls back the curtain on the writing world – its obsessions, its vulnerabilities and the way storytellers shape reality through narrative. Kitching proves herself a master of tension, delivering a thriller that's as thought-provoking as it is impossible to put down.' **Vikki Petraitis, author of *The Unbelieved***

'Gripping, twisty and perfectly plotted. A mystery that just demands to be devoured.' **Katy Brent**

'*The Secret of Strangers* is a juicy, razor-tense and cleverly crafted suspense. It's part Agatha Christie, with its cosy English village, writers' group and missing woman – but then darkly glam and sinister, too. Jess has crafted the whole complete thrilling package!' **Holly Craig**

'A clever, taut and twisty psychological thriller that had me turning the pages into the night. Jess Kitching has crafted a mystery that is both hugely compulsive and also full of heart.' **Emma Babbington**

'A blocked writer who investigates a mystery to avoid her manuscript? I've never felt so seen – or so enthralled. This is psychological suspense at its darkest and most propulsive.' **Jack Heath**

'*The Secrets of Strangers* starts with a bang and does not falter. This gripping, but very human, story of loss, friendship, jealousy and courage will keep you turning pages well past your bedtime.' **Kelly Gardiner**

'This book held me hostage in the best way. Gripping, twisty and emotional, it grabbed me from the first page – and even made me cry.' **Noelle W. Ihli, *USA Today* bestselling author of *Ask for Andrea***

'A compelling, unhinged tale that explores the moral ethics of turning a real-life crime into fiction, with a final twist that will blow your hair back.' **Camille Booker**

'Kitching delivers a thriller that is unrelenting, absorbing and delicately vicious. Using deeply emotional themes of loss and family as a vehicle for what unfolds, it will demand your attention until the very end.' **Luke Johnson, author of *King Tide***

'Jess Kitching is one of those rare talents who crosses genres with ease. Whether tugging at your emotions and making you ponder your life or keeping you up at night turning the pages because you "just have to know" what comes next, she is a master.' **Jo Dixon**

To Victoria – you have given me enough inspiration to make writing about the unbreakable bond between sisters easy . . . thank you!

PROLOGUE

Alexa

Alexa Clarke didn't feel her skull splinter at first.

Even the shudder-inducing crack of the initial impact took a few seconds to register with her.

Alexa's momentary ignorance could suggest how unexpected an act of violence was in her life. Maybe the hostile beauty of the late November morning had captured her attention. Maybe she suddenly remembered something – an appointment she had to attend or that she hadn't turned the iron off.

But the truth was, Alexa took a moment to acknowledge her attack because her mind was tangled in the thick forest of her darkest memories. Recalling them hurt more than a strike to the back of the head ever could.

In the moments before the hooded figure followed Alexa onto the field and inflicted their definitive blow, Alexa was in a trance. Barely one hundred metres from her home, but mentally a million miles away. Soaking in the silence that lulled her into believing everything would be okay.

Alexa was so absorbed that she didn't notice the grass rustling behind her.

She didn't hear the figure's anticipatory breathing as they drew closer or feel the atmosphere shift as their hands raised a heavy, blunt object above her head.

But then the impact came, and everything changed.

The shock was so stunning that Alexa carried on walking for one, two, three steps before the scream of agony reverberated through her skull.

Then, Alexa stopped.

Then, she realised something was wrong.

By the time the second hit came, a shrill ringing vibrated through Alexa's skull. Warm, sticky blood trickled down her forehead. Slowly at first, then faster, running past her eyebrows and mingling with her eyelashes until her vision turned red.

The last thing Alexa thought of as she crumpled to her knees was her husband handing her a pink polka dot mug. The first gift he'd ever bought her. So happy, so naive.

So blissfully unaware of what was to become of their story.

CHAPTER 1

The cursor flashes on and off, on and off. Its incessant blinking narrates the painful passing of each second I don't type. A haughty reminder that the Word document, not to mention the rest of the world, is awaiting my words.

Calling its bluff, I raise my hands above the keyboard to fire out the most groundbreaking opening to a thriller ever written. When inspiration doesn't strike, I lower them once more.

The cursor flickers.

At half past ten, I break from my desk to make a cup of tea, surprised it's taken me so long to use this excuse to leave my home office. Usually by this time, I'm three cups deep.

In the peace of my kitchen, I spot the bread Kamal propped in the toaster for me before he left for work. I see the pill he laid out, too. It sits beside the toaster, small and innocuous, but with a presence so loud it might as well be screaming.

Picking up the tablet, I roll it between my fingers. I wonder how much strength I'd need to crush it. Not much, I imagine, but a vision of Kamal's hope as I left the doctor's office with my prescription stops me from doing so.

My eyes glaze as they linger on the pill, then the bread. Witnessing how much Kamal tries to help me get 'back on track', as the doctor said, would be laughable if it wasn't so damned painful.

But Kamal doesn't know that the pills don't work. Or that as soon as the door closes behind him, the sadness comes for me anyway. It starts at my ankles, coiling up my body until it's wrapped around my throat. It stays there all day, choking and oppressive. Its grip loosens slightly when Kamal is home, but never enough to let me be.

Plucking the bread from the toaster and enclosing the pill in my fist, I open the bin and drop the items in there. Once I cover them with remnants of last night's dinner, I remember how to breathe. Marking that as a win, I select my favourite mug from the cupboard. Floral with a chip on the rim, it's the one I was using when I signed my first book deal. The generous offer was the result of a bidding war that was, to quote *The Guardian*, 'unheard of in recent years'. What luck the mug has brought me recently, though, I'm not so sure.

While the kettle boils, I look out across the garden, waiting for life outside to hit me with a distraction – or better still, a spark of inspiration. But what life outside? The neat garden, with its clipped grass glimmering thanks to a kiss of frost? The road to Bramblethorpe, which hasn't had a car drive along it for almost an hour, or the field beyond it that goes on with no break in sight?

I'd first come across Bramblethorpe on an episode of *Location, Location, Location*. Taken by how idyllic it seemed, I convinced Kamal we should check it out. It was close enough to Manchester that Kamal could commute for work, and far enough away that I felt I could breathe.

I remember standing in this exact spot the day Kamal and I first inspected the house. It was even colder then. A ghostly white sky threatened us with the promise of snow, the trees in the distance exposing their skeletal branches. But even with harsh weather surrounding it, the house and the grounds it stood on sang with beauty. I thought it would make the perfect writing location.

'Do you like it?' Kamal had whispered to me, his thick beard tickling my cheek as he wrapped his arms around me from behind.

'I love it.'

'And you're sure it's what you want, Janine? You're sure this is it?'

Turning, I'd looked into Kamal's eyes and seen it all – the worry, the stress, the strain. Everything we needed to escape.

Like a fool, I'd replied, 'It's everything I want and more. It's perfect.'

We put an offer in that day. Higher than the asking price, but I needed the fresh start the picture-perfect house promised. I would have sold everything I owned to have it.

Only now it transpires that the country dream was someone else's fantasy, not mine.

'I hate it here,' I hiss, then I say it louder because there's no one around to judge my bitter words. Exhaling, I push down my sadness with a biscuit, then another, and make my tea.

Drink in hand and throat thick with remnants of chocolate, I head to the foot of the stairs. There, I pause.

Being so behind on my latest manuscript, there should be no debate about going back to work, but my brain likes to pretend it has a choice in the matter. So much so, it enacts a daily tug of war about the pros and cons of reacquainting myself with Microsoft Word.

Six months ago, at the start of my writer's block, I truly believed that my writing alter ego, S. K. Atherton, would pull something miraculous out of the bag. But now? Now nothing can ease the gnawing in the pit of my stomach that tells me, quite cruelly, that a mere three books into my forever career as an author, I am out of words. And, with two weeks until my publisher, Tiff, expects a solid draft to land in her inbox, almost out of time.

'Take yourself off on another adventure if you need to,' Tiff said in her last email. 'Three weeks at a survival camp worked wonders when you were crafting your last book.'

As true as that might be, I don't have the heart to tell Tiff that my days of throwing myself into immersive experiences in the name of research are over. Especially if that research means leaving the house.

Sighing, I begin the ascent back to my office, but my pinging phone stops me. I check the message. It's from Katherine, sent to our writing group chat.

Another rejection. Tell me again why I bother writing . . . ?

I should sympathise. I've known Katherine for six months now. I know how much writing means to her and understand more than most people the all-consuming hunger of chasing a goal that seems out of reach.

Closing my eyes, I wait to feel something. Anything other than the constant hollowness that has narrated my days for months now. But nothing changes.

As my phone pings with Natalya's reply, I slip it in my pocket without responding and climb upstairs. There, I retake my seat at my desk and continue to berate myself for not knowing how to kill off a fictional person I've yet to invent. My alarm interrupts my self-loathing at twelve-thirty, warning that our writing group session starts at one.

As is the case with most good things in my life, I have Kamal to thank for finding the group. Fresh from our move to the country, we were out for a walk when he saw a flyer tacked to a noticeboard in the village square.

'A writers' group!' Kamal exclaimed, pointing to the bright yellow piece of paper. 'What a great way to make friends.'

My nose wrinkled. 'I already have friends.'

'I know, but they live over an hour away. It would be good for you to know someone local, too.'

I was too busy studying my husband's excitement to reply. It had been so long since I'd seen him look so happy. My brain warned me why that was. *If you make friends here, it means someone else can share the burden of being around you,* it said darkly.

Kamal took a photo of the flyer and didn't stop talking about the writing group until I caved and messaged its founder, Katherine. Part of me hoped she would say the group was full, but half an hour later she added me to a group chat with the other members. There were nine people in total, a number which surprised me. How many aspiring authors could live in one rural village, after all?

The group's first meeting was a casual 'get to know you' chat at the local café, Coffee and Cake. The twee establishment sits alongside the equally inventively named bed and breakfast, Bramblethorpe B&B, and is decorated unironically in stereotypical tearoom style.

As well as myself, four aspiring authors attended the first meeting instead of the promised nine.

Alongside Katherine and Natalya were retired teacher David and new mum Vicky, but they didn't come back. I got the feeling that the intensity of Katherine's passion for writing may have scared them off.

The rest of us stuck it out, though. We meet weekly, sharing snippets of our work and asking for feedback. Even though the only things I've shared are old, half-baked ideas, it's been nice. Fun, I'll begrudgingly admit. But even if it wasn't, that group is the one reason I have to leave the house. I owe it a lot.

Still, I'm trembling so much at the thought of the outside world that it takes me three attempts to button myself into my yellow coat. The switch from hiding out at home to being out in the bright, busy world often hits me like this. All my mind can think of is how many things could go wrong in the day. How many scary unknowns I wouldn't have to face if I just stayed inside.

But every week, I push myself to go. For Kamal's sake. Maybe even for my own.

A steady hum of nerves fuels me as I drive to the high street. Or what the locals call the high street, anyway. To me, the term means bustling boutiques and an abundance of cafés, but Bramblethorpe's high street can be walked in less than a minute. And once you've visited the post office, the pub and the village store, you've pretty much seen it all.

'Quaint,' my sister Beth said when I drove her through the village after we put an offer in on the house. It was Beth's polite way of saying, 'What the fuck have you done?'

Pulling up outside Coffee and Cake, I can't help asking myself the same thing.

Katherine and Natalya are at our usual table when I enter, their appearances at odds with the overly floral decor.

Katherine is a tweed-jacket wearing ex-economics lecturer in her mid-fifties. Sporting wild grey hair and carrying dreams of writing the next great love story, she's spent her life trying to hone her craft amidst work and family responsibilities. With a string of rejections behind her, it hasn't been easy, but when her husband Eddie passed away in March last year, Katherine left her job to chase her dream.

A twenty-year-old goth, Natalya's heavily studded outfits make her stand out in the pared-back simplicity of Bramblethorpe, although I quickly learned that standing out is not something Natalya is comfortable with. She has a habit of hiding behind a curtain of long black hair, but nothing about her should be hidden. She is beautiful inside and out, and very talented. It will only be a matter of time before we're attending the launch of her debut.

As I move towards our table, I catch the eye of the café owner, Margie. She must have been eligible for retirement twenty years ago, but Margie's always here. She's also the most inappropriate person I've ever met. The first time I spoke to her, she asked if I had children. When I said no, her response was, 'Tick tock.'

'The usual?' Margie calls, holding a teapot in the air.

'Please,' I reply, before taking a seat. 'Sorry I'm late. I would say there was heavy traffic, but you'd know that was a lie.'

'You never know, Gerald's sheep could have blocked the road again,' Katherine jokes.

Laughing, I slip my coat from my shoulders. 'How are you both?'

'I've been better,' Katherine admits.

'Because of the rejection?'

'Got it in one.'

'I'm sorry,' I reply.

Katherine offers me a sad, acknowledging smile. 'Thanks.'

'What was the reason this time?' Natalya asks, oblivious to how the phrase *this time* makes Katherine bristle.

'Apparently, my idea isn't strong enough to sustain a novel. That old chestnut. I've now had over four hundred rejections, can you believe it?' Shaking her head, Katherine grips her coffee cup. 'I hate being made to feel so useless. Eddie's not here, yet I'm still failing him.'

'You're not failing him!' Natalya cries. 'You've done what you set out to do. You've written books! So what if a publisher doesn't want them? Do you know how many people say they want to write but never do? You've done more than most. You don't need external validation to prove that.'

Natalya's speech shines with passion, but the look on Katherine's face says, actually, she does need the validation.

A beat rings out in the conversation, one I know I should fill. As the only published writer here, my words carry a weight that I'm not always comfortable with. But life has taught me better than to make empty promises, and the world of publishing is notoriously unfair. I don't want to be the one to say that sometimes, some dreams are just for dreaming.

'Excuse me,' I say, standing abruptly. 'I need the bathroom.'

Katherine's eyes bore into me as I leave the table. She expected better from me, I know that without looking at her. I expected better from myself, too, but it's like there's a block inside me, preventing me from being the supportive person I once was.

In the bathroom, I splash my face with water, only now noticing the sleep crusting my eyes. Once upon a time, I'd have been mortified at leaving the house looking like this.

Gripping the sink, I glare at my reflection. 'Come on,' I hiss. 'Do better.'

Commanding myself to be present, I plaster on a smile and push my body away from the sink.

When I re-enter the café, I plan to go back to the table, but a tall, imposing man enters Coffee and Cake. The fraught, frazzled energy he radiates stops me in my tracks.

I don't need to hear him speak to know that what happens next will change everything.

CHAPTER 2

My focus glues itself to the man as he goes straight to Margie. The tension he rattles with seems at odds with the smart clothes he wears. I imagine usually, he walks into a room and commands it with his aura alone. Now, the only thing filling the air is his nerves.

'Margie, can I have a word?' he says. His voice is stripped so bare by raw emotion that my skin prickles.

Glancing up from the coffee machine, Margie nods. 'What's wrong?'

'I was just – it's – have you seen Alexa?'

Margie blinks, dressing her features in an expression that looks like concern, but I know her too well to believe it's genuine.

'Alexa?' she echoes. 'No, dear. Not for a while. Why?'

The man swallows. 'She's – she's not at home. She's not been there since Saturday.'

I raise my eyebrows. So does Margie.

'Saturday?' she asks. 'Today is Monday.'

'I know, that's why I thought I'd ask if you knew where she was, what with … well, you know,' the man replies, scratching the back of his head awkwardly.

'She's not at the B&B this time,' Margie replies. 'Have you called the police?'

Horror fills the man's face. 'No, no, I don't need to do that. Lex is probably . . . she'll be cooling off somewhere, that's all.'

'Cooling off?'

It's only when hearing the judgement in Margie's voice that the man realises where he is. His eyes dart around the café, spotting me and then the curious gaze of Katherine and Natalya.

'I'm sure it's nothing,' he says, flashing a smile that would be dazzling if it weren't undermined by worry. 'Lex will be back before we know it.'

'I hope so,' Margie says, eyeing him. 'Shall I come by the house and let you know if I see her?'

'That would be great,' the man replies, pushing himself to be brighter. Backing out of the café, he waves a cheery wave. Margie's arm rises to wave back, but there's an undeniable glint in her eye.

As soon as the door shuts behind him, the man scurries towards a Tesla that's parked on the high street. His distress keeps me frozen, but Margie bursts into life.

'Did you hear that?' she asks, heading to Katherine and Natalya. 'Alexa Clarke is missing!'

Katherine frowns. 'Missing? Otis certainly seemed worried, but is missing the right word for it?'

'She's not been home for two days, what else could she be? Besides, with those two? It's got to be a scandal! There's definitely trouble between them,' Margie says, leaning closer like she's about to tell a secret and ignoring the jostle of my chair as I return to the table. 'Alexa's stayed at the B&B here a few times, did you know that? You've got to ask, why would someone leave their husband only to stay in the same village they already live in?'

'Wow,' Natalya marvels. 'If she's not here, maybe she's left him for good, then.'

'Has she left him, or has he done something to her?' Margie says, her eyes sparkling. 'You saw Otis's face when I mentioned the police. Never trust a man who owns an expensive car. Criminals, the lot of them. In fact, never trust a man full stop.'

I have to fight the urge to roll my eyes. It's common knowledge that Margie's ex-husband left her for a younger woman, resulting in a sour taste in her mouth when it comes to the opposite sex. Sometimes, she's so offensive with her sweeping statements, I wonder how she has any customers left.

Katherine, it seems, is as bored of it as I am.

'Margie, stop,' she warns. 'We don't know a crime has been committed, and we certainly don't know Otis had anything to do with it if it has. He just asked if you'd seen Alexa.'

'If you believe that, you'll believe anything,' Margie replies ominously. 'What if he came in here to act the concerned, loving husband, when really she's buried at the bottom of the garden? I'm calling it, ladies. This is a book coming to life.'

'Well, if something bad has happened, I'm not sure how proud you'll feel for talking about Alexa like this,' Katherine says, her brows furrowed. 'She's our neighbour. We should be concerned, not catty.'

Margie raises her hand to her chest. 'Of course I'm concerned about Alexa! I told Otis to call the police, didn't I?'

'Was that before or after your face lit up at the idea of having some new gossip?'

A taut silence stretches out and is only broken when Margie laughs.

'Oh, you are funny,' she says, waving a hand to dismiss Katherine's comment. 'Always keeping me on my toes.'

As Margie walks away, Katherine shakes her head. 'Sorry,' she mutters. 'I don't mean to snap, but my patience is shorter than ever today. Especially with people like that.'

'Don't worry,' I reply. 'You were right to call Margie out. It was almost like she delighted in that man's pain.'

My attention travels to Margie as she arrives back at the counter and reaches for her phone.

'Why do I get the feeling she isn't phoning around about that guy's wife out of concern?' I ask, strangely unnerved by the old woman's glee.

'Because Margie's not like that. No one in this place is. It's quite upsetting, actually,' Katherine replies, taking a sip of coffee. 'I know Otis and Alexa are fairly new, but a little community spirit wouldn't go amiss. I swear, ever since Alexa said no to helping out at that summer bake sale, their name has been mud.'

'The house they built didn't help matters,' Natalya adds. 'It's that big modern one on Maple Crescent. Surely you've seen it?' When I shake my head, Natalya continues. 'I think it's nice, but most people hate it. There were protests about the planning permission and everything. Ever since then, Alexa and Otis have been outcasts.'

'Do you know them well?' I ask.

'Not really,' Natalya admits. 'I've seen them when I go walking, but that's it. What about you, Katherine?'

'I'm the same,' Katherine replies. 'I've seen Alexa out and about; we've said hello, but that's it. Otis is the friendlier of the two. A nice man, by all accounts.'

'Doesn't everyone say that about the husband? Then they find the body,' Natalya mutters, then she shakes her head. 'Sorry, I know I sound like Margie. It's just writing 101, isn't it? Don't trust anyone or what they say. Although in a village like this, everyone knows everyone's business anyway.'

'You never know anyone's business, not truly,' Katherine replies. 'Alexa Clarke is the perfect example of that. I've seen that woman around countless times, yet I only recently found out that she's lost four babies in the last two years.'

My head snaps to face Katherine as if I've been slapped. 'Alexa miscarried four times?'

Katherine nods, her features melting with pity. 'They say she's devastated. It's put a terrible strain on her marriage. No wonder she's taken the odd night at the B&B to escape it.'

As Natalya makes sympathetic noises, the blood drains from my body, taking with it all assurance that I can get through the rest of the day without falling apart.

'She lost the first six months into the pregnancy,' Katherine adds with a shudder. 'It doesn't even bear thinking about. Apparently, Alexa is desperate to start a family. She left her job, changed her diet, did everything she could, but it still hasn't happened for them. Can you imagine how awful that must be?'

I can't bring myself to respond, but Natalya can. 'She must be in so much pain. They both must. I've heard all sorts about the Clarkes,' Natalya says, biting her lip. 'There's talk of Otis being involved in dodgy business, not to mention the rumours about him cheating.'

'That's what I've heard, too,' Katherine says. 'I'd hate to believe it, of course. They both seem like good people who are going through a hard time. It all started with the losses, apparently. They say Alexa couldn't face it anymore. That she hates being in that house with the reminders of what she's lost.'

'Maybe that's why Otis hasn't called the police,' Natalya theorises. 'He knows Alexa needs a break and left to get one. But I still don't get why Alexa would leave without telling him where she was going.'

Kathrine shrugs. 'People don't always think straight when they're grieving. We don't know Alexa's state of mind.'

'But if she's going through all this and no one knows where she is, then Otis should definitely go to the police. I mean, what if she's hurt herself?'

I jolt at the thought, but Natalya and Katherine are too engrossed in their conversation to notice.

'Do you really think she'd do that?' I ask.

'I don't know,' Katherine replies. 'But one thing I'm sure of is that Alexa Clarke needs help. Or, at the very least, a hug.'

We each get lost in the shadow of Katherine's words until Natalya sighs.

'I wish we could help, but we're not Janine,' she says. 'We don't have the skills to solve a missing persons case like she does.'

'Good point,' Katherine replies. 'I'd have thought you'd practically be a detective by now with all the research you'll have done over the years, S. K. Atherton.'

I open my mouth to reply, but Natalya groans. 'I hate research. Why can't we write whatever we want to progress the plot?'

'Because then our books wouldn't be realistic, and the basis of all books is reality,' Katherine replies. 'Even fantasy novels come from somewhere. Think of all the medieval and political references.'

'I'm sorry, I didn't realise there were dragons in medieval times.'

I take a drink, pretending to listen to Katherine and Natalya debate realism in writing, but my mind is with Alexa Clarke, wherever she may be.

CHAPTER 3

I cut my time with the writing group short by telling Katherine and Natalya I have a headache. It isn't exactly a lie. A mounting pressure has sat behind my forehead ever since finding out about Alexa Clarke.

Collecting my handbag, I make a move to leave, but Natalya commands our attention before I manage to flee.

'Should we keep an ear out for what's going on with Alexa?' she asks. 'Keep each other up to date in the group chat? I know it sounds bad, but Margie's right – this is like a book coming to life. It could be useful for our writing.'

'And it would be good to know that Alexa's okay,' I say.

A blush colours Natalya's pale cheeks. 'Of course. I meant that, too.'

With confirmation that we will listen out for news on Alexa Clarke, I leave Coffee and Cake, shivering on the walk back to my car. With each step, my brain replays the conversation. The more I think of everything I've been told, the more Otis Clarke's devastation lays heavy on me.

Sense tells me that, with no words achieved today, I need to crack on with writing, but as soon as I step into the house, a compulsion overcomes me. It ushers me to my office without allowing me time to remove my coat.

Throwing back the lid of my laptop, I type 'Alexa Clarke' into Google.

The results are random. A website belonging to a footballer with the same name; a webpage from a law firm announcing an Alexa Clarke as their new Executive Partner; articles about an Alexa Clarke who appeared on a now-cancelled reality TV show.

I amend the search, narrowing it down to 'Alexa Clarke missing'.

This time, I get a series of missing persons reports from around the world. All detail the disappearances of women called Alexa, but none appear to be our Alexa.

But who is our Alexa?

I've never met her. I've never even seen her. Or if I have, I didn't know who she was. How can you search for information about someone when you don't even know what they look like?

Abandoning Google, I hit Facebook and search 'Alexa Clarke' once more. Hundreds of profiles are listed in the results. I refine my request by adding 'Bramblethorpe' to the criteria, but nothing comes up.

Pivoting to a new tactic, I look up Otis Clarke instead. This time there are fewer results. When I add 'Bramblethorpe' to the search criteria, he appears.

The first thing that catches my attention is Otis's profile picture. How could it not when it's a photo of him and Alexa on their wedding day?

When I blow up the image to fill my screen, it's like being struck by lightning.

Alexa Clarke is both nothing like I expected and everything I imagined. Stunning in an unconventional way, she has a willowy build, a wide mouth and thick eyebrows much darker than her icy blonde hair. Her silk wedding dress is fitted and simple, the kind of gown made for someone so content in their body they're happy for fabric to cling to every curve. A gorgeous emerald ring sits on her ring finger, a symbol of the love she vowed to uphold for the rest of her life.

But more than Alexa's beauty, I am struck by the fact that the woman in the photograph is not a stranger to me. It turns out, Alexa Clarke is someone who's been on my mind every day for the last eleven months.

CHAPTER 4

Eleven months ago

I know I'm staring at her, this woman sitting opposite me, her hand cradling her belly to protect a growing bump. Her lips lift into a small, content smile she's probably too blissful to be aware she's making.

My eyes pinch. I want to be happy for her, I do – but I can't be. My envy is too strong.

'It's cruel, isn't it?' someone beside me says.

I jump, my focus darting to the stranger. I didn't even notice her entering the waiting room, never mind sitting beside me. As soon as I see her, I realise that must be rare. The woman is so beautiful, she probably turns heads everywhere she goes.

'What is?' I ask, coughing to clear the croak in my voice.

'That they make us wait for scans in the same room as people who are carrying to full term.' As soon as she finishes speaking, the woman looks at me empathetically. 'Sorry, you probably don't want to talk about it. I never do. But I saw the look on your face and I . . . well, let's just say I know that look. I understand it.'

My head bows as I curse myself for being so transparent. I thought I was holding it together better than that. That's all I do every day – wake up, move through life, hold it together. Cling on, really, even though I'm hanging over a cliff's edge.

'I'm sorry,' the woman says softly. 'We can talk, if you want?'

Despite myself, I laugh. 'I don't even know if I *can* talk anymore. These days, it's like I've got no words in me.'

'Well, I think we both know that silence isn't the worst companion in the world,' she replies, then she pauses before speaking again. 'I was carrying a little girl. Before that, another girl, and another. I like to think that they're all together somewhere. Probably arguing over clothes and toys like sisters do. And loving each other fiercely.'

My lips twist into a knowing smile. 'That's sisters summed up in a few sentences.'

'Do you have one?'

'I do. Beth. She's younger than me.'

'And she has a child?'

I blink, surprised. 'Two. How did you know?'

The woman's sad smile is back. 'Sometimes, there's a tone we use when we talk about people who have what we wish we did. Even when it's people we love.'

'Do I sound jealous?' I say, noting the edge of bitterness creeping into my voice.

'No, not jealous. Wistful.'

In the silence that follows, I stop and reflect on how I sound when I speak to Beth. I wouldn't really know. I've not spoken to my sister properly in a long time, or anyone else for that matter. Kamal says he understands, but I'm not sure he does. He still suggests we invite Beth and my nieces over or attend dinners with his family, not registering how painful I find those interactions. How they do the opposite of making me feel loved and included.

I'm debating saying all this when the woman asks me a question. 'Who do you reckon they'd have been? Your baby, I mean.'

I lift my eyes, meeting her gaze.

'If you want to talk about something else, let me know,' she says. 'I'll understand. But I couldn't help wondering if maybe you were like me – a woman staring out at the world, wishing that someone would ask her about the little person she thinks of every day, but no one ever does.'

My mouth dries, my hands jerk to cover my ears, but somehow, I speak. 'I think this one would have been a boy,' I whisper. 'A loveable little boy with eyes like his dad's. Hopefully his brains, too. But my creativity. I'd have wanted him to inherit that.'

'An undervalued trait,' the woman says, reaching into her handbag for a tissue when she sees I'm crying. 'I carry them at all times now.'

'Thanks,' I reply, dabbing my tears self-consciously. I swallow hard when I spot the woman opposite politely looking away, pretending she hasn't noticed my emotional outburst.

Suddenly, the woman beside me turns to face me, head on.

'I don't want to be that person who tells you what to do, especially at a time like this,' she says, 'but try not to cut off the people who love you, okay? I know it's easy to do. Hell, sometimes I shut my husband out so much it's like we're strangers.' The woman shakes her head at this. 'But we need the people who love us. The people who see us underneath all the sadness. They're the ones who can help us get through this.'

Instinctively, I grimace. 'Do you think this is something you can get through?'

'What a question,' the woman replies, lifting her gaze to the ceiling. 'Truthfully? I don't know anything anymore, but we have to hope, don't we? We have to believe.'

'I don't know if I can,' I admit, my voice scratchy once more. 'It feels like all my belief has dried up.'

From the corner of my eye, I see a nurse enter the room, ready to call out the name of the next person heading for their ultrasound.

'That's when you need belief the most,' the woman whispers, squeezing my hand. 'Happiness will find you again. It always does.'

My mouth opens to reply, but then I hear my name.

'Janine Rai?' the nurse repeats, scanning the room until I stand. She turns and walks away, expecting me to follow, but my body hovers beside the stranger who saw me at a time when I couldn't even recognise myself. I want to thank her, to sit and talk about all the things I haven't shared with anyone else, but she nods at me.

'Go on,' she says. 'Scan time. Just know, whatever happens, it will be okay.'

I don't know how my head manages to nod or my legs manage to walk. It doesn't feel like I told either of them to. But they do, one step after another. All the while, the stranger's words ring in my ears.

Whatever happens, it will be okay.

CHAPTER 5

My vision blurs as I stare at the photograph of the woman I now know to be Alexa Clarke.

'Fuck,' I say, choking on tears. Instinctively, I raise a hand to my stomach as if to cover a tiny set of ears, but of course, there's nothing there.

My head bows. Alexa had so much hope the day we met. So much presence. Her kindness and genuine understanding have stayed with me for almost a year. Helped me. Told me that no matter how dark my thoughts got, I had to have hope.

Hope, the thing that, if I listen to Katherine, Alexa had lost.

That idea is almost too awful for me to bear.

Sniffing back tears, I lift my head to look at the photo of the Clarkes on their wedding day. My vision blurs as the image transforms into one of me and Kamal on ours. We don't look anything like Alexa and Otis, but we carried ourselves in the same way. We were excited for the future, too, back before we knew the trajectory it would follow.

But grief changes you. It warps you, turning you into someone you never thought you would become. I know that better than most, but I don't want that for Alexa. I want her to be the woman I met that day at the hospital. A stranger who handed me a tissue and told me that life would find a way to become good again.

Suddenly, the image of Alexa and Otis captured in confetti-covered bliss takes on a new significance.

Maybe I can help. While I might not know Alexa Clarke, I know her story. I know she feels like she has no place in this world. I know that disappearing probably feels like the most appealing thing to do right now, even if it breaks the hearts of those who love her.

'It's okay,' I whisper. 'I'm going to help you.'

That all starts with finding her.

Luckily, there's enough information visible on Otis's Facebook account to provide a window into his world. I learn that he was born in London and has two brothers, Nathaniel and Leo. He owns a business called Archi-Tech, and a quick Google search informs me that Archi-Tech employs almost fifty people and logs annual profits in the millions.

Then I spot something that makes my heart leap. Alexa's Facebook account is linked to Otis's via his relationship status, although her name comes up as Alexa Larson.

Her maiden name, perhaps? I click the link. When Alexa's profile loads, the ache in my chest grows.

Her profile picture is one of her and Otis, but an older one. The photo looks like it was snapped at an informal outdoor event, maybe a barbecue or a garden party. They're sitting on striped folding chairs, Otis's hand resting on Alexa's knee as she laughs at something.

A lump forms in my throat. *Social media is curated. We only share the good bits,* I remind myself, but my mind dismisses that thought.

I want the photo to be real. I want the people in it to be as happy and as in love as they seem. I want Alexa to come home and for everything to be okay.

Before emotion gets the better of me, I skip to Alexa's 'About Me' section.

I learn that she was born in Denmark. She left her home country to travel, holding jobs in New York and Sydney before coming to England. Her location is still set to London, where she worked as a lifestyle journalist and editor before going freelance a few years ago.

Heading back to Google, I search the name 'Alexa Larson'. And just like that, Alexa's journalistic career is at my fingertips.

For the next few hours, I read everything I can find that has Alexa's name attached to it. I soak in each word as if the truth about where she is can be found in an article from four years ago. The more I read, the more something strikes me: the tone of Alexa's writing is upbeat. So much so that after reading her work, I feel like I could write an entire novel in the few hours I have left of the day. The fact that the woman who could inspire such determination in me is the same person checking herself into a B&B streets away from her home because she was so pained distresses me.

When I've exhausted Alexa's articles, I rake through information about Archi-Tech more thoroughly than someone would research the company if they were applying for a job there. Despite the rumours, I find no evidence to suggest that Otis runs his business with anything other than integrity.

That doesn't mean it's the truth, though, my brain warns.

The room darkens as I research Alexa and Otis. My eyes burn from hours of screentime, but I keep going, desperate to find something, anything, that might give me more insight about Alexa's state of mind. The information online is outdated and hidden behind social media gloss, but at least it helps bring the Clarkes to life.

Time must slip away from me because before I know it, Kamal calls me from downstairs.

'Janine?'

Glancing at the time, my heart plummets when I see it's almost seven-thirty. Snapping my laptop shut, I dash for the stairs, but halfway down them I freeze.

Kamal stands in the hallway, stretching his stiff neck. He hasn't noticed me yet, so for the first time in a long time, I see my husband as he is when he's not holding everything together. His thick hair looks dishevelled, his beard in dire need of a trim. There's a heaviness to him that sets my nerves on edge, but when he senses my presence, joy lights his face.

'Stressful day?' I ask before Kamal glosses over his tiredness completely.

'Aren't they all?'

As Kamal shrugs his coat from his shoulders, a crinkling sound rings out, making me take note of the colourful poppies in his hand.

'Before you say anything, they're only from the village store,' he says. 'I know you say flowers are a waste of money, but I never know if that's a masterstroke of reverse psychology.'

Forcing a smile, I accept the bouquet. 'They're a pretty waste, at least. Thank you.'

I notice the moment Kamal wonders if the thawing between us might mean a hug is on the cards. It's the same moment I head to the kitchen to put the poppies into a vase. A masterstroke of mistiming, the way all our movements seem to be these days.

Pushing past my accidental snub, Kamal follows me. 'What's for dinner?' he asks.

'Right now, nothing,' I admit, cringing as I'm forced to admit I haven't started it yet. With the countryside move taking us further away from Kamal's work, cooking is the one job I insisted on having.

'Don't worry,' Kamal says, grinning as if my lapse in self-appointed responsibility is something to be pleased about. 'We can make dinner together. An impromptu date night.'

'Kamal, please. You look exhausted and—'

'I'm fine. Come on, let's see what we can conjure up together.'

Knowing from Kamal's chipper tone that he won't budge, I drop the poppies into a vase and watch Kamal hunt for ingredients. Guilt nags at me with each movement, the feeling growing when Kamal stifles a yawn.

'So, how many words did you write today?' he asks while analysing the contents of the fridge.

'Almost two thousand.' These days, I don't even flinch when I lie to my husband.

'That's incredible! You'll be at the finish line in no time. I can see the headlines now: "S. K. Atherton has done it again!"' Kamal's shiny eyes stare ahead as if looking into a brilliant future that only he can see. 'Were there any tricky scenes to iron out?'

'Oh, it was just another day at the office.'

'Does that mean, "I'm so done with these fictional people, can we talk about something else?" or am I reading your tone wrong?'

'Exactly,' I reply, feigning a grimace.

'Fine by me, but if you need a sounding board for gruesome crimes or witty comebacks, you know I'm always happy to help. How was your writing group?'

'It was all right,' I reply noncommittally. 'Poor Katherine got another rejection from a publisher, though.'

'Oh dear. I hope she took it better than the last. Shall we do a stir-fry?'

'Stir-fry's great,' I reply, opening a cupboard to grab a chopping board. 'To be honest, we spoke a bit about writing, but most of the conversation was taken up by talking about a woman from the village they think is missing.'

'Alexa Clarke?'

My eyebrows arch as Kamal joins me on vegetable prep. 'You've heard about her?'

'It was all anyone could talk about in the village store,' Kamal replies. 'Then again, I suppose we live in arguably the sleepiest place in the north of England. I wouldn't be surprised if until today, the biggest story in Bramblethorpe was a chicken escaping a coop.'

I laugh. 'You're right, a missing woman trumps a lost chicken,' I reply, but my smile soon fades. 'What were people saying?'

'Lots of stuff,' Kamal says, sinking the blade of his knife into a mushroom. 'Mostly that she's left her husband and disappeared, leaving him frantic.'

'Her husband is worried. I saw him today at the café. He looked awful.'

'Poor guy. He must be going out of his mind, although half the village is practically ready to arrest him for murder.'

My spine ices over at those words. 'They think he's killed her?'

'Can you blame them? The situation is a little odd. Alexa Clarke hasn't been seen by anyone since Saturday, but her husband hasn't even called the police. Apparently, her car is at the house, too. Franny Henderson drove by to check it out. Weird, don't you think?'

Again, my body reacts viscerally as I imagine the worst. 'Maybe, but we don't know anything bad has happened.'

'We also don't know it hasn't. Put it this way – if this was the storyline of your next book, I'd be itching to read it. Penned by you, it would only end in the most gruesome of murders.' Kamal grins, unaware of how much the idea of Alexa being hurt makes me want to vomit.

'This isn't a book, though,' I point out.

'I know, but it's set up like one. Apparently, Otis Clarke is some big tech hotshot, which means Otis and Alexa are rich. As in, richer than anyone we've ever met. Also known as the perfect victims for extortion.'

Setting down my knife, I fight the urge to roll my eyes. 'In the space of a minute, we've gone from Alexa being missing to her being killed to being kidnapped and held for ransom.'

'Rich people are famous for doing dodgy stuff to get richer. Who knows what gambles the husband has taken? Maybe he didn't expect one of them to be with his wife's life.'

'That's a tad dramatic.'

'Maybe, but it's all so mysterious. Otis Clarke didn't go to the police but went to the neighbours. That's weird. I'm not sure I'd be as chilled as him if I were in his shoes. No good can come from someone disappearing on you. We both know that.'

The kitchen falls into a stunned silence as Kamal registers his words. He freezes, realising the error of what he said. The at-ease mood we've fostered teeters on the brink. I'm seconds away from destroying it altogether by storming out of the room, but Kamal saves the night by clearing his throat.

'All I'm saying is, a woman hasn't been seen in days. Her husband seems concerned but not concerned enough. So, I thought I'd ask the expert regarding mysteries like this and see what she thought.'

Swallowing my humiliation, I force myself to reply. 'The expert?'

'You're a thriller author. You know twists and lies and people's dark sides better than most. So, tell me, what's your theory?'

Picking up my knife once more, I shrug. 'I don't know.'

'Come on,' Kamal teases, the sound of our chopping rhythmical in the quiet of the kitchen. 'From what your friends said, does Otis Clarke seem like a good guy? Does Alexa Clarke seem like the type to leave her husband?'

'I don't know. They've never really spoken to her.'

'Ah, someone else in Bramblethorpe who keeps to themself,' Kamal jokes, but the comparison between me and Alexa punches me in the gut. 'Well, if she has left Otis, I'm sure everyone will be ready to share their theories as to why.'

Selecting another mushroom from the box, I thumb a grey-brown dent in the side of it.

'It's sad to imagine that Alexa might have run away, don't you think?' I say. 'To think that however tough things were for her, she felt like her only option was to disappear.'

'If she left, we don't know that it's because things were tough. She could have been having an illicit affair or been offered the job of her dreams.'

'I don't think that's the reason she's gone.'

'Oh yeah? What makes you say that?'

'I don't know,' I reply, but I do know. It's the same reason I stay in this house, dodging invitations from friends and calls from family. It's the same reason Kamal worries about me, and the same reason I was prescribed those pills.

'Please,' Kamal begs lightly. 'Switch on your creative brain and tell me your theory. I'm dying to hear it.'

'I don't have a—'

'Janine Rai, usually you can overhear a snippet of an entirely innocent conversation and come up with the most twisted story. I know you have a theory on this.'

The truth bursts from me, if only to make Kamal stop talking about how easy stories came to me once upon a time.

'They lost four babies,' I blurt.

The suddenness and horribleness of my words combine to create a vacuum that sucks the air from the kitchen. Kamal's shoulders tense, his hand paused above a bundle of spring onions. My arms ache to hold him, but sadness pins them to my sides.

'I think she lost four babies and couldn't take the pain anymore,' I whisper.

Kamal pauses before slowly pressing his knife into the onions. 'That's … that's terrible for them.'

I nod, fighting back tears before Kamal sees them, but of course he notices I'm upset. He notices everything; that's why his worry never switches off.

As my husband moves towards me, I back away from his sympathy.

'I'm fine,' I say, more abruptly than I mean to. Kamal flinches, and the guilt I was already feeling doubles. Choking on it, I leave the room because leaving is easier than facing it.

Hurrying back upstairs to the peace of my office, I swear, here and now, that I will find Alexa Clarke. Whatever it takes, I will find her, and I will help her.

CHAPTER 6

Alexa

Two days gone

Alexa Clarke was undoubtedly the most fascinating thing in the small, white room she had been laid in. The choice to position the five-foot-nine woman on a single bed gave the impression of her being an overgrown child, one who was simply too big for the space she occupied. To the left of Alexa was a bedside table and a lamp giving off a dim light. Beside that was a long, narrow window. Its curtain was drawn, the hem kissing the window ledge. No light seeped around the edges, a sign that it was night-time.

Dried blood matted Alexa's blonde hair to her skull and stained her pale skin. The hoodie Alexa had been wearing when she went for her walk was gone, as were her trainers. The rest of her outfit was intact, although mud now caked the knees of her leggings.

The tatty nature of Alexa's appearance was made even more shocking by how starkly it contrasted with her surroundings. The pristine room suggested that whoever owned it was neat, verging on obsessive. There was no junk under the bed, no excess furniture cluttering the space. Just a bed, some bedding and a woman named Alexa Clarke.

A woman whose flickering eyelids suggested that, after forty-eight hours of slipping in and out of consciousness, she was finally awake. More than that, she was trying to open her eyes.

Not that the process was easy. It couldn't be when the blood that spilt from Alexa's head had coated her lashes, drying to form a crust that welded her eyes shut.

Her eyelids screamed as she tried to pry them apart. The struggle reminded Alexa of times when she had forgotten to take her make-up off before she slept. The jarring thought stopped Alexa's mind in its tracks. Why had she been wearing make-up? Alexa hadn't used cosmetics in a long time. A beauty regime required effort, and recently all her effort had been taken up by getting out of bed.

But if Alexa hadn't gone anywhere that warranted a cosmetic cover-up, then why were her eyelids stuck together?

As Alexa's blood ran cold, she ordered herself to focus on facts, not fear. Scrunching her forehead, she tried to conjure her last memory. While her brain was pounding like she had the mother of all hangovers, no party came to mind. In fact, when Alexa tried to remember anything, thick clouds of confusion clogged her thoughts.

A low moan escaped Alexa's lips when, finally, the corner of her left eye ripped opened.

As soon as it did, Alexa wished it hadn't. The onslaught of light burned her retina, even though the room could hardly be described as well lit. She winced, but the facial movement only made the throbbing in her head intensify.

Clenching her teeth, Alexa forced the rest of her eyelids to open. The task was brutal, but she didn't stop until the top eyelashes broke free of the bottom ones. But even with her eyes open, Alexa still couldn't see. Her entire field of vision was blurred as if smeared with a sheen of Vaseline. Blinking, she waited until the world around her became clear enough that she could make out fuzzy shapes.

Shapes she didn't recognise.

With her heart hammering, Alexa ordered herself to stay calm and assess the situation. There was something soothing about the practical task that lulled her into believing things might not be quite as bad as they seemed.

Tilting her head to survey the strange room she found herself in, it was then that Alexa realised she was lying on a bed with crisp white sheets. She didn't know whose sheets they were. They certainly weren't hers.

As the pain in her head screeched louder, Alexa scanned her surroundings for clues as to where she was, but other than the bed and the bedside table, there was nothing in the room.

Nothing but a grey hoodie hung on the back of the door.

I have a hoodie like that, Alexa thought as her gaze settled on it. It was one of Otis's old ones, baggy and worn at the hem.

Alexa had been wearing the hoodie a lot recently. There was comfort in the way she could lose herself in the roomy material, the soft fabric providing the hug she had given up asking Otis for. Once upon a time, she would have only worn something as scruffy as that at home, but these days Alexa wore it outside, too. Especially when she was walking.

That's it, she thought. *A walk. That's the last thing I remember doing.*

She had gone for one after breakfast, and after the argument she'd had with Otis. Alexa remembered ignoring him to try to avoid the showdown, but he'd commanded her attention by shouting.

The next memory she had was of her walk.

I wore the grey hoodie, Alexa thought. She remembered dropping her purse into one of the oversized pockets but leaving her phone behind. Abandoning the thing that tethered her to the world had been freeing. Now the decision just felt foolish.

Frowning, Alexa tried to think of what came next. The route she conjured from her memory was hazy, but it came to her. Sliding open the bifold doors and stepping out into the garden. Hopping over the fence and walking through the trees that bordered the land her home was built on. Reaching the fields behind the house. And then . . .

And then . . . What?

Chewing the inside of her cheek, Alexa focused on the hoodie once more, waiting for it to confess the truth. That was when she noticed the red-brown splashes.

The red-brown splashes that looked an awful lot like blood.

Suddenly, a tsunami of memories swept over Alexa, obliterating her beliefs that quiet countryside areas were safe and that bad things didn't happen to nice, law-abiding people like her.

I was out walking, and I was hit over the head.

Alexa repeated the words in her mind, willing them to make sense, but how could she ever understand such a violent, unprovoked attack?

With a wobbling chin, she ordered herself to stand, but her heavy limbs barely twitched. Worse still, her minuscule movements sent ripples of agony rolling through her.

But through the pain, Alexa heard something. A strange, foreboding clanging noise.

Searching the vault of her memories, Alexa tried to place the sound, but it was too hard to concentrate when her attention was absorbed by the sensation that something was weighing her down. Brow furrowed, she peeled her head from the pillow to look down at her body.

As soon as she saw why she couldn't move, Alexa Clarke froze.

Chunky metal handcuffs encircled her wrists and ankles, attached to chains so thick it would take a chainsaw to cut through them. Alexa's blurry vision followed the links to the metal bedframe they were locked to, leaving her immobilised.

Leaving her captured.

Terror like nothing Alexa had ever felt before pressed against her throat. Peeling her fuzzed tongue from the roof of her mouth, she opened her pale, cracked lips.

'Help!' she screamed into the silence. 'Someone, please, help me!'

CHAPTER 7

Kamal makes a cup of tea for me the next morning, but I'm downstairs before he has to use it to lure me out of bed.

'You're up,' he says, unable to hide his surprise.

'I heard the kettle. Besides, I've woken up feeling like I could run a marathon. You know, if I actually enjoyed running.'

'Does that mean lots of words are brewing in you?'

'Something like that.' A lie, but it feels safer than admitting the only thing brewing in me is the desire to find Alexa Clarke.

Kamal grabs his lunch and goes to leave, but then he stops. 'Before I forget, we're out of milk. Could you swing by the shop and get some?'

My pulse flutters at the base of my throat. Reading my silence, Kamal shakes off the question.

'Don't worry, I can go on—'

'No,' I interrupt. 'It's okay. I'll go.'

He hovers. 'You're sure you want to?'

'Yes, I'll go. I'll make friends with the locals.'

It's hard not to be upset by Kamal's happiness, given that it highlights the severity of my isolation. Once upon a time, which one of us would do such a simple chore wouldn't have been up for debate, but that was before tiny village stores and small talk made my palms damp.

When Kamal is gone, I swill the tablet he left out for me down the sink and stand at the kitchen window. Sparkling frost glimmers as far as the eye can see, while a dark sky peers down on the frozen wonderland. The perfect day to stay indoors and avoid the harsh world.

But you're not doing that, I remind myself. *Today you're going out, and you'll be fine when you do.*

The assurance is enough to calm me down. Marginally, at least.

Draining the last of my tea, I check my phone. A notification from Natalya is waiting, one I open quickly when I see it's an update on Alexa Clarke.

Apparently, she's still not home. Surely it's time for Otis to go to the police now?!x

The words 'Katherine is typing' appear at the top of the screen, but I close the conversation. I don't have time to chat when there are more useful things I could do.

Things like looking for Alexa myself.

Fuelled by that thought, I dress and leave the house. My throat is tight as my car draws closer to the centre of Bramblethorpe, passing people who waved when I first moved here but soon learned not to when I didn't return the gesture.

When I slow at an intersection, I spot Jim Marshall in the distance. His faithful dog, Bernie, trots alongside him. Despite having never interacted with him, Jim is one of the few people in Bramblethorpe I can name, but only because Katherine and Natalya have shared so many stories about him.

Thanks to his fiery temper and prolific career as a professional boxer fifteen years ago, Jim is well known around here. Half-hated, half-feared, his territorial attitude towards the farm he runs alone after his wife left him is legendary. He has a reputation for setting up booby traps to warn trespassers away. It's even rumoured that he once threatened a group of teenagers with a shotgun because they were camping on his property.

Usually, I never pay attention to gossip, but whenever I see Jim's scowl and the bulky outline of his physique, his rumoured aggression is all I can think of.

With no other car approaching the intersection, I set off more quickly than I would if Jim and Bernie weren't there. Minutes later, I reach the safety of the high street.

I'm psyching myself up to enter the village store when my sister calls. Knowing that if I let the phone ring out, it would be the fourth of Beth's calls I've ignored this last week, I force myself to pick up.

'Beth, now isn't a good time,' I say.

'Why not? You work from home inventing stories. You have all the time in the world.'

Once upon a time, my sister's mock ignorance about what I do for a living was something we laughed about. Today, it's only insulting.

'I'm not at home,' I reply.

'Really? But you're always at home.'

Insult number two nestles like a knife between my ribs. 'Well, today I'm not.'

'Where are you?' Beth asks, fighting to be heard over my nieces squabbling in the background. A single parent to a thirteen-month-old and a three-year-old, Beth assures me she has the hardest job in the world. I don't doubt her assertion, but it's a job I'd kill for.

'I'm out running errands,' I say, picking at the leather of my steering wheel.

'I'm glad you're out of the house. And is everything okay? Is today a good day?'

I force a sigh. 'Beth, you don't need to check up on me. What do you want?'

'Okay, grumpy, I won't keep you long, but Mum and I were thinking we should meet for lunch next weekend.'

Inwardly, I groan. It's hard enough keeping up the pretence with Kamal that I'm working on my book, but add Mum and Beth to the mix and I have a nightmare on my hands. All Mum ever says is how her book club is eagerly awaiting the next one, as if that doesn't pile on the pressure.

'I'll check with Kamal, but I think we have plans,' I lie.

'Well, we're flexible. If you're with Kamal Saturday, we can do Sunday.'

'Sorry, it's a whole weekend event.'

Beth pauses. 'If I call Kamal, will he say the same thing?'

There's something about her tone that ruffles me. 'What did I say about not checking up on me?'

'What you're calling checking up on, some would say looking out for.'

'I'm the big sister. It's my job to look out for you, not the other way round.' When a beat of stung silence rings out on the other end of the line, I wince. I don't mean to snap at Beth. I don't mean to snap at anyone. I just can't seem to help myself.

'Janine—'

'I've got to go. I'll call you later, okay?' I say, even though we both know that I won't.

I hang up before I hear Beth's reply. It takes me a second to get myself moving afterwards, with some small, niggling part of my conscience warning me that how I just spoke to my sister was not okay.

When I enter the village shop, the bell above the door dings to announce my arrival. Not that the cashier notices. She's too busy chatting to another middle-aged woman, a customer who has already paid for her shopping but is in no hurry to leave.

'Apparently Alexa walks out on him all the time. Terrible, isn't it? There's obviously something wrong with her mental state,' the customer says. I flinch at her cutting analysis, but keep listening.

'We don't know if this has anything to do with Alexa's mental state. Otis could be a narcissist. It wouldn't surprise me, with all that money. Besides, whenever someone steps out on their marriage, there's always more to it.'

'Well, I think I've got the scoop on that. Want to hear?'

Intrigued, I busy myself searching the range of apples on display.

'Mary, don't be daft! Of course I want to know,' the cashier squeals.

'Rumour has it that Alexa was spotted a few weeks ago in Saddleforth looking cosy with a handsome man. A man who was most definitely *not* Otis Clarke.'

My eyes widen, but my reaction is tame in comparison to the cashier's audible gasp.

'Who told you that?' she cries.

'Franny Henderson.'

'Oh, well, if Franny said it then it must be true,' the cashier scoffs, her disappointment palpable.

'Say what you like, but Franny said she double-checked it was Alexa because it was such a shock to see her away from that horrible house.'

'Come on, Mary. You know as well as I do that Franny is as accurate with the truth as the prime minister is.'

A bubble of laughter escapes me at the comment. The two women jump and turn to face me at the unexpected sound. Under their scrutiny, I burn with embarrassment.

'I—' I begin, but the cashier smiles warmly.

'Don't worry, love. I spend my day eavesdropping on customers' conversations. It's only fair you listen back.' Suddenly, she narrows her eyes, then an even brighter smile overcomes her. 'You're the new woman, aren't you? The writer?'

'That's me,' I reply. 'I'm Janine.'

'Welcome! Although I suppose you're not so new here anymore. Still, it's lovely to finally meet you. We were all very excited to hear we had a famous author living in the village. Mary's got all your books in paperback.'

'I'll have to get you to sign them,' Mary chips in.

'I'd love to,' I reply, approaching the counter with an apple. When I set it down, I notice it's bruised, but I daren't swap it. The cashier, whose name badge reads Renee, takes the apple and weighs it.

'I'm sorry you had to hear our gossiping,' she says. 'Although I'm sure you've heard all about what's going on with Alexa Clarke.'

'I have. It sounds very mysterious.'

Renee grimaces. 'It does. Whatever the outcome is, I suspect it won't be good.'

'Especially now we know cheating is involved,' Mary adds.

Renee shoots her a warning look. '*If* Franny Henderson is telling the truth.'

'I don't think Franny would be wrong about something this important,' Mary says, hoisting her shopping bags onto the crook of her arm. 'I should go, but it was lovely to meet you, Janine. Or should I say, lovely to meet you, S. K. Atherton!'

When Mary leaves, I purchase my apple even though I need a single apple as much as I need a hole in the head. I pay by card and head for the door.

'It was nice to chat, dear,' Renee calls before I leave.

My lips twitch into what I hope comes across as a friendly smile before I dash outside. It's only when I get back to my car that I realise I forgot to buy milk.

Sighing, I lean my head on the steering wheel and listen to the blood pound in my ears.

This level of distress makes no sense. Going to the shop shouldn't be a big deal for someone who has been on stage in auditoriums that fit thousands, but somehow it feels like the hardest thing I could ever do. Sadness claws at me as, yet again, I'm reminded that I've lost part of myself.

I want to hate myself for it. In fact, most days I do. I should be stronger than this. Better. The person smiling on the back cover of her books, who people queue to meet. But I'm not. I'm a walking disappointment.

Lifting my head, I stare ahead as if the answer to my problems can be found on the high street, but all I see is Margie leaning in the doorway of Coffee and Cake, chatting away. From her animated expression, I'd bet money it's about Alexa Clarke.

My brow furrows. So many people are talking about what's going on like Alexa's life is entertainment. They're swapping theories and sharing stories, but no one is *doing* anything.

I can't be like them.

As soon as that thought registers with me, it's like a lightbulb switches on. Forget milk, forget apples – Alexa is the reason I am out of the house today.

I decide to start where I would start if this were a book – with Alexa's last known whereabouts.

Typing Maple Crescent into Google Maps, I set off driving. The further I get from the high street, the more I come alive with purpose and the less I listen to the voice in my head warning me that what I am doing is borderline insane. By the time I reach Maple Crescent, checking out Alexa's house doesn't seem inappropriate. If anything, it feels entirely sensible.

Driving down the leafy street, I think back to Natalya's words about Alexa's home: *That big modern one*, she'd said.

As I make my way down the road, I can see why a modern structure would cause a stir somewhere like this. It's a narrow, winding road with uninterrupted fields running along one side and beautiful period properties on the other. Everything is as I imagine it was one hundred years ago, with the pretty ivy-fronted houses dotted around like something from the front of a Christmas card. Or, if I listen to the cynical side of my brain, a documentary about a remote, off-grid cult.

I pass four well-proportioned cottages with sweeping gardens, then an ornate home set back from the road. Slowing, I study the bold brickwork and design, then shake my head. This house looks like it comes straight from the pages of a Victorian Gothic novel. Natalya called Alexa's house modern. This house would have only been considered modern in 1859.

Continuing onwards, I creep past a subtly signposted entrance to a public footpath, a cute cottage and another grand period property before reaching a T-junction with Oak Avenue.

My forehead scrunches as I read the street sign confirming I'm on Maple Crescent.

Spinning my car around, I travel back down the road, slower this time. I pass the last house and the cottage, the Gothic dream home, the first four cottages – but no modern masterpiece.

Pulling up on the side of the road, I reach for my phone. My plan is to see if Google Maps can help me, but my hands are shaking with so much nervous energy that the phone slips out of my grip.

Bending to retrieve it, I rummage around the embarrassingly dirty footwell of my car. My fingers brush against scraps of leaves and dropped mints, but no phone. Reaching under the seat, I continue the hunt until out of nowhere, a shadow falls across the window, shrouding me in darkness.

CHAPTER 8

'Fuck!' I shriek.

I whip upright, moving so fast that I smack my head on my steering wheel. My teeth clench at the thud of impact, my face scrunching as a clout of pain ricochets through me.

The elderly woman standing beside my car looks as shocked at my outburst as I was by her sudden appearance. She holds her hand to her chest and for one horrifying moment, I panic I've just scared one of Bramblethorpe's oldest residents to death.

'What a fright we've given each other,' the woman shouts, fighting to be heard through the closed window. 'I didn't mean to scare you, dear. I saw you driving up and down and thought you might be lost.'

Acting as if my pulse isn't pounding in the base of my throat, I wind my window down. 'That's so kind, thank you.'

'Oh, it's no bother. I was gardening when you drove past, you see. It's never too early to prep for spring,' the woman says, waving a trowel in the air as if I'll want to fact-check her story. 'I'm Dorrit Holbeck. Nice to meet you.'

Stepping out of the car on wobbling legs, I shake Dorrit's trowel-free hand. 'Janine,' I reply.

Introductions made, the well-worn smile lines on Dorrit's face come to life. I memorise her features should I ever need to describe a character who is the epitome of a wholesome grandmother.

'This here is Magnus,' Dorrit says, nodding to a small Scottie dog by her feet who looks almost as old as she does. 'He came to say hello. He's terribly nosey, although his arthritis will make him suffer for that. Now then, how did you end up getting lost on Maple Crescent?'

'I'm not lost. I'm looking for . . .' I trail off as my attention finds itself being drawn back along the street, searching for the Clarkes' home and the secrets it contains.

'Let me guess, you're here about Alexa?'

My focus snaps back to Dorrit. 'How do you know?'

'You're not the first car that's driven along here today, believe me.'

'Right,' I reply, cringing as I realise I must seem like another nosey local. 'Do you know the Clarkes?'

'I'm their neighbour, dear. Of course I know them.'

I force a smile. 'Of course! Sorry, I moved here from central Manchester. I barely knew what my neighbours looked like, never mind their names.'

Dorrit grimaces at the sorry admission. 'Things aren't like that around here. Folk tend to know each other well. Some people don't like that, but I think it's nice to have people keeping an eye out for you, especially at my age.'

'I imagine it's a comfort for you.'

'It is, dear, although I must admit, I don't know Otis and Alexa well.'

'I take it that means you don't know where Alexa is?'

'It sounds like no one does,' Dorrit replies, unable to keep the creep of worry out of her voice. 'Otis said when he came home from work on Saturday, she was gone.'

Hearing the truth so close to Alexa's home brings a new level of eeriness to it. I find myself once again staring along the road Alexa must have walked along, wondering if it could talk, what would it say?

'I can't understand why anyone would work on a Saturday,' Dorrit continues, shaking her head. 'And with computers too! But Otis is a busy man. When he came round yesterday to ask if I'd seen Alexa, I offered him a cup of tea, but he said he didn't have the time.'

Even though I know it pushes my presence here to borderline rude, I can't help asking, 'Did Otis say anything else?'

Dorrit shakes her head. 'I'm sorry, I wish I could be more help, but I don't know anything. Otis said there's no reason to worry, but I'm not so sure.'

'Do you think something's happened to Alexa?'

Dorrit takes a second to think how best to reply. 'I would hate to start a rumour like that, but Alexa and Otis . . . they've been arguing recently. A lot. My house is close by. You hear things. You see things.'

'What did you see?' I ask, dry mouthed.

'Oh, this and that. Shouting on the doorstep, Otis driving away in the middle of the night. Alexa spending more time alone or crying in the garden. I never went over to ask if she was okay – I didn't want to intrude – but maybe I should have.'

As guilt sweeps over Dorrit, I say, 'You weren't to know what would happen.'

'Maybe, but I knew things weren't right. Someone crying like that – it's never a good sign, is it? Otis always looks so sad these days. A little angry, too. You never know what can happen when you feel like that.'

The loaded analysis of the Clarkes' life squirms inside me. 'Are you saying that you think Otis has hurt Alexa?'

Dorrit's expression twists. 'I don't know. Accusing someone of that isn't nice and Otis usually seems like such a nice man. I never saw any evidence of him hurting her, but all that arguing ... Things can't have been good between them, can they?'

'Do you know what they were arguing about?' I ask, but at that moment a car passes on the road beside us. Dorrit jumps at its sudden appearance then takes a step backwards.

'I shouldn't have said anything,' she rushes to say. 'It's probably nothing and, like I said, I never saw anything. Not really. Besides, all couples argue, don't they?' She backs away from me before I can say yes, they do, but not so frequently that one of them spends most of the day crying. 'I should get back to my garden. I've so much to do.'

'Wait,' I begin, but Dorrit shakes her head.

'I'm sorry, dear, but I've already said too much. If you have more questions, you need to speak to Otis. His house is just next door,' Dorrit says, pointing to what looks like a hedge. When she sees the confusion on my face, she explains, 'The driveway curves from behind the hedge. It was designed to be deceptive. Some landscaping they arranged after people complained about the house. From the road, you can't see it head on, but the start of their driveway is just there.'

I go to say thank you, but Dorrit has already started to walk away.

'Dorrit,' I call, stopping her. 'What if Otis can't answer my questions?'

She blinks, chewing the inside of her lip. 'Then I think you should take them to the police.'

With that, Dorrit hobbles away. Magnus follows, his stilted walk mirroring his owner's until they disappear into a garden up the road, leaving me alone.

CHAPTER 9

Sense tells me to drive home. Dorrit's analysis of Alexa's marriage verged on chilling, and that's without mentioning the eerie atmosphere bathing this isolated, frost-bitten street. But my eyes can't help wandering to the hedge that leads to the Clarke house.

I know what I'm thinking of doing is wrong. I know that, technically, it's trespassing. But I'm the kind of person who loves a puzzle or escape room. The kind of reader who can't not finish a book, even one I'm not enjoying, because I have to know how the story ends. I can't walk away not knowing where Alexa Clarke is or if she's okay.

Besides, Alexa helped me when I was at my worst. I'll be damned if I'm not going to help her too.

Leaving my car on the street, I move towards the hedge. There, I find the start of a driveway, curving back behind the hedge and so well hidden I missed it before. Craning my neck, I hunt for a better view of the building at the end of the driveway, catching a glimpse of an imposing modern structure.

'Bingo,' I whisper.

My brain itches to move, but sense makes me pause. *This is madness,* it tells me. I should go home to my manuscript. I shouldn't even *be* here. But before I can talk myself out of it, I set off down the gravel.

The first thing that strikes me as I make my way towards the house is how silent it is here. If where I live is isolated, then Alexa Clarke's house is another level of remote. Even though I know a public footpath runs close to the house, it feels like I'm the only person left in the world.

Shuddering, I wrap my arms around my waist and force myself to focus on the crunch of gravel beneath my feet, not the buzz of my nerves.

The further I walk, the more details of the house I see, and the more it takes everything in me not to drop my jaw. The building is like something from an architectural TV show, all sharp edges and metalwork contrasting with highly polished wood. Sitting in the middle of landscaped gardens, it's both intimidating and stunning at the same time. I can't help but wonder how much it's worth.

To the right of the house is an impressive garage, designed to mirror the architectural style of the main building. Beside it sits a smart, grey car – Alexa's car. I know this already thanks to the village gossip. My legs move of their own accord, pulled towards the vehicle by curiosity.

The car is so dirty, I notice the grime from a distance. Despite clearly being an expensive model, it looks unused. Unloved. Peering through the windows, I find that the interior is bare apart from a parking ticket stub perched on the dashboard. The date on it reads April 11, cementing the idea that Alexa's car hasn't been driven in a long time. And, with it still in her driveway, it definitely wasn't used the day she disappeared.

As the sound of a car passing along Maple Crescent registers behind me, the hairs on my arms stand to attention. I should leave now, before I'm caught, but instead I duck around the side of the building, out of sight should the driver look this way.

Chewing my lip, I walk the perimeter of the building until I come to a glass façade at the back of the property. Its wide windows invite me to look into the main living area of the house. The space is plunged in darkness, indicating that no one is home. My pounding heart can't help but feel relieved, although if I was writing this scene, Otis's absence would mean one of three things.

One: he is with the police.

Two: he is out looking for Alexa.

Three: he is doing something normal, like working.

The first option can't be right because, at least as far I know, Otis hasn't gone to the police. The second might be true, but if Otis were out looking for Alexa, Katherine or Natalya would likely have heard about it through the village grapevine and messaged.

Which only leaves option three. The worst option. With his wife missing, surely Otis being at work is an indication of one thing: guilt.

Gulping, my eyes trace over the darkened living space.

A large open kitchen sweeps across the back wall, looking upon a dining table with chairs for twelve guests and a luxurious living room. Three plush sofas face a log-burning fireplace that looks like it would be at home in an exclusive spa resort.

But the main thing I notice is the mess.

There are discarded cups and dirty plates scattered around the place, but the thing that's caught my attention is the dining table. It's in disarray, the surface covered entirely in papers. From my position, I can't see what's written on them, but that doesn't stop my imagination from running wild. Maybe they reveal that Otis's business is in trouble, or that he has recently taken out a life insurance policy for Alexa. Maybe they're divorce papers.

Curious, I step closer to the window to get a better view, but in doing so I catch sight of a photo on a side table. It's a cosy shot of Otis and Alexa, wrapped in each other's arms. Their smiles pummel me enough that I step away from the window.

These are real people, not characters in a book. I'm not doing creative research. I'm trespassing. I'm breaking the law.

'What the fuck are you doing?' I whisper to myself, heading back to my car, without another glimpse at the house. My steps are slow at first, but they pick up speed as I become increasingly aware of the stillness of my surroundings. Even though there's no one else here, I can't shake the feeling that I'm being watched. By the time the road comes back into view, I'm tempted to break into a run.

Gripping the sleeves of my jumper, I order myself to walk on calmly, as if I am not petrified. I stare at my feet, counting my steps to keep me going. It's only when I register the sound of gravel crunching that I look up.

As soon as I do, my heart stops.

There's a car driving down the driveway, coming straight towards me.

CHAPTER 10

My eyes lock onto a stern-faced Otis Clarke behind the wheel of the car.

I want to run, but where can I go? There's nowhere to run and nowhere to hide. I am in the centre of Otis's driveway, and his frown tells me that he has well and truly spotted me. Through the windscreen of his car, I watch his frown turn into fury. I can't say I blame him.

When Otis reaches me, he brakes sharply then exits his car.

'What the hell are you doing on my property?' Otis's voice doesn't sound like it did yesterday. Instead, it's strong and forceful, filled with an anger that has my heart hammering.

My dry mouth opens and closes, too terrified to form words.

Otis's brows furrow. 'You were in the café yesterday, weren't you?' he snaps.

'I . . . I'm sorry?'

'You were there, when I asked Margie about Alexa.'

I could kick myself. Of course Otis saw me. I was right in front of him, hanging on his every word.

Before I can think of how to respond, Otis's expression morphs into one of heartbreak, interrupting my train of thought.

'Do you know something about Lex? Is that why you're here?'

I study the man before me, taking in his designer stubble and fancy suit, and the skin under his eyes that's greyed from a string of sleepless nights. He's handsome in a way that instinctively makes me wary. Charming, I'm sure – not used to being told 'no'. I know I should be scared of him. Half the things I've heard paint Otis out to be the big bad wolf, after all. But looking at Otis Clarke, I don't see the man behind the terrible rumours. I see a man frantic with worry. It's confirmation that invading his privacy like this is inexcusable.

'Do you know where Lex is?' Otis asks, his voice cracking.

I swallow the knot in my throat. 'No, I don't. I'm sorry.'

My reply crushes Otis, I can see it in the way his shoulders cave and his head bows.

'If you don't know where she is, then why are you here?' Otis asks.

I could make an excuse. Maybe I should, given the fact that Otis is a stranger with a multitude of concerning rumours swirling around him, but something about his collapsed frame tells me Otis Clarke doesn't need another riddle in his life.

'My name's Janine Rai,' I begin. 'I live in Bramblethorpe, too. I'm here because – well, I'm here because I want to help find Alexa.'

Otis looks up, confused. 'Do you know her?'

'Not really, no. I've met her, but only once.'

Otis analyses me suspiciously before slotting a composed mask over his upset. 'And you think that qualifies you to figure out where she is?'

'No, but it qualifies me enough to want to help.'

'Help how? By stalking me at my house? By leaving fingerprints on my windows?'

I blush at Otis's verbal slap, a well-deserved blow.

'You don't know me and you don't know Lex, so why are you really here? For gossip? To run back to the village and tell them you've seen the awful husband for yourself?'

'No, it's nothing like that,' I protest, but anger has taken over Otis.

'Lex always says people here treat a stranger's misery as if it's cheap entertainment. It looks like she's right! I know what you're all saying about us, about me, but you're wrong. I'd never hurt Lex. You can tell all your friends at the village shop that.'

'That's not why I'm here,' I say, but Otis only laughs.

'Why else would you be here? You should be ashamed of yourself. Spying like this is a violation of my privacy. I could report you for it.'

'I – I'm not spying on you,' I protest, my cheeks flushing.

'You're trespassing on my property! If that's not spying, what is?' Otis's furious eyes sparkle, dangerously close to tears. 'My wife is nowhere to be found and all you fuckers can do is talk about it over dinner.' Otis runs his hand through his hair before heading back to his car. 'You should leave,' he calls over his shoulder. 'I'm not in the mood to talk.'

Panic absorbs me as I watch Otis walk away. All I want is for something, anything, to stop him from shutting me out.

'I know what it's like!' I shout. 'Losing a baby. I – I know what it's like.'

As my response echoes in the stillness of the morning, Otis turns back to me, both of us as shocked as each other to hear those words out in the open.

'People are talking about the miscarriages?' he croaks.

'They are,' I admit. 'That's how I met Alexa. We were at the hospital. We had appointments on the same day. Alexa, she … she told me things would be okay.'

Otis's chin wobbles, as does my own. I fill my lungs with air, a task that's been getting harder with the weight of grief compressing my chest.

'I know what it's like to lose a child and feel like life will never be the same again,' I say. 'I know how awful it is to wake up every day and find yourself in a world you no longer understand. I know that losing a child is the worst thing to happen to a marriage, and what it feels like to be Alexa. That's why I'm here. I want to help her, like she helped me.'

Furious with myself for welling up in front of a stranger, I dry my eyes with the sleeve of my jumper, but witnessing my upset seems to defrost Otis.

'The day we met, Alexa talked about you,' I continue. 'She told me she shut you out of her life so much it felt like you were strangers.'

Otis's expression pinches. 'She said that?'

'She did. She also told me not to do that to my own husband. I don't think she wants to do that to you, Otis. I think maybe she's just . . . lost.'

Dropping his head, Otis nods. 'Lex has been that way for a while now,' he says softly. 'We both have. When she wasn't home, I thought she'd gone to stay with a friend or gone to the village B&B. She's done that before. I thought . . .' Otis trails off, then shakes his head. 'This is crazy. I'm not offloading my life to someone I've just met.'

'But I want to help,' I push, but Otis continues to back away.

'Look, you seem nice and I'm sure Alexa would appreciate you reaching out, but right now I need to focus on finding her and making sure she's okay. I don't have time to go through everything with a stranger.'

'But I can help. I'm a thriller author.'

Otis blinks at my random revelation. 'So, what, you want to send me a free book or something?'

'No, but missing people, unreliable narrators, twists and turns are in my wheelhouse. I have a talent for imagining every possible scenario. My husband won't let me watch a detective show with him because I always give away the ending.' I hope my smile makes my outburst appear less odd, but I'm not immune to how strange my presence here is.

Otis's bewilderment proves he most definitely finds me odd. 'You really think that because you've written a few books, you can help find my wife?'

'I do.'

There's a split second where I think Otis might accept my offer, but as quickly as it arrives, it disappears.

The second I sense him withdraw, I step forward. 'I'm known for going all in on my research. I've shadowed a team of detectives working on missing persons cases. I learned all about profiling. I know how to create timelines and look at the bigger picture to find someone. Alexa helped me when I most needed it. Please. I want to do the same for her.'

Otis studies me for what feels like the longest time. 'You're really not here for gossip?'

'No, I swear. I'm new to Bramblethorpe. I barely speak to anyone. I'm practically the village recluse.'

Otis laughs, but sadness tinges the sound. 'I thought that's what they were calling Lex?' he says, then he shakes his head. 'This is insane. I'm not asking a random writer if she can pretend this is a book and imagine where Lex might be.'

'I ask questions,' I say, a little too loudly, but my outburst stops Otis from turning away again. 'Too many questions, my husband jokes, and I never give up until I find an answer. Please, Otis. I have skills that could be of use.'

Otis hovers. 'You really think you can find Lex?'

'I do.'

'I guess you'd better come in then,' he says.

CHAPTER 11

A CCTV camera stares down on us as Otis unlocks the front door. I gulp as I imagine it watching me before, skulking around like a woman possessed. Shame bathes me, increasing when Otis shoots a wary look in my direction before opening the door.

When we step inside the house, it takes everything in me not to react.

The entrance of the Clarkes' home is as impressive as the exterior suggests it would be. A grand staircase sweeps up the centre of the foyer, leading to a mezzanine with a cosy seating area and tall doors that must lead to the bedrooms. I don't have to see them to know they will be more luxurious than any hotel I've ever stayed in, even the fancy one my publisher put me up in for my London book launch.

While I try not to gawp, Otis leads me through to the open-plan living area. My attention shifts to the messy table, but Otis is clearing the papers away before I can get a look at them.

'You have a lovely home,' I comment, my adjective of choice a poor description of such modern splendour.

'Thanks. Lex and I designed it. The project was a nightmare. Two years of meetings and builders and mud, but it was worth the late nights and extra cost. Do you want a drink?'

As Otis indicates to the tap, I shake my head. An awkward silence rings out, one I'm not sure how to fill, and not just because these days I seem to have lost all my social skills. Part of me can't believe that I really am here, inside Alexa Clarke's house. The opposite of where I should be on a random Tuesday when I have a mountain of work waiting at home, I'm sure.

'The place is Lex's dream house,' Otis says eventually to fill the silence. 'She lost her parents when she was seven. She's dreamed of her own family home ever since. When we got married, I promised her we'd build the perfect one.'

Otis's voice catches when he speaks about his wife. To stop himself from falling victim to his upset, he gestures to the vast expanse on the other side of the glass bifold doors. The garden is well designed but clipped back at this time of year. Dead leaves litter the frost-bitten grass, making me shiver.

'Lex loves the garden. She's even more obsessed with the view past the trees. Fields that go on forever, she describes it as. Not my kind of thing, but Lex would sleep under the stars if she could.'

'Was Alexa getting out much before she disappeared?'

Otis turns from the garden, but he doesn't meet my gaze. 'I don't know. I'm at work for most of the day. Weekends, too. Lex is at home at the moment, but I don't know what she does with her time.'

Politely ignoring the resounding sadness of Otis's admission, I take in my surroundings once more. My eyes come to rest on the papers, now neatly piled up.

What was Otis looking at? What doesn't he want me to see?

When I sense Otis watching me, I force myself to look away from the table.

'We should start by making a timeline of the day Alexa went missing,' I say.

'Sure, but I can't add much to it. Once I left for the office, I don't know what she did.'

'I noticed a CCTV camera on the way in,' I say, burning as I think of how it will have tracked me snooping around the property. 'Does it show Alexa going out on Saturday?'

Otis nods. 'CCTV shows her leaving the house at eleven through the bifold doors in here. She goes into the garden.'

My eyebrows arch. 'The garden? But it's the middle of November.'

'I thought it was weird, too, but that's what happens on the recording.'

'Do you see where she goes from there?'

'No. The cameras only show points of entry to the house. I don't know if Lex sat outside, if she went for a walk, if someone came to see her. I don't know where she went.' Otis's shoulders slump, the words knocking the life out of him. 'The next person you see is me arriving home from work at seven. It's like Lex steps outside, then she vanishes.'

An eerie chill tickles my bones at those words. 'Could she have dodged the CCTV?'

'Maybe,' Otis replies, but he doesn't sound sure. 'The cameras are only on the doors to the house and garage. To be honest, when we moved here, we thought installing CCTV was excessive. I know the house is near a public footpath, but it's on the edge of a village where nothing happens. You've as much chance of something exciting kicking off here as you do a UFO landing on your roof.'

I smirk at Otis's assessment of Bramblethorpe. 'Did you check CCTV from the days before Alexa left to see if anything unusual happened?'

'I did, but there's nothing. Every day is the same. I go to work, I come back. Lex goes out once a day, every day. She's never gone for more than an hour. Judging by her clothes, she's out for a walk, but that's a guess.'

'Does she meet anyone?'

'I told you, I don't know how Lex spends her time. I wish I did, but I don't.'

While Otis deflates over how little he knows his wife, a dense sorrow clogs the air. I try not to be affected by the sadness, but I can't avoid breathing it in. Part of me wants to judge Otis for knowing so little about the woman he married, but I can't. If someone asked Kamal what I did all day, his answer would be just as clueless.

'It's not that I don't care what Lex does,' Otis says as if he can hear my thoughts. 'I just thought that leaving her to grieve was for the best. She goes to a miscarriage support group once a week, but other than that it's like she doesn't want anyone around her at the moment. Especially me. Everything I do or say is wrong. Eventually I just... stopped speaking, I guess.'

Otis's shame quadruples under my gaze. I want to comfort him, but I can't when his words mirror my own life a little too closely for comfort.

'We both want a baby, but since losing her parents, all Lex has wanted is a family,' Otis continues, leaning against one of the bifold doors as if it's the only thing holding him upright. 'If Lex isn't crying, she's researching how to make sure she doesn't miscarry again. Supplements, exercises, prayers. You name it, she's doing it. She left her job because she thought stress might be to blame.

The doctors said that wasn't the reason she miscarried, but still, she blamed herself.'

'Still, she'd try anything if it meant she could be a mother.'

'Exactly. A few months ago, Lex fell pregnant again. We really thought it was going to work out for us that time.' Otis doesn't need to say what happened. The gut-wrenching end of the story is ingrained into his every pore.

Pushing himself away from the door, Otis looks across the garden, scouring the scenery as if searching for something. His wife, his child, a reason why this is happening.

'Okay, so external CCTV is drawing a blank,' I say. 'Are there cameras in the house?'

Otis blinks. 'Are you asking if I spy on my wife?'

My cheeks burn. 'That's not what I meant.'

'No, we don't have them in the house,' Otis replies, his tone more spiked than before. 'Like I said, they're only near points of entry. They'd have picked Lex up if she went down the driveway or to the garage, but she didn't go near those places. Her car is still here, too.'

The unusualness of the situation prickles my skin. There's no denying Otis is devastated. My gut sympathises with every word he says. If I were a betting woman, I would put money on him telling the truth. But a person doesn't just vanish. And if Alexa is in as bad a way as he says she is, then simply waiting for her to come home isn't enough.

'Otis, I have to ask, why haven't you gone to the police with this?'

Otis sighs. 'Right now, I don't know. The choice made sense a few days ago. After all, I've been in this position before. Lex taking off when things get too much isn't unheard of. She once stayed away for almost a week and didn't contact me the entire time she was gone. What if that's what's going on here? What if she just needs space? She'll be mortified if she comes back to a big fuss. She was livid when she found out I'd asked if anyone had seen her last time she left. It's going to hurt her even more when she finds out that everyone in the village is talking about the babies.'

The thought of how I would react to everyone knowing about my struggles makes me wince. I can't exactly blame Otis for not wanting to give the gossips of Bramblethorpe even more to talk about. But still, this is the third day where Otis has had no contact with his wife. He doesn't know where she's sleeping. What she's eating. If she's okay, hurt, or worse.

Fighting a shudder, I force myself to speak. 'You said Alexa retreats when things get too much. What situations make her feel like that?'

I expect Otis to reply with a retort about me knowing what Alexa's going through, but instead, he gulps. 'Lex takes off like this whenever we . . . well, whenever we argue.' Casting his gaze to the floor, Otis continues. 'We had a row Saturday morning. That's why I wasn't surprised when I came home and Lex wasn't here. I almost expected it. I let myself be angry all weekend, but when Monday rolled around and I'd cooled off, I . . . well, I realised how ridiculous I'd been. I thought I'd better check on her.'

There's a layer of guilt to Otis's words that I don't have it in me to appease, because he's right – he should have checked on Alexa. Tough times and personal frustrations or not, she is his wife, and she is not okay. Clearly.

'What did you fight about?' I ask.

'Me thinking we should stop trying for a baby,' Otis admits.

The words plough through me. The thought of Kamal coming

to me and saying that . . . I can't imagine my reaction. I try to keep my composure, but my face doesn't lie.

Otis shrinks. 'Lex looked at me like that, too, but you have to understand – I can't stand seeing her like this anymore. It's killing me.'

'And that's what you said to her on the morning she disappeared?'

'That's what I tried to say, but Lex shut me down. That's why when I came home to an empty house, I left her to it. I didn't even message around to see where she was until Monday.'

As Otis stews in regret, it's hard not to draw parallels between him and Kamal. Kamal, who moved his entire life to the countryside because I said fields and clean air were what I needed. Kamal, who gives me all the space I need, even though the distance between us crucifies him.

'I know how it sounds. A grieving woman alone all the time, married to a husband who doesn't know where she is – how can they be happy? But I swear to you, Lex and I might be in a bad place, but we've never stopped loving each other. It's the losses that are killing us, but we'll get through it. We just need a fresh start.'

I wrestle my thoughts into submission, even though they warn me that Otis might be too close to the situation to face the truth. I'd never admit it out loud, but there have been many times when I've thought about leaving Kamal. Not because I don't love him, but because walking away from our shared heartache seems easier than living with it.

Maybe Alexa Clarke felt the same. But how do I tell her husband that?

'You said you thought Alexa might have gone to a friend's house or to the B&B,' I push. 'Have you asked anyone if they've seen her?'

'I have. Everyone's said they haven't heard from her, and she's not checked into the B&B, either. Something I'm sure you, and the rest of Bramblethorpe, already know.'

My sheepish expression tells Otis the answer to that. 'And I'm guessing you've tried asking Alexa yourself? Called her, texted her?' I ask.

'There's no point.' Otis opens a drawer in the kitchen and reaches inside for something. When he holds the object in the air, my eyebrows dart upwards.

'Alexa left her phone?'

'It's not as suspicious as it sounds if you know Lex. She hates technology, especially social media. Thinks it's ruining society. She often leaves her phone when she goes out. That's why I didn't panic when I found it.'

An icy wave rolls from my head to my toes at the strangeness of Otis's explanation. 'But leaving home with no phone and no car? And no one's seen or heard from Alexa in days? It doesn't make sense that you haven't gone to the police yet.'

'I know it sounds bad, but—'

'Bad? Otis, it sounds more than bad.'

Suddenly, I'm painfully aware that I am in a stranger's house and no one knows I am here. That a knife block stands on the kitchen counter, closer to Otis than to me.

With that thought ringing in my ears, I can't help thinking that, despite a long list of recent stupid decisions, the choice to come to Maple Crescent today might have been my most stupid choice of all.

CHAPTER 12

'Are you okay?' Otis asks, frowning at me.

'Me? I'm fine,' I fluster as my eyes dart around the kitchen for an exit. Gulping, I open my mouth to make an excuse to leave, but Otis speaks before I can.

'There's a reason I didn't go to the police,' he says, reaching into his back pocket for something I can't see and won't until it's too late.

'I – I've just remembered,' I stammer as I back away. 'I have to go home.'

Otis's eyebrows shoot towards his hairline. 'You're leaving already?'

'Yes. I'm sorry. I – I have something on.'

'But you said you wanted to help,' Otis presses, moving closer and bridging the gap I created between us. 'I'm only telling you any of this because you said you'd help.'

My eyes widen at the proximity of Otis's impressive arms. One look at their size and I know I would be defenceless against this man. The thought has me moving quicker until I'm practically dashing for the exit and the safety it promises.

'Lex is using her bank card,' Otis calls after me.

My footsteps slow until I come to a stop. I turn back to him.

From his back pocket, Otis pulls out his phone. 'We have separate bank accounts, but I know Lex's bank login, she knows mine.' He types something, then approaches me. 'I didn't go to the police because of this. Here, see for yourself.'

With shaking hands, I accept the phone and flick through the transactions. Relief spreads through me as Alexa's spending habits since Saturday prove that she is alive and well.

'You think the same as me, don't you?' Otis says. 'You think that if she's using her card, then she's got to be okay.'

Too relieved to speak, I nod.

'I don't want to find Lex for any reason other than to check she's all right,' Otis continues. 'She can stay away for as long as she needs to. She can go on holiday, move in with a friend, whatever. I just want to know she's okay.'

'We'll find her,' I say, my tone so confident that it melts the edges of Otis's tension.

Looking back at the phone, I study the transactions made since Saturday. Sure enough, Alexa's card has been used every day. The purchases aren't big, no more than twenty pounds each time, but they happen a few times a day.

Expanding the details on each transaction, my head tilts as names of various Manchester establishments flick by. Some are fast food places, some are supermarkets, some are bars. Clearly, Alexa Clarke left this house and let loose.

'Okay, this is great,' I say. 'Using this information, we can narrow down Alexa's location. All of her purchases have been made in Manchester. Does she know someone who lives there?'

'We know a few people, but they've all said they haven't seen her.'

'Could she be with someone you don't know?'

Otis's forehead creases. 'Maybe? I don't know when or where she'd have met them, though. Lex hasn't been the best at socialising recently.'

'Well, she's eaten out most days. At least we know she's eating.'

'I know, but who is she eating with and why isn't she eating at home?'

As Otis crumbles, I look back to the statement to give him a moment's privacy. I reread the expanded transaction information of the purchases, checking the times and locations. When I look at the details of a £3.52 purchase made on Monday, something catches my eye.

'Wait, there's something interesting about two purchases,' I say.

Otis's head snaps up. 'What?'

'Sunday and Monday, around one o'clock, Alexa bought something at the same place. Variety Food Store on Albion Street.'

Otis snatches the phone, his eyes wide. 'Why didn't I notice that?' he whispers.

'Maybe you were too busy being relieved she was using her card,' I reply with a shrug. 'But if Alexa has used her card at the same time and place twice, it suggests she'll do it again.'

Otis looks up, his eyes locked on mine. 'I need to go there,' he says.

We don't have to speak for us both to know what we're going to do next. Readjusting my handbag on my shoulder, I follow Otis out of the house, ready to visit Variety Food Store.

CHAPTER 13

Otis leads me towards the sleek car he had been driving earlier. The vehicle suits him, or the man I imagine he is when he isn't crippled with worry.

'It should take about thirty-five minutes to get to Manchester at this time,' he says, unlocking the door. 'Then I say we wait outside the store and look out for Lex. What do you think?'

'Sounds like a plan,' I reply, but I pause by the passenger door.

'Janine, we have to go. It's almost lunchtime already.'

'I know, I just . . .' I trail off. It's clear at one glance that I haven't made the most sensible choices today. With all the rumours swirling around about Otis, part of my brain wonders if I should get into a car with him alone.

Otis must be able to read my thoughts because he sighs. 'Look, you showed up on my doorstep, not the other way around,' he says. 'You don't have to come with me to Manchester if you don't want to – I'm not forcing you. All I care about is getting there as soon as possible. If it makes you more comfortable, follow me in your own car. I don't mind. We just need to go. Now.'

Making my choice, I slip into the passenger side of Otis's car without another word. I've barely clipped my seatbelt in place before he powers the vehicle down the driveway, leaving a flurry of gravel in our wake.

Bramblethorpe blurs past us as we fly down a string of country lanes. Part of me debates asking Otis to slow down, but I don't think he would pay attention to me even if I did.

As we zoom past the 'Welcome to Bramblethorpe' sign, a call comes through to Otis's phone, connecting to the dashboard thanks to Bluetooth. The name Sonya West appears on the screen, but Otis declines it abruptly.

'So,' he says before I can ask whose call he was dodging, 'you said you're an author?'

'That's right.'

Otis takes a left so sharply I need to hold onto the dashboard to stop myself from sliding out of my seat. 'What's your last name? I'm not the biggest reader, but maybe I've heard of you.'

'I write under a pen name. I'm published as S. K. Atherton. My parents' initials and my maiden name.'

Otis shoots me an impressed glance. 'S. K. Atherton, eh? I took one of your books on holiday last year.'

I hold my hands up. 'Please don't tell me you hated it. In fact, don't tell me anything you thought about it. I'm barely comfortable with people knowing I write, never mind the idea that they've read my work.'

Despite the reason for our drive, Otis manages to laugh. 'Can I tell you I didn't get around to reading it because I took work on holiday too?'

Now it's my turn to laugh. 'Yes. That's the kind of feedback my fragile ego can take.'

'Lex is a big fan of yours, though. She's the one who told me I had to read your book.'

I smile in response because smiling is easier than speaking now another tie between me and Alexa has come to light.

Pressing my lips together, I focus my attention on life outside the window. Bramblethorpe is now far behind us. Otis's driving makes a mockery of speed limits, but I find myself soothed by the intensity of the motion. Moving this fast, it feels like nothing can catch me, as if all my problems are far away.

Of course, a person can put as much distance as they like between themselves and their problems, but they always catch up. As the grey-skied edges of Manchester come into view, everything I want to outrun does exactly that.

Before being here again breaks me, I look back to Otis. 'Have you thought about what you'll say to Alexa when you see her?'

A look flickers over his face, gone before I can put a name to it.

'Honestly? I think I'll be so relieved, I won't say much. I'll just want to give her a hug.'

My lips part to ask Otis what he'll do if Alexa doesn't want to hug him, but as his hands flex against the steering wheel, I decide better of it. I don't want to make him more tense or put words to thoughts he's probably already thinking. But even if I'm silent, there's no denying that Otis needs to face the fact that maybe Alexa hasn't left for some space. Maybe, for her, this is the end of their relationship.

I glance at him, then settle my attention on the road ahead. The tarmac is filled with cars now, central Manchester's hustle and bustle well and truly around us. Red-brick buildings mingle with glossy high-rise offices and ornate Victorian façades. Shopfronts advertise sales and must-have purchases, shouting that the path to happiness is through spending more, more, more. Everywhere I look, I see colour, signage and people.

Dark spots dance in my vision as I remember who I used to be when I lived here. A woman who went for cocktails with friends. Who loved to listen to live music. I haven't done any of those things in so long. I haven't been back here in a long time, either. Not since the last loss pushed me out. The panicked tingling in my head tells me I was wise to stay away.

'The car park is up ahead, a few buildings down from the university,' Otis says, his steady voice freeing me from the jaws of anxiety. A few moments later, he swings into the four-storey concrete structure, going so fast he almost clips his wing mirror.

With a nervous glance at Otis, I wonder what's going through his mind right now. I wonder how he will feel when he sees Alexa.

Let's just hope she wants to see him, I think.

While Otis searches for a parking spot, an awful worry undermines my confidence. Alexa's disappearance is strange – stranger than even the village gossip suggested – but maybe she designed it to be that way. Maybe by helping Otis, I am doing the opposite of providing the help I want to give her.

The decision to assist a man I don't know in hunting for his wife might not be the wisest choice I could have made, but as Otis parks, it's too late for me to back out now.

'Ready?' he asks.

'Ready,' I confirm.

Together, we head towards Albion Street. The crowds are even more intimidating now I'm out of the car. Walking through the mass of people, I make my body as small as possible, but shrinking can't protect me from the sensory overload.

I'm preoccupied with putting one foot in front of the other when Otis comes to a sudden stop.

'There it is,' he says, pulling me into an empty doorway and pointing to a shabby building ahead with Variety Food Store written above the door in fading red letters. Otis can't hide his shock. 'Is this really where Lex has been going for the last few days?'

'It must be.'

'But look at it. The place is a crumbling wreck! It's not the type of shop Lex would be drawn to. So why is she?'

'I don't know, Otis. Your guess is as good as mine.'

Otis lets out a long, steady breath before glancing at his watch. 'It's half-twelve now. What should we do?'

'We should wait.'

So, that's what we do. We perch on a bench opposite the store-front, observing the people who enter the nondescript building. With it being around lunchtime, there's a steady stream of customers. Two men in business shirts buy a soft drink each and a man in a tracksuit purchases a pack of cigarettes. A herd of students stop for snacks. The customers make their purchases and go, but none of them is Alexa Clarke.

My bum is numb from sitting in the cold by the time Otis checks his watch again.

'It's after three,' he says. 'Where is she?'

'I don't know,' I reply, scanning the street to see if Alexa has miraculously appeared. 'Maybe she didn't come here today?'

'But Lex has gone to this shop at one o'clock for the last two days. Why would she stop today?'

'Maybe she isn't in Manchester anymore, or maybe she saw us waiting outside and walked away.'

'Why would she do that?'

'Because she might not be ready to see you, Otis,' I say softly, but my answer only upsets him further.

'No, that can't be it.' Otis pulls out his phone and logs into Alexa's bank. He chokes when the page loads.

'What?' I ask.

Otis is so distressed, he can't reply. Instead, he turns the phone to me. Sure enough, there's a transaction logged at Variety Food Store two hours ago.

'How did we miss her, Janine?' he croaks. 'How?'

'I don't know.' I reach for the phone so I can check the transaction, mistrusting of its validity even though it's written in black and white. 'I don't think we did. We couldn't have.'

'But there's a transaction here, on her card.'

'I know, but maybe …' My voice wobbles, wishing I didn't have to be the person seeing the situation as it is, not as they wish it would be. 'Otis, have you stopped to think that maybe Alexa isn't the person using her card?'

Otis's head jerks back as if he's been slapped. 'Who else would be using it?'

'I don't know. Maybe it was stolen. Maybe someone Alexa is with is using it on her behalf. Either way, Alexa hasn't used her card today, no matter what her account says. Maybe she never has.'

As those chilling words hang in the air, Otis pulls back.

'That's bullshit,' he says, taking the phone from me. 'Lex has to be using her card.'

'Otis, we've sat here for hours. We haven't seen Alexa.'

But no matter how calmly I speak, my words inspire a fear in Otis that he can only handle by being defensive.

'Fine, maybe someone is buying food for her,' he snaps. 'Maybe she's given her card to a friend, I don't know. But something weird is happening here, and I'm going to prove it.'

With that, Otis sets off towards the store.

'Wait! Where are you going?' I shout, chasing after him, but he's too enraged to answer.

An electronic chime rings out to announce our entry to Variety Food Store. I'm unsurprised to find the shop is as small and worn as its exterior suggests. Confectionery and carb-based snacks fill the head-height shelves, and a stand of gossip magazines lines the back wall. In the corner, a dated drinks fridge emits a low humming noise.

Otis doesn't stop to take any of this in. Instead, he walks to the teenager texting behind the counter, clearing his throat to command his attention.

'Have you seen this woman?' Otis asks, holding up his phone to show a photo of Alexa.

The teenager shrugs, barely looking up from the message he's typing. His rudeness provokes Otis enough to slam his hand on the counter.

'I said, have you seen this woman?' he barks at the now wide-eyed teenager.

'Hey, let's take this down a notch,' I say, pulling the phone from Otis's hand. 'I'm sorry about my friend. His wife hasn't been home in a few days. I'm sure you can understand why he's upset. That's why we need to know if you've seen this woman in here recently?'

This time when he's shown Alexa's photograph, the teenager studies the image. His eyes narrow, but then he shakes his head. 'Sorry, never seen her before.'

'Please, think carefully,' I urge. 'She might look different than she does in this picture. Maybe she's cut her hair, maybe she's not wearing make-up, maybe—'

The teenager shakes his head to cut me off. 'I told you, I've not seen her.'

'That's impossible,' Otis says, taking the phone back and holding it closer to the cashier. 'Look again. Look at Lex's face.'

'I've seen it, but I've still no idea who she is.'

'You're lying!' Otis cries. 'My wife's bank statement says she's been coming here every day at one o'clock. It says she was here today, so you must have seen her.'

'Mate, I'm telling you, I've never seen that woman before.'

Stumbling backwards, Otis's jaw slackens. 'You must have,' he whispers. 'Otherwise, what the hell have I been doing for the last few days?'

As Otis's upset takes over, I make the mistake of reaching for him. 'Otis,' I begin, but the sound of my voice wakes his self-consciousness.

'Forget it. He doesn't know anything,' he sniffs before fleeing the store.

Pained, I watch him go before facing the cashier once more. 'You're sure you haven't seen Alexa?'

When the teenager shakes his head, I follow Otis out onto Albion Street.

It's started to rain while we were in the store. People scurry past us, desperate to reach the comfort of their workplaces. I follow Otis as he ploughs through the damp streets with reckless abandon.

'Otis, stop!' I demand when he knocks into yet another bewildered stranger.

Otis takes a few lurching steps onwards before sense tells him to follow my instructions. When he turns to face me, there's a weariness to his movements that's haunting.

'Where is she, Janine? Where's Lex?'

'I don't know,' I reply, even though I know from the manic air surrounding Otis that he wasn't really wanting me to answer – he simply needed to get the words out in the open.

'I never should have left when she was so upset,' he groans, bending at the waist with his hands clamped to his thighs. 'What if she went out in a state and something bad happened? What if she got hurt? What if—'

'What ifs don't help right now,' I cut in. 'You need to calm down and call the police.'

Otis flicks his attention to me, his expression tight with terror. 'The police?'

'Alexa isn't using her card. And the fact of the matter is that no one has seen or heard from your wife in days. The police need to know what's going on, Otis. It's time.'

CHAPTER 14

Alexa

Three days gone

Delirium. That was the point Alexa had been driven to. Hollering for help until she passed out. Hallucinating that strange creatures with gnarled features were in the room, drawing nearer and nearer. Weakened and dehydrated to the point she was sure death would come for her.

But each time Alexa closed her eyes, certain it would be the last thing she ever did, she would still wake up. More than waking, she would wake to find a needle in the crook of her arm. Attached to it was an IV drip. Alexa didn't know whether to laugh or cry at the sight.

The drip proved one thing: Alexa was not meant to die here. Not yet. Someone out there wanted to keep her alive.

The worry was: what did they want her alive for?

In all her time in captivity, Alexa had not seen her attacker. Her injuries meant she wasn't conscious for their visit, but she knew she wasn't alone in the building. She'd heard someone moving around beneath her. She'd heard their car start and their TV blaring. She'd even woken up from a delirious slumber to the sound of the door to the white room closing.

One thing Alexa never heard, though, was the pound of footsteps running to her aid.

'What do you want from me?' she had roared when she first saw the drip embedded in her arm, but there was no answer. Whoever had captured Alexa did not want to speak.

But what *did* they want?

Alexa had no idea. She had no idea about anything. Why her? What had she done to deserve this? The questions rattled around in her aching skull, but no answer came alongside them. Only more pain. More fear.

And as more time passed, more uncertainty that she would leave this room alive.

CHAPTER 15

I drive us through the rain-soaked streets of Lancashire, back to Bramblethorpe. Even though driving Otis's expensive car terrifies me, I have no choice but to take over. He's too numb from shock to be behind the wheel. Plus, he has an important phone call to make.

With my teeth embedded in my bottom lip, I focus on the road as he speaks to the police, informing them about Alexa's last known whereabouts. My features remain impassive as if I'm not listening, but I can't help it. I mine Otis's every word for details.

How does a woman go into her garden and simply disappear?

Was Alexa really going for a walk, or was something else going on?

Does Otis sound defensive over the fact that he waited so long to call the police, or is it shame?

I don't know the answer to any of my questions. All I know is my fear that something bad has happened.

Eventually, Otis hangs up. 'They're sending someone to the house,' he replies. 'They said it shouldn't be too long.'

I glance at the route displayed on my phone map. 'We're only ten minutes away from your house.'

Otis grunts in response, and I leave him to his thoughts.

When Bramblethorpe comes into view, a self-conscious prickle ignites my skin. People out and about watch Otis's car pass, whispering to one another as soon as they see it. But it's when they notice me driving, not him, that their whispers really kick up a notch.

'Uh-oh,' Otis mutters darkly. 'The Bramblethorpe bitching brigade have spotted us. According to the locals, we'll be having an affair before you know it.'

My heart lurches, praying for Kamal's sake as much as my own that that's not the case. I've no idea how I could ever explain what I've done today in a way that would make sense to my cool, collected, rational husband.

When I reach Maple Crescent, Dorrit is in her garden, bundled in layers to protect herself from the chill. Magnus sits by her side. She straightens as I pass, but I don't wave. The less attention I can bring to myself by Otis's side, the better.

Spinning the steering wheel, I turn Otis's car into his driveway. There, I find a white four-wheel drive already parked outside the house.

I've barely parked before an attractive woman leaps out of the white car. She's in her mid-thirties, although the cosmetic injections she favours try to suggest otherwise. That's not to say they're not well done, though. They're subtle, just the right amount to plump here and tighten there. Her auburn hair hangs in long, flowing curls, and her lips are graced with the lightest touch of nude lipstick. But what strikes me most is how she frowns when she sees me, and how relieved Otis is to see her.

'Gabby,' he exhales, slipping out of the car and falling heavily into the woman's arms. The familiarity of their embrace tells me that they have a longstanding relationship, but the positioning of Otis's hands at the top of Gabby's back suggests it's friendly, not romantic. Still, I hesitate, uneasy at intruding, especially when Gabby takes Otis's head in her hands to speak to him.

When I exit the vehicle, the woman pulls back, her stance protective. 'Who are you?'

'This is Janine,' Otis replies on my behalf. 'She's helping me look for Alexa. Janine, this is Gabby, my best friend.'

'Nice to meet you,' I say, sticking out my hand. Gabby shakes it, but her expression remains cool.

'Are you a friend of Alexa's or . . .' Gabby's voice trails off in a way that's loaded.

'Not exactly,' I admit. 'I mean, I knew Alexa. Well, I met her once. I—'

'Once?' Gabby echoes, shooting Otis an alarmed look. He shakes it off.

'Gabby's a lawyer,' Otis explains. 'The best there is, but a little prone to paranoia.' He nudges his friend with his elbow to lighten the comment. 'Janine's here as a friend, Gabs. She writes thrillers under the name S. K. Atherton. She works with the police when researching for her books. I thought she'd be a good person to help. You know how everyone else around here has been.'

As Gabby nods, eyeing me with shrewd curiosity, I shift awkwardly on my feet.

'I can't believe you came,' Otis says to Gabby.

'Where else would I be? You need someone by your side right now.'

Otis smiles gratefully before looking at me. 'I told Gabby Lex had left again. She's taken a few days off work to help me through it all.'

'What are friends for?' Gabby chimes in, but from the way she's looking at Otis, I can't help thinking that the label *friend* isn't one she wants.

'I need a friend more than ever now,' Otis says, his voice cracking. Instinctively, Gabby reaches for him.

'What's happened?'

I wait for Otis to speak, but he's too upset to do so.

'Alexa's bank card,' I say, clearing my throat. 'Otis was under the impression that Alexa was okay because she's been spending on her card.'

'Let me guess, another shopping spree?' Gabby mutters. 'If she's not punishing Otis by walking out, then she's hitting the plastic – hard.'

'Not quite,' I reply. 'We traced Alexa's purchases to a convenience store in Manchester. We went there to see if we could find her, but she never showed up.'

Gabby grunts like she expected as much, but her already stiff features freeze further when I continue.

'We think Alexa's card might have been stolen. We're waiting for the police now.'

'The police?' Gabby echoes, her mouth agape.

'Something's going on here, Gabs,' Otis croaks. 'I don't know if I think that Lex has just gone away for a few days anymore. I think . . . I don't know what I think, but it's not good.'

Otis's head has barely ducked before Gabby's arms find him. She holds him steady, whispering that it will be okay. All the while I watch her, wondering how someone who has turned so pale can make such a bold promise.

CHAPTER 16

When we enter the house, Otis goes straight to the kitchen and pours himself a whisky. He offers one to me and Gabby, but we both decline. We watch Otis down his drink, check the time, then excuse himself to go to the bathroom. His watery eyes tell me that's more to compose himself than for a bathroom break.

As soon as Gabby and I are alone, she turns to me. 'Why are you really here?'

The question is so direct, I can't help but flinch. 'I want to find Alexa and make sure she's okay.'

'But why? You don't know her. You don't know Otis.'

'Can't someone want to do a good thing?' I say, but as Gabby's already sceptical expression increases, I shrink. 'There's nothing weird to it, I promise.'

Gabby lets out a small scoff then folds her arms. 'You do know she leaves him all the time, don't you? That this is just what she does? Makes everyone worry, breaks his heart, then comes back and expects us to act as if nothing happened?'

A defensiveness prickles my skin. 'From what I've heard, she's going through a lot.'

'And so is Otis. The miscarriages crushed him, too, you know, not that anyone talks to him about it. They just expect him to be okay. To carry on as if he isn't cut up on the inside.'

My cheeks fire into life, thinking of how in all our losses, people always ask how I am. Very rarely do they do the same to Kamal.

Glancing at the door Otis just exited from, Gabby moves closer. 'Look, I don't want to sound like a bitch, but you need to leave. You can say you being here isn't weird all you like, but it is. And if the police are coming over soon, they won't want random people hanging around.'

'But I—'

'No,' she cuts in. 'Do you have any idea how hard things are for Otis right now? Lex has left him *again*. He can't take another hit like this. He's hanging on by a thread. He doesn't need you here, stirring up trouble.'

'I'm not stirring trouble. I'm just offering to help.'

'If you want to help, then leave.'

'I can't. I was there when Otis realised Alexa wasn't using her card. The police will want to speak to me.'

Gabby's nostrils flare, but she can't deny that I am right. Turning away, she leaves me to wander around the impressive room while we wait for Otis to return.

I find myself being drawn to the wall facing the sofas, which is a giant built-in bookcase. It has been expertly styled, with vases and small sculptures that probably cost more than most people's monthly salaries sitting alongside beautifully framed photographs. One is from Otis and Alexa's wedding. It's a snap I didn't see on social media, but it's just as stunning as the ones I did. Alexa's emerald ring sparkles even more in print. The only thing more beautiful than it is her smile.

Further along the shelf, I spot another shot from the wedding. This time, it's an image of the entire wedding party. Sure enough, Gabby is in it, standing two people away from Otis.

'That's one of my favourite photos,' Gabby says, coming up behind me. 'Otis bucked convention and had me as a groomsman. Fun idea, right?'

Looking at the image again, I notice Gabby's dress is the same grey as the groomsmen's suits. I wonder how much it stung her, to be part of Otis's big day as a friend when she wanted to be his bride.

'Are you and Alexa close too?' I ask.

Gabby doesn't react, almost as if she was anticipating this question. 'Not as close as I am to Otis, but that's to be expected because we grew up together.' Her tone is guarded, almost as if she's challenging me to read more into her relationship with Otis.

Otis enters the room at that moment, carrying an empty whisky glass.

'Gabs and Lex get along great,' he says, sinking into one of the sofas wearily. 'I'm lucky. I know how awkward it can be when your spouse doesn't get on with your friends. One of our other friends, Drew? His wife hates me.'

'Only because you got him so drunk on his stag do, he missed his flight home,' Gabby says.

Otis laughs, but his smile soon fades. 'Lex was so unimpressed with me that day. I'll never forget the look on her face when I got home.'

Wordlessly, Gabby slides from my side and goes to him, taking his hand in hers.

'What if something's happened to her, Gabby?' he croaks. 'I left for work on Saturday and didn't look back once. I just wanted peace from it all, you know? But now...'

'You don't know anything bad has happened,' Gabby soothes.

'No, but I know nothing good has.'

Gabby's lips open, a perky distraction on the tip of her tongue, but one look at Otis and she knows it won't cut it. She falls silent. We all do, glancing at the time because until the police come, all we can do is wait.

The atmosphere before their arrival is tense. The wind whistling outside breaks the oppressive absence of conversation, but no one comments on it. Never have I witnessed weather mimic a mood so perfectly – a dark, brooding sky and rainfall lashing the windows, landing like teardrops. It's almost poetic.

When sitting becomes too much, Otis paces the room, fizzing with manic energy. His phone ringing interrupts the silence, but every time he sees who is calling, he looks like he wants to throw his phone at the wall. By the sixth call, Otis shuts his phone in a kitchen drawer.

While there, he pours himself another whisky, but before he takes a sip, he pushes the glass over and walks away. Amber liquid pools across the counter, trickling onto the floor.

'Otis, sit down,' Gabby instructs, hurrying to the scene to tidy the mess.

Otis follows her command. He slumps onto a seat at the dining table, absent-mindedly running his finger back and forth across the edge of it.

'Lex hated this table,' he says. 'Mum got it for us as a wedding present. Well, I paid for it, but Mum picked it. A family table, she called it. Twelve seats. Lex said, "What family has ten children?", but Mum wouldn't budge. She was adamant that a dining table is the heart of a home. A place where happy memories are made.'

I think of the dining table in my own home, the wood chipped and stained by glasses of red wine from nights with friends I've allowed to slip out of my life. That table was where I wrote my first novel, back when I saw myself as too much of a novice to buy a desk.

With the money I received from my book deal, I purchased one as a sign of commitment to my new career, but sometimes I find myself pining for the life I had when I was at the dining table. Back then, there was a simplicity to writing I'll never have again. There was no pressure, no expectation, just the flow of someone who had a story to tell.

'I should have put my foot down,' Otis says, pulling my focus. 'Said no to the table and the expectation that we'd be able to fill it with a big family. Maybe Lex would have been happier then. Maybe things wouldn't have ended up like this.'

'Otis,' I begin, but he ignores me and looks at Gabby.

'How long has it been since I called the police?' he asks.

Gabby's expression tightens as she checks the time on her phone. 'Not long, you've only been home an hour and a half.'

Otis groans. 'Great. Who knows how long they'll be? It's one of the perks of living in the middle of nowhere – the worst police presence known to mankind.' Defeated, Otis drops his head in his hands. His fingers curl, his nails pressing into the top of his skull like he's about to tear the skin free from the bone.

'Otis,' Gabby begins, but when he looks up, a fierce determination has taken over him.

'I can't sit here. It's driving me insane.'

'Don't be silly. You need to be here when the police arrive.'

'I can't do it, Gabs. I can't sit and act like every second isn't torture, thinking of all the times I was opposite my wife and never tried to make things better for her.'

'What are you doing?' Gabby asks, her voice rising an octave when Otis stands up.

'I'm going out.'

'Out? Out where?'

Otis leaves the room without answering.

'Otis, you need to be here when the police arrive!' Gabby shouts, rushing after him. I stay put, more aware of my position as an outsider here than ever before.

Seconds later, Otis storms back into the kitchen wearing a raincoat over his clothes. 'Lex left the house from this room. If I retrace her steps, maybe I'll find something.'

'But you don't know where her steps took her,' Gabby argues.

'She left through that door,' Otis says, pointing to the bifold doors. 'She had to have gone somewhere from there.'

'But you don't know where!'

'Do you think I don't know that?' Otis cries, his distress rising until it sounds like it's tearing his throat. 'Do you think it's not killing me that for the last few days when I should have put everything into finding her, I listened to my stung pride and did nothing? It's all I can think about! But I have to try, Gabby. I have to try.'

Gabby follows Otis, her face the picture of confusion, but I understand him. Otis knows that when he leaves those doors, he won't find Alexa. That's not what matters, though. Hunting as if he will find answers will burn off the energy flowing through him – and ease his guilt.

Ignoring another plea from Gabby to stay inside, Otis stomps towards the rain-splattered doors, pausing when he reaches them.

'Are you coming, Janine?' he asks.

Gabby's jaw drops, but I don't need to think twice. I grab my coat and follow Otis out into the garden, joining the hunt for Alexa Clarke.

CHAPTER 17

Wind howls through the trees as we set off across the manicured grounds surrounding the Clarkes' home, the torches on our phones lighting the way. The dense curtain of fog that has threatened to fall for the last few hours has descended fully now, blanketing the area in an eeriness that makes me long for the comfort of the warm fire at home.

Home, the place I should be now that darkness has fallen. But I can't leave now. Who knows what we might find out here. Who knows if the next few minutes will lead us to Alexa Clarke.

Otis walks ahead, his purposeful pace one I have to jog to keep up with.

'What's the plan here?' I call after him.

'I don't know,' he admits, wiping raindrops from his face. 'I thought if we retraced Lex's steps, something might come to us.' He stops in the centre of the garden. 'The problem is, we don't know what her steps were. We don't know where she went. CCTV shows her going into the garden, then we lose her.'

Otis's shoulders drop. Barely ten steps from the door and he's already lost confidence in his search. Wind batters his body, nature's attack doing little to elevate his spirits.

I step forward, fighting to be heard over the feral cry of the weather. 'Are you sure there's no way Alexa could have gone to the front of the house without being seen by CCTV?'

'That's right. She'd have gone out here and then … well, then I don't know.'

I look around the darkened garden. Encased by towering trees, it's a beautiful spot filled with raised flowerbeds and seating options for outdoor dining. On a summer's day, I imagine there aren't many nicer places to recline with a book. The problem is, it's not summer. It's November, and imagining anyone lounging outside at this time of year is impossible.

'Is there a way to get out of the garden without using the driveway? Maybe through the woods?' I ask, pointing to the trees ahead.

'I mean, you can climb the fence and cut through the trees to the fields, but why would Lex do that when she could use the public footpath?'

'Maybe she fancied an adventure?'

Those words are enough to send Otis over the fence and into the thick of the wilderness. I follow close behind, clambering over the waist-high horizontal slats and landing clumsily on the other side.

The strip of woodland we trek through is beautiful in a mysterious, other-worldly way, but it's surprisingly narrow. When we emerge through it on the other side, we're confronted by a field of long grass. *Fields that go on forever* – that's what Alexa calls them, according to Otis. The time of day and the weather make it hard for me to confirm the accuracy of that. The fog is even thicker here than it was in the garden, the world before me barely visible through the mist.

'I feel like we're trespassing,' I confess, glancing around.

'Don't worry, this is public land,' Otis says. 'Anyone can walk here.'

Although the words were said to put me at ease, I can see that they spark a worry in Otis that anyone could have been here with his wife. Someone she didn't know.

Someone who might have hurt her.

'Lex!' Otis roars, the boom of his voice lost in the vast nothingness. He powers forward, swatting the long, wet grass to form a path. 'Lex, where are you?'

The fact that only the weather responds to his call is crushing.

Together, we push on through the field, delving deeper into the grey-veiled world while scouring the grass for clues. With the help of my phone's torch, I find an empty crisp packet, a child's lost glove and a squashed plastic bottle. Signs of life, but not signs of Alexa Clarke.

The rain falls heavier, pelting down around us. Each droplet makes a dull pattering sound as it splats against Otis's raincoat.

'Lex!' he shouts, moving faster. The act of searching for his wife rather than waiting for her to return has awoken something animalistic in him. 'Alexa!'

Hearing Otis scream into the abyss and knowing there is little chance that a response will come to him breaks my heart. I search for something to say before he tears his vocal cords.

'Tell me about this field,' I call, pushing grass aside to catch up to him. 'If she went this way, knowing more about the area might give us an idea of where she could have gone from here.'

Otis gulps then studies his surroundings once more. 'There's not much to say. These fields don't lead anywhere other than to more woodland.'

'How do you know that?'

'We walked them all the time when we first moved here. We'd do a loop around the fields then go back to the house. A few times we even...' Otis looks back at me, suddenly shy.

'It's okay, Otis. Two consenting adults having sex outdoors doesn't make me blush.'

'Perks of living in the country, eh?' Otis quips, swallowing the memory. 'I don't think the fields mean anything to Lex, though, other than them being somewhere she likes to walk. I told you, she loves nature.'

Standing in the cold and damp, it's hard to see why anyone would love this place, but then I think of Alexa alone in her house all day, and the freedom of this open space seems more appealing than anything.

'How did we get here, Janine?' Otis whispers. 'Lex goes out every day, yet I have no idea what she does or where she goes.' I hang my head at his painful admission. 'I thought I was doing the right thing by leaving her alone. It was ... it was easier that way. Easier than arguing. Easier than seeing her in pain.'

So much is said around those words. So much regret, so much anger – all of which Otis aims at himself. I open my mouth to say something comforting, but Otis sets off again before I get the chance.

'Lex!' he hollers.

I use the lull in conversation to take in the scenery as far as my torchlight allows me to see. My pace slows as once again I note how isolated it is where Alexa and Otis live. Anything could happen here, but who would be there to witness it?

The question makes me shiver, but then I notice Otis striding further away, so far ahead I almost lose him in the fog.

'Otis!' I shout, scurrying after him. 'Maybe we should go back to the house?'

If he can hear me, he pretends he can't.

'I said maybe we should go back?'

Suddenly, Otis stops and faces me. He looks utterly dejected.

I approach slowly, giving Otis the time he needs to feel his pain. Out here is probably the only time he will be able to do so. We both know that as soon as we go back to the house, Gabby will be on hand with forced brightness to stop him giving in to his hurt.

'This is ridiculous,' he says. 'I'm trawling a field in the dark for clues about someone who might or might not have been here days ago. What am I hoping to find, a map telling me where Lex is? Unlikely, so what am I looking for? Grass? Mud? Litter?'

Otis breathes in a ragged breath and prepares himself to speak again, but something on the grass catches his eye. My heart pounds as Otis stares at whatever he has spotted, but then he scoffs.

'A tennis ball. My wife is missing, and a tennis ball is all I can find.'

Otis bends to retrieve the ball, then spins on his heel and launches it through the air. The neon sphere soars across the field, swallowed by the fog before I can see where it lands.

'Let's hope I find Lex before that dog finds its missing ball,' he mutters.

I continue my approach, slower than before but more concerned. When I reach Otis, I rest my hand on his forearm. 'Come on. Let's go back. We've seen enough.'

Otis doesn't argue. He just trails alongside me, taking in fraught gulps of air as he walks away from the hope that somewhere in the grass, there's a clue about where his wife is.

CHAPTER 18

Gabby opens the doors as soon as she sees us trudging through the garden.

'They're here,' she calls.

Otis breaks into a run, reaching the house before I'm even halfway down the path. By the time I make it to the open doors, Gabby has wrapped a towel around his shoulders and steered him towards a sofa.

Two formally dressed strangers stand beside the dining table, silently observing the goings on in the room. I can tell by their expressions that they see what I see when I watch Otis and Gabby. The familiarity of their touch, the intimacy they share. But what strikes me most about the two new people I am faced with isn't their curious observation but their commanding presence. When Otis called the police, I assumed uniformed officers would be sent to take preliminary statements, but the strangers in Otis's house are most definitely not regular on-the-beat officers.

I gulp as the seriousness of the situation sinks in. One of them looks at me – the female of the duo. Her gaze is penetrative, and every bad thing I have ever done comes bubbling to the forefront of my mind. I'm about to confess that when I was seven, I stole a chocolate bar from the supermarket, but she speaks before I get the chance.

'Please, come in,' she calls.

Obediently, I slip inside the house and slide the doors shut behind me.

Over the years, I have spoken with officers at all levels of seniority for research purposes, but this isn't research – it's real life. Being confronted by the officers' closed but curious expressions makes my bones freeze, and not just because of the icy rain that has seeped through to them.

While I move towards the dining table, I make notes in my mind of their appearance. The woman is in her early forties. She wears an ill-fitting, cheap suit, but her natural aura of authority compensates for her shabby outfit. While her expression is businesslike, the lines around her eyes confess she is someone who laughs a lot when not in situations like this.

The man beside her is a little younger, with round cheeks and a receding hairline. His creased white shirt tells of a long day behind a desk. He doesn't command the same respect the woman does, but from the way he stands, I can tell he possesses an attitude that does its best to overcompensate for that.

'Mrs Rey, is it?' he says.

'It's pronounced "rye", actually, but you can call me Janine,' I reply.

'Janine Rai, also known as S. K. Atherton. Gabby here has filled us in. We're big fans,' the woman replies. 'I'm DS Fatima Rani. This is DS Christopher Mullins.'

Gabby leaves Otis's side to hand me a towel. 'I thought you might need this.'

'Good thinking. It's torrential out there,' DS Rani says, nodding to the world outside the window. My stomach plummets as I realise how dark it is – and therefore, how late.

Kamal.

I glance at the clock on Otis's oven. It's well after six o'clock already. Kamal's anxious face flashes in my mind. I am never not there when he comes home, not since we moved to Bramblethorpe. Not since what happened in Manchester.

'Do you need me to stay, or . . . ?' I ask awkwardly.

'It's my understanding that you were with Mr Clarke today, is that right?' DS Mullins replies.

'That's right.'

'In that case, it would be better if you could. We will need to ask you a few questions.'

I debate asking if I can make a quick call first, but the way the detectives move without waiting for a response silences me. Pulling my phone from my pocket, I fire a quick text to Kamal.

I'll be home in a bit. Will fill you in when I'm back x

I have no idea what I will say, but as I press send, I'm just grateful I got the chance to message my husband some kind of reassurance.

The detectives sit on one sofa, Gabby and Otis on another. I take the third, burningly conscious of the mess my sodden clothes will leave on the fabric.

While DS Mullins pulls a notepad from his pocket, DS Rani leans forward to address Otis. 'Mr Clarke, your call earlier said that you would like to report your wife as missing.'

Those words supercharge the atmosphere with electricity.

'Report my wife as missing,' Otis repeats, then he dissolves into tears.

Panicked, Gabby glances at me, but I'm as clueless about what to do as she is. DS Rani and DS Mullins, on the other hand, don't look alarmed. They sit calmly, waiting for the story to unfold.

'Alexa hasn't been seen since Saturday morning,' Gabby says, her voice faltering at the responsibility of being the one to recall this twisted tale. 'She left the house while Otis was at work. We've no idea where she is.'

DS Mullins cocks his head. 'Today is Tuesday. Is there a reason why you're only just reporting Alexa missing?'

'Alexa tends to go away whenever she argues with Otis, then returns a few days later,' Gabby explains. 'We thought that's what was going on here.'

'And were you arguing with your wife the day she went missing, Mr Clarke?'

Gabby's cheeks colour, but Otis is so defeated he barely even notices her distress.

'Lex … we've … we're not …' As Otis drops his head, Gabby reaches for his hand. She squeezes it tight until she spots the detectives watching her every move.

'We thought Alexa was taking time away after a difficult few months. She was using her bank card, so Otis and Janine went to Manchester to see if they could find her. They never saw Alexa, but her account recorded a transaction. Janine thinks the card might have been stolen,' Gabby blurts.

Her distraction tactic works. Every eye that was on her and Otis is now on me.

'It's just a theory,' I say, swallowing hard.

'May I ask, Mrs Rai, how did you become involved in this situation?' DS Mullins asks. 'As a childhood friend, Miss Findlay's role here is one I understand, but as far as I can tell, you're a stranger.'

There's something in DS Mullins's tone that ruffles me, but getting into a battle of wits with a dismissive authority figure is what a sassy protagonist in a book would do, and I am most definitely not one of those. I'm just a woman, seemingly in way over her head.

'I heard Alexa Clarke was missing,' I say, furious with my voice for betraying how dry my throat is. 'I thought I might be able to help.'

'And why's that?'

'Because I write about things like this.'

DS Mullins's lips twitch with ridicule.

'Well, by the sound of it, it's a good job you joined the search,' DS Rani says, shooting her colleague a warning look. 'Otherwise, who knows when we would have been called.'

Gabby's cheeks burn on Otis's behalf, but I'm too busy justifying myself to care about how he looks in all of this.

'I'm only here to help,' I say. 'I looked at the information Otis had and pieced together the clues. It's all there on Alexa's bank statement – the day and time her card has been used at Variety Food Store.'

DS Rani turns to Otis. 'May I see the statement?'

Otis nods and loads the transaction history on his phone. When he leans across the coffee table to hand it over, I notice he's trembling.

DS Rani looks at the screen, scrolls a little, then hands the phone to DS Mullins for him to inspect. 'You mentioned earlier that Alexa would leave after arguments,' she continues. 'How often would you say that happened?'

'Every few months or so,' Otis admits. 'It hasn't always been that way. Just over the last eighteen months. Ever since ... ever since the second miscarriage.'

The sad silence that follows Otis's words drains the room of colour. DS Mullins goes to speak again, but DS Rani gives him a subtle shake of the head. In the extra pause she provides, she allows Otis room to process having to admit his most personal grief to two strangers.

'I'm sorry to hear about your losses, Mr Clarke,' DS Rani says. 'I appreciate you telling us about them. Context like that is vital for us to assess Alexa's wellbeing before she disappeared.'

Otis nods, his chin wobbling at the mention of Alexa's wellbeing.

'When Alexa left, where would she usually go?'

'To a friend's house. She's stayed at hotels before, too, and the village B&B.'

'Have any of Alexa's friends seen her since she left?'

'Not that they've told me, no,' Otis replies, sinking into the worry of the words.

The detectives exchange a look before DS Mullins takes over the questioning. 'Before the discovery of the stolen card, was there any reason to suspect that Alexa might not have simply gone away for a few days?'

Otis shakes his head.

'Are you sure about that?'

When Otis doesn't reply, DS Mullins turns Otis's phone back around to face him.

'How about the fact that Alexa Clarke withdrew two thousand pounds in cash from her account the day before she went missing?'

CHAPTER 19

Gabby and I jerk our heads in Otis's direction, but he avoids our gaze. DS Mullins, on the other hand, can't take his eyes off us.

'I see you've not been broadcasting that information,' he replies, handing DS Rani Otis's phone. As she flicks through Alexa's statement, her concern deepens.

I curse myself for not examining Alexa's transactions before she disappeared. Otis had been so open about his marriage, I felt inclined to believe him. Judging by this news, I was wrong to do that.

Otis rubs his lips together nervously before speaking. 'What are you doing?'

DS Rani ignores him, then lowers the phone. 'Mr Clarke, over the last four months, your wife has repeatedly withdrawn large chunks of cash from her account. Is this something you were aware of?'

Gabby opens her mouth to reply on Otis's behalf, but when he nods, she is silenced.

'I only found out about the money when Lex was gone,' he croaks. 'That's the first time I checked her account, I swear.'

The blow of Otis's admission collapses my lungs. He told me there was nothing unusual about Alexa's activity around the time she disappeared. From the look on Gabby's face, I can tell he told her the same, too.

'Do you know how much money Alexa has withdrawn in total, Mr Clarke?' DS Rani asks.

'Just over – just over twelve thousand pounds,' Otis admits.

Floored, I lean back against the sofa cushions.

'Twelve thousand pounds is a lot of money,' DS Mullins states.

'I know. I mean, I know *now*. Lex was already gone when I found out what she'd been doing.'

'To clarify, you say you didn't know your wife was making large cash withdrawals from her personal account until after she disappeared?'

'Yes. No. I don't know.' Otis rests his head in his hands. 'I just want Lex back. I just want her home.'

As Otis crumbles, DS Rani and DS Mullins exchange a glance.

'Okay, I think it's best we take statements from each of you individually now,' DS Rani says. 'Is there a space we could use for this?'

'Take this room,' Gabby replies, her shock concealed as she once again adopts the role of Otis's protector. 'There's a snug next door. Otis and I can wait in there while you talk to Janine. I'm sure she needs to get home soon.'

The reminder of home makes my heart ache. I can only guess how late I'm going to be after this bombshell, but I'm too nervous to ask if I can send Kamal another reassuring text.

As Gabby puts her arm around Otis and leads him away, I watch them go. There's a stiffness to their movements I hadn't seen earlier, and unease clings to me accordingly.

When they've gone, the detectives turn to me and smile. Their smiles aren't unkind, but I wouldn't describe them as friendly, either.

'Well, what a strange situation this is,' DS Rani says. 'Without you, who knows when the police would have been involved. It doesn't seem like Otis was in a rush to contact us.'

Hearing DS Rani verbalise my own nagging thoughts makes them scream louder. I press my hands together, as if praying for Alexa Clarke.

'When you first met Otis, did it concern you that he hadn't gone to the police about his wife's disappearance?' she asks, a question so loaded with implication that no amount of light tone could lift it.

'A little,' I admit, 'but Otis's explanation made sense at the time, and we thought Alexa was okay because it looked like she was spending money. Otis was upset, so I didn't question him too much, but maybe I should have.'

'Looked for the plot holes, eh?' DS Mullins jokes, but his words highlight how strange he finds my presence here.

'I'd like to hear your take on what's happened,' DS Rani says. 'Would you mind going back to the start of how you became involved? Try to include as much detail as possible, no matter how small. Mullins here will note down what you say, and I might butt in with a question, but for the most part we'd like to hear the story from your perspective.'

'An S. K. Atherton exclusive, if you will,' DS Mullins comments.

Ignoring him, I recite the events of the last two days. While I speak, DS Mullins makes notes. DS Rani, on the other hand, watches me. She nods and asks the odd clarifying question, but for the most part she lets me run through what's happened in my own words, at my own pace.

When I've finished, I sit back, spent. Out of the corner of my eye, I notice that the world outside is well and truly wrapped in night-time now. The knotting in my stomach tightens as I think of Kamal, clueless as to where I am and no doubt worried.

'Thank you for your time, Janine. You've been a great help. If you could provide DS Mullins with your contact details in case we need to get in touch again, that would be great. But for now, I think it's time we let you go home.'

'Are you sure?' I ask, but I've already risen to my feet.

I write down my phone number and address, then DS Rani walks me to the kitchen door. 'Can I give you a word of advice before you head off?' she says. 'Look after yourself, okay? However good your intentions are, unusual situations often have unusual solutions. Ones you don't want to get involved with.'

With that, DS Rani opens the door for me to leave. I don't hesitate on taking her up on that offer. Ducking out of the kitchen, I hurry down the hallway while she goes to get Otis.

I hear DS Rani say, 'Mr Clarke? We're ready for you now.'

I hear Otis follow her.

I hear the kitchen door close as he is taken into the kitchen to deliver his statement.

Not once do I turn to look at him.

My fried nerves jangle as the front door draws closer. A desperation to flee this house and the deception trapped within its walls takes over my body, but someone hissing my name stops me in my tracks.

Emerging from the snug, Gabby scurries towards me. She grabs my arm and pulls me further away from the kitchen. Her nails dig into my flesh, but she's too irate to care.

'Did you know about Alexa syphoning money?' she asks.

I shake my head. 'Did you?'

Gabby shakes hers, too. 'It doesn't look good, does it?'

'What part, Alexa syphoning money or Otis hiding the fact that she was?'

Gabby opens her mouth to defend Otis, but she stops because, really, what can she say back to that? 'I don't know why Otis would lie. It's a strange detail to hide.'

'I don't understand, either, but I only met Otis today.'

Gabby meets my eye, and I see the question she's asking herself: childhood best friends or not, how well does she really know Otis Clarke?

CHAPTER 20

Unease over Otis's financial revelation clings to me, but thoughts of Kamal's inevitable worry crush it. I can almost picture the lines on my husband's forehead deepening as he wonders where I am, imagining the worst. Kamal deserves better than that.

After saying a quick goodbye to Gabby, I dash out of the house, through the rain.

Before I set off for home, I check my phone. There are ten missed calls from Kamal and a queue of increasingly concerned messages. Mum and Beth have called, too, suggesting that my panicked husband has contacted my family to see if they know where I am. Now everyone is worrying together.

I'm about to throw my phone onto the passenger seat when I catch sight of another message, this one from Natalya to the group chat.

The police are apparently at Otis's house! What do you think that means? Is this a real missing persons case?!?! x

The message tangles me in knots. I wonder how long it will take for everyone in Bramblethorpe to find out about Alexa's card, and what rumours and theories will become public discourse when they do.

But as another worried text from Beth appears on my screen, I push those thoughts aside.

After firing a quick text to Kamal to say I'm on my way home, I spin my car around and speed away. My agitated fingers drum against the steering wheel as I race through Bramblethorpe, cursing the fact that in one poorly timed evening, I have shattered the illusion that all is well with me. The pent-up energy only intensifies when I see my home in the distance, with Kamal's car in the driveway and every light in the house on. Grimacing, I slow down as I get closer.

My brakes have barely announced my arrival when Kamal runs out of the house. He almost buckles with relief when he sees me, but adrenaline sustains him enough to reach me. Wrenching open my door, he pulls me out of the car and straight into his arms.

'Are you okay? Is everything okay?'

Kamal's questions bowl me over, rolling away before I get a chance to register them, never mind provide an answer.

He holds my face in his hands. 'I came home and you weren't here. You weren't picking up your phone. It was just like before. I thought . . . I thought . . .'

I hug my husband so he doesn't have to finish his sentence. 'It's fine, I'm fine,' I soothe, saying the reassuring platitudes out loud for my own benefit as much as his.

'It's late, Janine. Where were you?'

'I was . . . I was out.'

'Out where?'

I could lie, I realise. Lie to protect Kamal from further worry and myself from further questions. But as I look at my husband's tired eyes, I'm suddenly exhausted by the thought of more lies. The truth about Alexa's cash withdrawals has already left a bitter taste in my mouth.

'I was with Otis Clarke,' I admit.

Kamal pulls back, frowning. 'The man with the missing wife?'

When I nod, Kamal studies me, waiting for more.

'Come inside,' I say, slipping my fingers through his. 'I'll explain everything.'

Kamal moves in slow, jerking steps as if afraid of what he'll find out when he walks through the front door. His fear grows when we step inside and he sees my mud-caked shoes. Glancing at Kamal's feet, I notice he has no shoes on. His socks are wet from rushing out to meet me on the driveway without a second thought for his comfort.

As the walls of my throat constrict, I wrap my arm around my husband and lead him to the living room.

'Why were you with Otis Clarke?' Kamal asks as he takes a seat on the sofa opposite to me. 'What were you doing?'

'It's not how it sounds,' I begin, but Kamal shakes his head.

'I don't care how it sounds, Janine. I just want you to be honest. What were you doing with Otis Clarke?'

'We were looking for Alexa.'

Kamal blinks. 'What? Why?'

'Because I want to help find her. Something strange has happened there, Kamal.'

My words have the opposite effect of reassuring my husband. 'What do you mean, strange?'

'Otis was worried about Alexa, but he thought she was okay because her bank card was logging transactions. Only Otis and I went to Manchester today and—'

'Wait, you've been in Manchester today with a man whose wife is missing?' When I nod sheepishly, Kamal's eyebrows dart towards his hairline. 'Were you alone together?'

'It's not like that,' I protest, but Kamal's eyes widen as if he can't believe what he's hearing.

'Janine, I'm not asking if you're having an affair! My concern is that you're spending time alone with a man you know nothing about. A man whose wife is missing. For all we know, he could have something to do with it.'

'We don't know that's the case,' I protest, but the question, *If Otis Clarke is a good man, why was Alexa syphoning money?* niggles in the back of my mind.

'We don't know that it's not the case, either,' Kamal reasons. 'Why would you get involved in this?'

'Otis Clarke needed help,' I say, struggling to justify what, in the cold light of the truth, looks and sounds like absolute madness. 'I had time to provide that.'

'I thought you were at home, working on your book?'

'I am,' I reply, my cheeks firing at the lie. 'But writing doesn't have set hours. I had time spare to help.'

My words do little to calm Kamal. 'You're explaining your decision to get involved in this as if it's rational, but it's not. This isn't a book you're working on, Janine. Otis could be dangerous. You could have got yourself in real trouble.'

'I thought you loved my ability to find a story in everyday life?' I try to joke, but as Kamal frowns, I know my words have hurt him.

'This isn't about not loving you or the way your mind works. It's about you being safe. It's sad what's happened to Otis Clarke, but it is not your responsibility to fix this for him.'

'I'm not doing it for him. I'm doing it for Alexa.'

'But you don't know her.'

'So? It doesn't mean I can't be concerned about her. It looks like she's missing, Kamal. No one knows where she is.'

Kamal sucks in a breath, my words worrying him more. 'We all want Alexa to be alive and well, but that doesn't mean you need to run around Lancashire with a man you know nothing about.'

As my head dips, Kamal leans forward and takes my hands in his.

'Janine, you have a big heart. It's only natural you would want to help, but finding Alexa is a job for the police, not you. Look at it this way – what if she doesn't want to be found by her husband?'

I struggle with the potential truth in Kamal's words. A truth that seems increasingly likely after recent revelations. 'Maybe, but something about this doesn't feel right. What if something bad has happened to Alexa? She doesn't have her phone. She isn't the one using her bank card. For all anyone knows, she's completely vulnerable.'

'Then that's all the more reason to walk away and keep yourself safe,' Kamal says, but he sighs when he sees my dubious expression. 'I understand why you're worried, I do, but my priority is your safety and your wellbeing. After everything that's happened, that's where your focus should be, too.'

My gaze lowers at the truth in Kamal's words. A truth that bears eerie echoes of DS Rani's advice.

'I'm assuming that after what happened today, Otis called the police?' Kamal asks.

'He did, yes.'

'Good, then your involvement in this can end.'

'But Kamal—'

'Janine, you've done more than enough to help. It's time to let the police do their job. No good comes from meddling in other people's business, not when the stakes are this high.'

'But we need to find Alexa.'

'And that's exactly what the police are going to do.'

'Really? They seem more bothered about Alexa secretly taking money from her bank account than finding her.'

Kamal pounces on my statement. 'Alexa Clarke was hiding money? Well, that settles it – you should get out of this now. Otis and Alexa Clarke are strangers who clearly have some messed up secrets. That's not a situation to get mixed up in. Alexa might be in trouble, hurt or even dead because of her husband. I'd rather find out if he's guilty or not when the police solve this, not when they're asking me to identify your body.'

As my shoulders sag, Kamal draws me towards him.

'Janine, I love you more than life itself. I don't want you sleep-walking into a dangerous situation.'

'But I need to find Alexa,' I whisper.

As a tear rolls down my cheek, Kamal studies me. 'Nothing I'm saying is unreasonable, but you don't want to hear it. Why does it matter to you to be part of this?'

'I told you, I want to help.'

'That's not the truth, Janine, I know it's not. Why are you looking for Alexa Clarke?'

A dangerous wobble takes over my lower lip as I twist my hand free of Kamal. He sees it, and he knows what it means. He reaches for me again, breaking down the walls of my feeble resistance.

'I think I know why you're doing this. I understand, too, but please listen when I ask you to put your safety first. I know you and Alexa have lost babies, but that doesn't mean you know her. It doesn't make an unknown less risky.'

'I just want to find her,' I croak. 'I want her to be okay.'

'I know, but I need you to ask yourself: is this about Alexa Clarke, or is this about you? Who are you trying to find in this? Because I'm not so sure it's Alexa.'

A curtain of hair falls across my face as I bow my head further to block Kamal from seeing the effect of his words.

'I'm only saying this because I care, Janine. You've been doing so well with getting back to a place of happiness. Don't let this distract you from all the progress you're making.'

I curl in on myself to dodge Kamal's compliments, ones he has no right showering on me when I have been doing the opposite of what he thinks.

'Promise me something?' he says. 'Promise me you'll stay away from Otis Clarke, at least until the police confirm if he's a suspect or not. Please?'

Lifting my head, I look into the eyes of the man I love, now pooled with worry. I have seen that emotion in him so many times. I have been the cause of it for so long now. I hate myself for doing it to him, to us.

'I promise,' I nod, but even when I say the words, I know it's likely to be a promise I won't keep.

CHAPTER 21

Alexa

Three days gone

The patter of raindrops didn't bring Alexa Clarke the same comfort it usually did. As a child, whenever it rained, she would grab a blanket and lie under her bedroom window, listening to the droplets land. The ritual was almost meditative. But silenced, starved and bloodied in the white room, the sound of rain was anything but soothing. Every drop hitting the windowpane landed like a hammer cracking Alexa's skull.

She opened her eyes, and the dim room came back into focus. How long Alexa had been in here, she couldn't guess, but the increasingly pungent stench of stale urine and the mounting weakness in her body warned her it was too long.

Alexa knew that if something didn't change soon, her story would not have a happy ending. It couldn't. Her head was an open wound. She was laid on a bloodstained pillow, no doubt inviting infection to take hold. And she was so, so tired.

Opening her mouth, Alexa went to shout for help, but what was the point? Her voice was gone, lost to the pain of her situation.

Worse still, every dry-mouthed swallow was comparable to digesting a packet of razor blades.

The closest thing Alexa could compare it to was the final day of a music festival, when the series of late nights screaming along to her favourite songs announced their impact. Alexa had experienced that gruff vocal legacy many times in her twenties. Somewhere in her home was a box of wristbands from each one, kept for when she needed reminding that sometimes life was simply dancing in a field with your best friends.

There were other things in the box, too. Polaroids from dinner parties and boarding passes from trips abroad with her husband. So many memories. It was laughable that she tried to condense them all into one box.

But the things in there were only tokens of happy times. Alexa knew the reality of her marriage was far more complicated than a strip of black-and-white stills from a photo booth suggested.

Remembering her husband, Alexa opened her mouth to allow her useless voice to call for help once more. But, as she dragged her weary gaze to the door and saw the shadow underneath it, she froze.

Someone was there.

Someone was standing outside the room.

Alexa blinked three times to check her unreliable vision wasn't playing a trick on her, but each time she opened her eyes, the shadow was present.

'I know you're there,' she called, the barely audible words tearing her sandpaper throat. 'I can see your shadow.'

When there was no response, panic fluttered in Alexa's chest. Her fate was pinned on getting help. Leaving this room, righting her wrongs, surviving – none of that could happen unless someone set her free.

'I can see you,' she rasped. 'Please, help me.'

Still, the shadow was motionless.

'Please,' she called out, the torn walls of her throat catching against each other. Forcing herself to stare at the shadow, Alexa waited until the awful truth hit her.

There was no one there.

There never had been. She had simply succumbed to delirium.

Pressing the back of her head into the pillow, Alexa cried out as the wound roared, but nothing hurt as much as the realisation that this was it. There would be no apologising. No happy ending, no turning things around.

This.

Was.

It.

But then, out of the corner of her eye, Alexa watched as the unthinkable happened. The door handle started to turn, slowly, until eventually it clicked open.

Alexa choked on a disbelieving laugh. *They're coming into the room*, she cheered, but then the reality of that thought ploughed through her.

They were coming into the room.

The person who clubbed her over the head and dragged her here in the first place – they were coming into the room.

Voiceless or not, that realisation was enough to make Alexa scream.

CHAPTER 22

For the rest of the evening, Kamal and I walk on eggshells. Every few minutes, I catch him looking at me. I know he's questioning my motives, my judgement – maybe even my sanity. I can't blame him. When I look back over my choices today, I question my own, too.

But still, something in me says that I can't give up.

As I brush my teeth, I try imagining what Alexa is doing right now. Where she is. If she's safe, if she's okay. I'm so lost in my thoughts that I almost don't notice a message come through from Natalya.

Apparently, Otis was seen in his car with a woman who isn't Alexa today … He didn't wait long to move on, did he?! x

My heart lurches into my throat, imagining Kamal's reaction if he knew that the Bramblethorpe gossips are painting me out to be Otis's mistress.

Katherine's reply only worries me more.

I wonder who the woman was. Do we know if she's staying at the house?

My thoughts go to Otis, struggling with the burden of people's chatter as it is. And then there's Alexa, who could hear something along the grapevine. Would she know it wasn't true? Would this rumour push her to come home, or would it push her to do something reckless?

'Everything okay?' Kamal asks, entering the bedroom and spying my pale face.

'All good,' I reply.

If Kamal suspects I'm lying, he doesn't say. He just climbs into bed, waiting patiently for me to join him. Turning my phone off without replying, I do just that.

I know Kamal's hoping I'll turn around so we can have a pre-sleep chat like we used to. Nose to nose, we'd discuss the day, our dreams and anything that crossed our mind, until sleep came for us. It's been so long since we've done that. So long since I felt I could. Seeing Kamal's hurt up close has been too much.

It's still too much. I lie on my side, facing away from him, my body rigid.

Eventually, Kamal rolls over. A few minutes later, he falls asleep.

I can't say the same for myself. Every time I close my eyes, I see anger flash in Otis as he strikes his wife, knocking her unconscious. I see Alexa run from a shadowy figure at the top of the stairs, tripping and tumbling down them until her body comes to a stop in a twisted shape at the bottom. I see a well-built, hooded stranger bundle Alexa into a blacked-out vehicle then speed away. I see Alexa, bloodied, bruised and pleading for my help.

When Kamal's alarm shakes me awake, a dry-mouthed gasp catches in my throat.

'Bad dream?' Kamal asks, hovering in case I need I hug.

'Something like that,' I reply, swinging my legs out of bed and heading to the bathroom.

The previous day feels like a weight pressing against my back as I move about the house. The pressure only grows when I check my writing group chat.

Apparently, the police didn't leave Otis's house until after eight last night. That's never a good sign, is it?

Katherine's update and the cold light of the morning make Otis's deception about the money and his delay in calling the police seem even more sinister.

When Kamal leaves for work, an itchiness overcomes me. I roam the house, trying to ignore the feeling. I try even harder when I see another email from Tiff asking for an update on my book. I try harder still when I see a message from Beth that reads, *You gave us quite the scare last night . . . again*, but the scratching is persistent.

It reminds me of each time I have a new story idea. The moment inspiration sparks, there's a buzzing in the back of my head demanding I pay attention to what my subconscious is trying to tell me.

Right now, my body is doing the same thing, only this time it's not trying to push a book idea on me but thoughts of Alexa Clarke. Call it intuition, call it an overactive imagination, but I can't shake the feeling that she is not okay. And if the police are only getting involved now, then we are days behind where we need to be with finding her.

Opening my laptop once more, I look over Alexa's social media accounts, hunting for a clue about why she might be hiding money. The obvious answer is she's been planning to leave Otis, but I wonder if another reason could be hidden in plain sight. The problem is, Alexa hasn't posted on social media in a long time.

I want – no, I need – to know more, but so far, the only source I have is Otis. A man I promised my husband I would not see again, no matter how tempted I am to ply him with more questions.

I last a wordless hour and a half at my desk before I find myself once again heading to Maple Crescent.

Gabby's car is on the driveway when I get there. I wonder if she stayed over last night, and what other bombshells were dropped in my absence. Leaving my car behind, I go to ring the doorbell, but Gabby opens the door before my fingertip touches it.

'I saw you on CCTV,' she explains when she registers my surprise. 'Come in.'

She steps to the side, and I head inside.

'How's Otis?' I ask as we walk through to the kitchen.

'Not good, how do you think he is?' Otis jokes from the dining table.

I jump at the sight of him, then frown. Otis hasn't looked good in the short while I've known him, but this is the worst I've seen him. I'd be surprised if he had an hour of sleep last night. His skin is tinged grey, almost as if each day without Alexa is draining the life from his body.

'It's good to see you again, Janine,' Otis says, then he indicates to the rest of the dining table. 'Please, take a seat. There are enough of them to choose from.'

As I slip into the chair opposite Otis, Gabby brings me a glass of water before sitting beside him.

'How did it go with the police after I left?' I ask.

'Well, they're officially treating this as a missing persons case now. They're releasing a press statement at midday.'

Even though this news isn't unexpected, it still hits me like a blow to the chest. All that time Otis spent thinking Alexa was taking a break, he was wrong. All that time, wasted.

'That's good,' I manage to say. 'It means more people will be looking for Alexa now.'

'I know, but the label *missing person* …' Otis's body caves inwards. He goes to say something else, but then his phone bursts into life.

Everything about Otis's demeanour becomes hostile from the first ring. I glance at the name on the screen: Sonya West. A bell of recognition chimes somewhere in the back of my mind.

Gabby peeks at the screen too, then sighs. 'Sonya again?'

Otis nods. He watches the phone vibrate but doesn't pick it up. It's only when the ringing stops that he breathes again.

'Who's Sonya?' I ask.

'Alexa's best friend,' Gabby replies.

It hits me where I know the name from – in the car yesterday, driving to Manchester with Otis. Sonya had called then and, once again, Otis hadn't answered.

'How come you're dodging her calls?' I ask.

Gabby and Otis exchange a loaded look.

'Sonya is … well, she's a lot,' Gabby replies, not taking her eyes off Otis as she speaks on his behalf. 'Her personality is hard to deal with at the best of times, but now that she's going through a messy divorce and Alexa is missing, her flair for dramatics is even greater than normal. Right now, it's not fair on Otis to have to put up with her … hysterics.'

'Hysterics?' I echo.

'I know, I hate to use that word about another woman, but if you met Sonya, you'd understand.'

'Gabs, you don't have to sugar-coat it for Janine,' Otis says before facing me. 'I'm dodging Sonya's calls because she hates me.'

'Otis!' Gabby cries in protest. 'She doesn't hate you.'

'Come on, you know it as well as I do – Sonya hates me. Always has, always will.'

Gabby and Otis are too busy squabbling to notice my reaction to the news that Alexa's best friend hates Alexa's husband. It's a good thing, really, because it's not a positive one.

Gabby turns to me. 'Sonya doesn't hate Otis. She just hates that when Alexa fell in love with him, their marriage took her away. Sonya's very protective of Alexa.'

I'm tempted to ask if Sonya has reason to be protective of Alexa when it comes to Otis, but he speaks before I can. 'We've never seen eye to eye, ever. If I said something is black, Sonya would say it was white.'

'Alexa married Otis at a difficult time for Sonya,' Gabby continues. 'It was right after her father passed away and her mother got sick. They're hard things for a person to deal with, especially when the friend you rely on is now spending all their time with someone else. Sonya never forgave Otis for that. You know how it is when you're friends with someone and they fall in love. You're left wondering where you fit in the new picture they're drawing.'

'Sonya refuses to come to the house because I'm here,' Otis says. 'She'll only see Lex if she treks over to her.'

'Which Alexa hasn't been doing because of everything that's gone on,' Gabby adds.

I nod, but there's something about this exchange that's a little too rehearsed for me to fully believe that Sonya is simply a jealous friend.

'I'm sure Sonya guilted Lex a lot for that, never stopping to think that not visiting when things were so hard for Lex makes Sonya the bad friend,' Otis mutters.

As if overhearing her name, Otis's phone starts ringing again with a call from Sonya. We all look at the illuminated screen, but no one makes a move to answer the call.

Otis groans. 'I can't deal with Sonya shouting at me right now.'

'Maybe she just wants an update,' I say. 'She'll be worried about Alexa, too.'

'She's got a funny way of showing it,' Otis replies as he runs a hand through his hair. 'I thought I'd do the decent thing and answer earlier. Do you know what Sonya said to me? She said she can't believe she let Lex marry a murderer.'

The room falls silent. Gabby studies her palms while Otis holds my gaze, letting his disbelief at the accusation shine through. I also suspect he is watching my reaction, waiting to see if my allegiance has changed thanks to everything that was uncovered last night. I maintain composure, even though internally I am screaming.

'I thought you said the police are treating this as a missing persons case?' I ask. 'That's not the same as murder.'

'Try telling Sonya that. It's bad enough that my wife is missing, but to have people talk like there's no hope of finding her and accuse me of being involved? It's too much.'

'Otis, no one thinks you're involved,' Gabby soothes, but she can't look me in the eye when she says this.

'Why did you lie about Alexa hiding money?' The question leaves my mouth before I can frame it less bluntly.

Both Gabby and Otis stare at me, but Gabby is more shocked by the question than Otis. 'I've been wondering when one of you would ask me that,' he replies.

'Otis, it's your private business. You don't have to tell us anything,' Gabby says, but I don't agree. Otis accepted our help, yet all the while he kept a big part of the story to himself. Maybe he doesn't owe us answers, but an explanation as to why he lied would go a long way to stopping my nerves from chewing a hole in the lining of my stomach when I'm around him.

'I didn't say anything because I knew how it looked. It's easy to hear that Lex has been hiding money and think she's left me, but I know my wife. She wouldn't do that.'

'Lots of people don't want to admit their marriage is over,' I say.

Gabby's eyes widen at my bluntness. Otis, on the other hand, doesn't react.

'I am not one of those people,' he says. 'I don't have to be. Lex and me, we're in this for life.'

'But Alexa has been hiding money from you. She leaves this house every few months. You said so yourself.'

'Janine, yesterday when you told me you wanted to help, you said you knew what grief does to a marriage. Can you honestly tell me you don't have times when you want to walk away from the person you know is hurting as much as you are, even if only for a few days?'

Otis's analysis of life after child loss is so piercingly accurate it pains me. I know it, I live it. It's the reason I'm here, in this pretty village, trying to piece my life back together around the ugliness of what's happened.

Otis studies me before sitting back in his seat. 'Wow. You really do know.'

Coiling my fingers together, I nod. 'Before my husband and I moved here, I went out for some milk. I didn't come home until three a.m. the next day.'

Gabby's lips part, but Otis remains neutral like he knows exactly how this story goes.

'I wasn't doing anything bad. I just walked. I sat on a bench for a few hours, I think. It's all a blur, to be honest, but I remember thinking that if I kept moving, I would be too busy to focus on what I'd lost. So I walked and I walked, but what happened kept catching up with me.' I swallow, the pain of admitting the truth closing my throat. 'Eventually, I went home and saw the search party my husband had arranged. Family, friends, neighbours – you name it, they were looking for me. Kamal had even called the police. Everyone was so worried. They still are. No one seems to understand that I just wanted to walk away for a while. So yes, Otis, I get it, but that doesn't mean I understand why you lied.'

Otis sighs. 'I lied because I knew if you heard about the money, you'd think Lex was running from me. You wanted to help, Janine, and I needed you to trust me. I know it's hard when you don't know us, but Lex and I are soulmates, aren't we, Gabs?'

'Yes,' Gabby confirms. The response breaks her heart, not that Otis notices.

'The only thing I didn't tell you was that the day before she disappeared, Lex went to the bank and withdrew two thousand pounds in cash,' he says. 'She'd withdrawn similar amounts a few times before, too. It looks strange, I know, but there's got to be a reason she was taking money other than that she was leaving me.'

'You told the police you didn't know Alexa had withdrawn money until she was gone. Is that true?'

'I swear I didn't know before. I never checked Lex's bank account. I never felt like I needed to, but once I checked Lex's statement and saw the withdrawal, I took out all the documents in her office. I told you Lex is a technophobe, right? Well, she likes to have paper copies of everything. I went through all her bank statements, insurance documents, every scrap of paper she's ever kept. They covered the entire dining table.'

My face itches to react as it remembers the papers littering the table when I first came to Otis's house, but I force it not to.

'I found nothing other than that Lex has been withdrawing money every few weeks for the last four months,' Otis continues. 'There was nothing to indicate why or who that money was going to, but—'

On the table, Otis's phone vibrates again.

'For fuck's sake,' he snaps. He silences the call, then pinches the bridge of his nose. 'Sonya's going to tell the police I've got something to do with Lex vanishing, isn't she?'

'You don't know that,' Gabby says, but her reply lacks any conviction.

'I do, and so do you. You know what she's like.' Otis presses his face into his hands. 'The detectives said they'd be back today. I know what they're going to say. What they're going to insinuate.'

'But you haven't done anything wrong.'

'So? They don't care about that. They've already decided I'm guilty of something.'

'Otis, you had reasons for handling this the way you did,' Gabby says, taking his hand. 'All you need to do is explain that to them.'

'But they don't see them as reasons. Besides, you've seen this village – who else are they going to suspect? The lady at the post office? My elderly neighbours?'

Gabby doesn't try to soothe Otis this time. She lets her hair fall in front of her face, only looking up again when Sonya calls once more. Snatching the phone from the table, Gabby leaps to her feet.

'Sonya, hi,' she begins, her voice silky smooth and insincere, the same tone she used on me when we first met. I don't hear what Sonya says or how Gabby responds, because Gabby leaves the room before I can eavesdrop on the conversation.

When she's gone, Otis deflates. 'This is madness. How can Lex still not be home?'

'You've said it yourself, Alexa sometimes leaves,' I say feebly.

'I know, but this is different. Something in here tells me so,' Otis says, tapping his chest. 'I want her back, Janine. I need her. I love her. I love her so much.'

I comfort Otis as he descends into gut-wrenching sobs, but all the while I watch him through new, wary eyes. After all, loving someone doesn't mean you don't hurt them. Sometimes it's the people who claim to love us the most who hurt us. I just pray that Otis hasn't hurt Alexa in the worst way possible.

CHAPTER 23

Soon after Gabby returns from speaking to Sonya, I make an excuse to leave. 'I have an interview with a book club to prepare for,' I lie.

Gabby leads me out, maintaining her self-appointed role as Otis's minder when I ask if she'll keep me posted on any updates with Alexa.

'If Otis sees it fit, sure,' she says noncommittally. 'Let's just hope Alexa turns up soon. The more this drags on, the more I worry for Otis.'

'Well, maybe we're closer to the truth now he's being honest with us.'

Gabby looks at me, and something passes between us that I don't quite understand. I'm about to ask her if there's anything else I should know when she nods curtly and closes the door.

Once again, I find myself on the outside of this impressive house, but when I study its clean lines and sharp angles, any appeal it previously had fades. This house is a symbol of wealth, of making it in a world that does everything to try and make sure you don't. It's expensive, it's beautiful – but is it cherished?

Does the house reflect the lives of the people who live in it? I wonder.

Shuddering, I make my way back to my car, but I don't leave straight away. Instead, I sit in the driver's seat, my gaze lingering on the other vehicle on the driveway.

Gabby's car.

Gabby, whose bond to Otis clearly goes beyond that of friendship.

Gabby, who only found out about Alexa hiding money when I did, making me wonder if, deep down, she's starting to doubt Otis, too.

Raindrops drum on the roof of my car as I sit behind the steering wheel. Kamal's instructions to walk away circle my brain. I feel a glimmer of temptation to follow his advice, but I'm too invested. I see the strands of a story in the air around me. The rocky marriage, the best friend with a perhaps not-so-secret crush, the other best friend who hates the husband.

The characters of the story are changing, too, morphing the more I learn. Is Otis a worried husband, or someone else entirely? Is Gabby a loyal friend, or was she overtaken by a desire for more with Otis? Who is Sonya West, and what is her role in this twisted tale?

The question sits with me, beating in my chest like a second heart until I reach for my phone. I search through Alexa's friends on Facebook until I find Sonya West.

Sonya's profile picture is of her and Alexa. The timestamp tells me it was uploaded fourteen months ago. I can't tell where they are thanks to the dark background, but they're dressed up. Sonya has matched her lipstick to her pink dress. Alexa looks impossibly stylish in a boxy cream suit.

Moving past the photograph, I hunt for information on Sonya. Her 'About Me' section tells me she's thirty-eight and works in marketing. Her relationship status reads 'Separated', and a flick through her profile shows all evidence of a partner has been erased. A messy divorce, indeed.

If I suspected Sonya was worried about Alexa before, her profile only confirms it. This morning alone she has shared four separate posts about her friend. Desperation seeps through every word in the latest.

My darling Lex hasn't been home in days, and no one can tell me where she is! How is this okay?! Lex, if you're reading this, PLEASE get in touch. I love you xx

There are almost fifty comments underneath expressing concern and support. Sonya has replied to each one. Her responses are full of details about how tough the situation is for her and dramatic phrases, but who am I to judge? If Sonya wants to appeal to the internet for comfort, let her. It's not like she's getting much support from Otis.

Before memories of Kamal's warning talk me out of it, I send her a message.

Hi Sonya,
I'm a local from the village your friend Alexa Clarke lives in. I'm helping Otis look for her. To help do this, I'd like to know a little more about Alexa's life. I was just with Otis and noticed you'd been calling, so I thought I'd reach out. Anything you can tell me that you think might help would be great.
Would you be up for a quick call?
Janine

The 'Read' notification appears under the message almost immediately. Seconds later so does the ellipsis indicating that Sonya is typing.

Her response speed proves one thing: Sonya West is more than a little concerned about her friend.

You were just with Otis? What did he say? Did he explain why he was ignoring my calls?

I chew my lip, not wanting to discuss Otis like this when I'm already going behind his back to contact Sonya.

Otis has been busy talking to the police. I'm sure he'll get in touch soon. In the meantime, anything you can tell me about Alexa that could help with the search would be great.

My eyebrows dip, wondering if I need to explain more or if Sonya's worry for Alexa is greater than her desire for answers about Otis.

Her reply confirms the latter is correct.

Fine, but forget a call – can we meet? There's a LOT to talk about.

I've barely hit send on my response saying 'sure' before Sonya replies again.

The Blackwell Arms in Manchester, one hour?

Searching the pub online, I discover it's a forty-five-minute drive away. My heart rate elevates at the idea of being so far from home and walking into a pub I've never been to before. I'm about to suggest we meet somewhere nearer when Sonya sends another message.

Please.

One word, six letters, and a tonne of terror contained inside it.

Confirming our meet-up, I set off towards The Blackwell Arms, ready to discover the truth about Otis and Alexa Clarke.

CHAPTER 24

The drive to Manchester is uneventful, but being so far from home still has me shaking. By the time I reach The Blackwell Arms, I'm damp browed and have bloody, teeth-shaped imprints on my bottom lip. Hardly the first impression I was going for, but I don't have time for self-consciousness. Not when I see Sonya's latest message.

I'm sat by a window at the back of the pub. Thought out of the way would be best with what we're here to talk about. Hurry. Please x

I take Sonya's desperation as my cue to leave the confines of my car.

The Blackwell Arms is like most traditional British pubs. It has a dark oak bar sweeping through the middle of the room and a patterned carpet that style forgot. Commentary mumbles in the background from a television playing a football match, with the regulars glued to it. Unlike other pubs, though, The Blackwell Arms smells clean, no lingering scent of spilled beer and bad decisions.

I order a Coke then take it to the back of the pub, an area quieter than the front but no less stereotypically styled.

Sonya West jumps to her feet when she sees me. A halo of frizz surrounds her scraped-back hair, the style so poorly tied up that she might as well pull it loose from the scrunchie.

'Janine?' she asks.

'That's me. Nice to meet you.'

I don't know whether to go for a handshake or not, but Sonya takes the decision out of my hands by pulling me into a fierce hug. 'I'm so glad you're here,' she whispers.

When Sonya pulls away, I'm alarmed to see that there are tears in her eyes. She dabs them away while we settle into our seats. I study her. Sonya's wearing make-up, but it was hastily applied. Her clothes are well tailored but creased. In fact, there's a general air of chaotic dishevelment about Sonya that almost makes me want to pass her my doctor's details.

'Thank you for meeting me on such short notice,' I say.

'I should be the one thanking you. I'd have dropped everything for an update on Lex.'

'Has Otis been giving you any?'

Sonya stops chewing the side of her thumb to scoff. 'You were with him earlier. You'll have seen him ignoring my calls. He doesn't tell me anything, even though I'm Lex's best friend. I'm so worried. Disappearing without going to a friend or telling anyone where she is . . . it's not like her.'

'Otis said the same thing.'

'I bet he did,' Sonya mutters.

'I take it you're not a fan of his?' I ask, taking a sip of my drink.

Sonya pauses to study me before she answers. 'How well do you know Otis Clarke?'

'I don't. Not really. I met him for the first time the other day.'

'Have you fallen for his charms yet?'

When I pull back, Sonya laughs.

'Don't judge me for saying that. Otis has this way about him that gets people on side. He acts so self-assured that people don't get the chance to realise what he's saying is bollocks. He's a con man dressed in a nice suit. Don't let the fancy house and six-car garage fool you.'

'Well, you don't hold back,' I reply, a remark Sonya shrugs at. 'Have you always felt this way about Otis?'

'Maybe not as strongly as I do now, but I've never been his biggest fan.'

'Why's that?'

'How long have you got? One thing you should know about me, Janine, is that I'm a good judge of character. I see things most people don't. To everyone else, Otis and Alexa are the golden couple. How could they not be? Those looks, that house, that life? It's the dream!'

'But you don't see it that way?'

'No, and you wouldn't either if you knew what went on beneath that shiny exterior.'

It takes everything in me to not wrap my arms around myself as protection against the iciness of Sonya's words.

'Lex is the most wonderful person I've ever met,' Sonya continues. 'It's impossible not to love her. She shines on her own, but put her next to Otis and together they sparkle. Otis likes that. He grew up poor – I mean, *really* poor – so the ability to turn heads matters to him. Surely you've noticed that?'

I think of Otis, bleary-eyed and disintegrating more and more as time goes on. 'I don't know if I'd describe him like that.'

'Maybe not now he's playing the role of a distraught spouse, but you're not blind to the house, the car, the confidence.' Sonya's lips curl in disgust. 'From the moment Lex met Otis, she was enthralled, but I never fell under his spell. Lex told me things she told no one else. I know things about that man that would destroy his "good guy" image forever.'

Every hair on my body bristles. 'Like what?'

'Like how shitty a husband he is. He doesn't care about Lex at all. I'm guessing you know she's miscarried multiple times?'

It hurts to hear that question, never mind respond to it. The best I can muster is a small nod.

'She struggles, but Otis is never there for her. He hasn't been since the first one. When she needed him most, he threw himself into work and froze her out. Then, if he's not freezing her out, he's arguing with her over every tiny thing. What kind of partner would do that?'

I think of how many nights Kamal has stayed late at the office recently and how I lash out every time he mentions what we've been through. How our behaviour around each other is full of pretence because grief seeps into everything and no one gives you a handbook on how to deal with it.

I'm about to say all this when Sonya speaks again. 'Everything in Otis's life must be perfect. I don't think he can cope with the fact that this part of the picture isn't immaculate. He has everything on his tick list: a beautiful wife, an impressive business, a show home. Now he's ready for the perfect mini-Otis clones. The problem is, they've not arrived.'

'That's not Alexa's fault.'

'I know that, and you know that, but does Otis? Those miscarriages killed Lex, but he's never supported her like he should have. The day after they lost their last baby, he went away with work for a week. The *day after*, Janine. Can you imagine what that felt like for Lex?'

I bow my head. 'No, I can't.'

'Even if Lex said to go, he should have insisted on staying with her, and he should have been kinder. He once asked her, "What's wrong with you?" Lex said she couldn't tell if he meant what's wrong as in why are you crying, or what's wrong as in ... well, why can't you carry my children?'

I gasp, wounded as if the cruel comment had been said to me personally.

'Exactly,' Sonya nods, triumphant now she has successfully cast doubt on Otis. 'Lex isn't happy. She hasn't been for a long time. She was looking at properties in Denmark, did you know that?'

My eyebrows arch. 'Really?'

'Yes, and not for her and Otis to live in, let me assure you!' Sonya says, shaking her head. 'The last time I saw Lex, she was so thin I worried she was going to snap. I messaged Otis to say she needed help, but he never replied. Imagine your wife's best friend saying she's worried and you don't reply!'

Even if Sonya's assessment smacks of over-simplification, something in her words coils around my body. 'When was the last time you saw Alexa?'

Sonya bristles, a shamed flush reddening her cheeks. 'Longer ago than I'd like, but that's because of Otis. I don't want to be around his ugly house or dirty money, and I definitely don't want to be around a man who pretends to love my best friend.'

'Do you really think he doesn't love Alexa?'

'Do you think he does? She vanished and he waited days before contacting the police. There are only a few reasons for that, and none of them are good. My bet is that it's something to do with his business. There have been rumours for the last year that things aren't going well at Archi-Tech.'

My forehead wrinkles. 'When I researched Archi-Tech, it seemed to be doing well.'

'Otis has friends in high places. I'm sure he has the power to pull a few articles that could spell bad press.'

I try not to react to Sonya's suggestion, even if she sounds like a conspiracy theorist, but I mustn't do a very good job of it.

'Don't believe me, then,' Sonya says with a shrug. 'But if it's not about Otis's business, then the only other reason not to call the police is because he's hurt Lex and needed time to hide the evidence.' Sonya analyses me. 'You seem shocked, but you don't know Otis like I do. Trust me, he's loud, he's obnoxious, and he has a vile temper. Lex calls him a sulker. I call him an arsehole. He's never loved Lex like she deserves to be loved. If you ask me, he got rid of her.'

My heart drops, but sense tells me to keep a level head. 'Does Otis have a history of being violent?'

'Not that Lex has ever said so, but you never know what goes on behind closed doors. Especially ones as fancy as Otis Clarke's.'

Despite everything I've heard over the last few days, my lips still twist with uncertainty. 'I know you know him better than I do, but he seems lost without Alexa. Gabby said—'

'Gabby? Gabby is at the house?' When I nod, Sonya snorts. 'Oh, I bet she is loving this! She's got everything she ever wanted – Lex gone and Otis crying on her shoulder.' A smirk comes over Sonya's face. 'You know there's something going on between them. You must have picked up on the vibes.'

I shift in my seat. 'I mean, they seem to know each other well, but from what I saw, I think the attraction is more on Gabby's side than Otis's.'

'That's what Otis wants you to think. He's a good liar like that. They say they're "best friends",' Sonya scoffs, air quoting the phrase.

'But Gabby's always wanted more. Lex knows Gabby is just waiting to sink her claws into Otis. Otis denies it, but secretly I think he likes having the two women in his life fight over him.'

'And do they fight over him?'

Sonya purses her lips. 'Not directly. They're always pleasant in this fake, simpering way, but there's a nasty undercurrent there. Gabby has this way of making out that Otis has told her things he wouldn't tell Lex. It drives Lex insane. Whenever Lex and Otis get into a bad fight, one of them leaves. Lex goes to me or to a hotel, but Otis? Well, he goes to Gabby. One time he was with her for three days.'

Sonya watches me, waiting for a reaction.

'Janine, Otis went to another woman's house for *three days*. What do you think he was doing all that time?'

'A man and a woman can be friends without being romantically involved,' I acknowledge, but Sonya cackles.

'Don't be so naive! You've seen the way Gabby looks at Otis. I tell Lex all the time to leave and let the two of them get on with what's obviously already happening.'

As Sonya shakes her head like I'm clueless, the discomfort I feel in her presence quadruples. It's not that I don't see the point she is trying to make, but I don't agree with her black-and-white way of viewing the world.

'Look at it this way,' Sonya pushes, 'if your husband disappeared to another woman's house for three days, would you believe his pleas of innocence?'

When I say nothing, Sonya smirks as if my silence provides my answer.

'Otis denies anything has ever happened, but if my ex-husband could find the time to have an affair in his lunch hour, then Otis and Gabby can find the time to have one in three days. Men, they take a whole, happy woman and suck the life out of her. Anthony did it with me, and Otis did it with Alexa.'

Sonya's bitterness bites at my throat, although her rage makes more sense in light of the revelation about her own relationship. It's hard not to pity her, even if she is making such wild generalisations.

'The last time Lex let slip that she thought Gabby was too friendly with Otis, he said he was tired of the conversation and that Lex should trust him. Talk about gaslighting, right?'

'Maybe,' I reply, once again uncomfortable at Sonya's scathing analysis of Otis Clarke. Or maybe the thing I'm uncomfortable with is how willingly I got into a car with a man who, according to Sonya, is not to be trusted. Maybe my judgement isn't to be trusted either.

Misreading my discomfort, Sonya shakes her head. 'Whose side are you on, Janine? My best friend is missing and you're sitting there playing devil's advocate. Get off the fence and open your eyes to the truth about Otis Clarke!'

Out of the corner of my eye, I spot a young couple approaching a nearby table freeze when they hear Sonya shout. Sonya notices them, too. She offers what I think is meant to be a reassuring smile, but her tension makes it have the opposite effect. As the couple back away, Sonya deflates.

'I'm sorry, I didn't mean to shout,' she says. 'I'm just worried.'

'It's fine. Look, it's not that I don't hear your concerns. There are things about Otis that worry me too, but I'm just here to gather as much information as I can so I can help Alexa.'

Sonya's chin dimples, but she nods.

With an easing of the pressurised atmosphere, my shoulders unclench. 'Have Alexa and Otis stopped arguing about Gabby?'

Sonya nods again. 'Lex learned to pretend she was cool with their friendship, although it still bothered her. The arguments about Gabby stopped, but maybe that's the problem.'

'What do you mean?'

'I saw it in my own marriage. When you argue, it's because you care. It's because you've got something to fight for. As soon as the arguments stop, that's when you should worry, because that's when whatever was there between two people has died.'

Even though I know Otis and Alexa argued the morning she went missing, I still gulp. 'Do you think Otis and Alexa's relationship has died?'

'Think it? I know it.' Sonya leans forward, so close her breath tickles my cheek. 'Have you ever been around two people who were once madly in love but have lost the will to speak to each other? Two people floating around in a big empty house like ghosts?'

Kamal's face flashes in my mind. His hand reaching for me, me pulling away. The two of us side by side in the same room, but oceans apart. I shake my head to answer, and to rattle the vision from my brain.

'Well, that's Lex and Otis. The love between them hasn't been there for a long time. And that beautiful house they built? Let's just say, these days, it's more like a prison than a dream for Lex.' Sonya sits back, watching me absorb what she said.

Wrestling my anxiety into submission, I ask Sonya perhaps the most important question of all. 'Where do you think Alexa is?'

The change in Sonya is instantaneous. 'I really don't know. She's never vanished like this before. But if you ask me, I don't think leaving Otis was what she was doing that day.'

'What makes you say that?'

'She didn't call me. Lex and I talk as often as we can. Life gets in the way of big catch-ups, you know? But whenever Lex took a break from Otis, she always called. Sometimes it was to check it was okay to stay with me, other times to say what had happened – but she always, always called. The thing is, I've not heard from Lex in two weeks.'

A dense silence follows Sonya's admission.

'If Lex had walked out, she'd either be home by now or with a friend. Plus, she'd have told me if she was thinking of leaving Otis. A decision this big is *not* something she would keep to herself.'

'What about the cash Alexa's been syphoning?' I ask, but the way Sonya's features shift tells me this is news to her. 'You didn't know about the money?'

'I had no idea.' Sonya's face crumples even further. 'How much did she take?'

'Twelve thousand pounds.'

Sonya gasps. 'Twelve *thousand* pounds?'

I nod. 'Her last withdrawal was the day before she disappeared.'

Sonya's watery eyes flood with fear. 'Maybe she was leaving him, then. Maybe Otis found out and stopped her. Janine, I'm more worried than ever now. Where is Lex? What has he done to her?'

'We'll find her,' I reassure Sonya, but she reaches across the table to grab my hand. Her grip is too tight, her bones pressing too hard against mine – but even if I tried to pull away, I know I wouldn't be able to.

'Don't include Otis in that "we",' she begs me. 'If Lex was hiding money, something was wrong. If Lex was building a secret escape fund, he has to be the reason why.'

Sonya's words send a shiver down my spine, a reaction she leans closer into.

'I can see it in your eyes, Janine. You don't trust Otis. Don't ignore your gut. There's more to this than meets the eye, I can feel it. Can you?'

Sonya's question stares at me like a loaded gun, asking if I dare pull the trigger and provide an honest answer.

CHAPTER 25

After promising to keep in touch with Sonya, I leave The Blackwell Arms. In the quiet cocoon of my car, I pause to unwind from the intensity of our conversation, but Sonya's dark hypotheses embed their claws into me.

Sighing, I check my phone. A missed call from Beth and a message from Natalya to our group chat await me.

> *Please can we meet?! I need to talk all things literary agent. Maybe at the pub, if that's okay? Sorry Katherine, I know you don't drink, but this calls for more than a cup of tea! x*

My eyes widen at the words *literary agent*. I suspect this can only mean good news for Natalya's writing career. Instantly, my mind goes to Katherine and how she will react, but she's already replied saying she will be there.

Even though visiting another pub is the last thing I want to do, I confirm my attendance.

By the time I arrive at The Admiral, Bramblethorpe's most popular (and only) pub, the empty glasses around Natalya indicate she's on her third gin and tonic.

'Janine, you made it!' she cries, throwing her arms around my neck. 'I'm so glad you're here. Having the opinion of a real writer is going to make such a difference!'

As Katherine's cheeks colour, I do my best to gloss over Natalya's carelessness. 'I can't wait to hear what this is about,' I say, eyeing Natalya's half-finished G & T and Katherine's water. 'Anyone want a drink?'

When Katherine and Natalya shake their heads, I head to the bar and order a gin and tonic for myself. While the barman makes it, I spot a young couple in a corner booth, talking deeply. The man's hands rest on the woman's stomach, round and full of life.

'I remember all that excitement with my first,' the barman says, spying what I'm looking at as he hands over my drink. 'Back before I knew the pain of sleepless nights. There's nothing like that tiredness, is there?'

The question embeds like an axe in my chest, the comment made all the crueller by the barman's unwitting, friendly smile. I don't know how to react. Offended that he thinks I look exhausted enough to be caring for a newborn or devastated that he assumes I am a parent.

'How much is that?' I reply curtly, paying and walking away before he sees my hurt.

I take a long gulp of my drink to steady myself before joining my friends.

'So, what have I missed?' I ask.

'Nothing. Nothing yet, anyway,' Natalya says, barely able to contain her excitement. 'I was waiting until you got here to tell the story. Basically, you know how a few weeks ago, I told you I'd sent a draft of my crime novel to a few literary agents?'

Katherine and I both nod.

'Well, one messaged back. Sophie Hyatt. She wants to read my full manuscript.'

My lips stretch wide, impressed but unsurprised. Natalya is talented, and Sophie Hyatt is known for discovering the next big thing.

'This is huge!' I cry, throwing my arms around Natalya. It takes me a few seconds to realise that I haven't reached out to hug someone in so long. It feels nice. Alien, but nice.

Pulling back, I turn to Katherine.

'Wow,' she says, two pink dots colouring her cheeks. 'Well done, Natalya. I'm happy for you.'

I watch as Natalya hugs Katherine gratefully. There's friendship to the move but tension, too. However much Katherine meant her congratulations, I know that there's no pain quite as sore as watching someone else living your dream. Every time I see my sister and her daughters, there's an edge of torture to it.

'What's Sophie said?' I ask, taking a sip of my drink when they pull apart.

'Just that she loved the idea and can't wait to read the rest of it. Then she – well, this is where I need your advice,' Natalya says, chewing the corner of her lip. 'Sophie asked about my future book ideas.'

'That's a good sign,' I say. 'Publishers will want to know if you're a one-hit wonder, or if you've got more ideas in the bank.'

'Sophie said that, too. The problem is, I don't have any more ideas. Not fully formed ones, at least, and not ones Sophie liked.'

'Did she say that to you?'

'Not exactly, but when I went through stories I've made notes on, she was silent. That's when I told her about Alexa Clarke.' Natalya dips her head, shamefaced.

I look from Natalya to Katherine and back again. 'Am I missing something?'

'I said one of my ideas is to write about the disappearance of a local woman and how it impacts a community,' Natalya explains. 'I told Sophie about what's happening here, and she loved it. She said people love reading about how people turn on each other in trying times. Plus, she said a novel inspired by a real-life case would be a great hook for promotion.'

'If Sophie's talking like this, that's great,' I reply. 'She clearly sees a future for you as an author.'

'I know, it's amazing! It's just ...' Natalya bites her lip, looking as young as she is underneath the heavy eyeliner. 'Is writing fiction about someone who's actually missing ethical? I mean, the story I pitched is exactly what's happened to Alexa Clarke. Missing wife, mysterious clues, a husband the police think is a suspect.'

'Is that what Otis is now?' I ask, but Natalya barely hears me.

'The worst part is that Sophie asked how the story would end and I ... well, I said it ends with Alexa Clarke dying.'

I'm not prepared for the effect Natalya's words have on me. It's like a ghost passes through my body. Of course, a part of me has wondered if Alexa could be hurt – or even worse – but to hear it out loud, as if it's been confirmed, makes me shudder.

'I feel awful,' Natalya confesses. 'I've essentially killed Alexa Clarke.'

'Stop,' Katherine says. 'Unless this is you confessing to her murder, you've hardly done that. You're just using reality as a source of inspiration, something all writers do. Besides, who gets to decide what's ethical and what isn't? Publishers think it's ethical to release a book pretending someone famous has written it just to sell a few extra copies. If they're happy to dupe the general public, they can't suddenly grow a conscience and say you can't write about a real crime.'

'Uh-oh,' Natalya teases. 'Not this rant again.'

'I'm right to be angry after spending years working for something that probably won't happen because I'm not a self-appointed social media guru,' Katherine snaps.

A blush singes Natalya's cheeks. 'I'm sorry, Katherine. I didn't mean to upset you.'

Katherine inhales to steady herself. 'No, I'm sorry. I shouldn't get annoyed. I just don't want you to give up on your dreams because of a few insecurities, that's all. Besides, being creative means pushing boundaries. If that means blurring the line between fiction and reality, then so be it.'

'I guess,' Natalya replies, but she still looks uncertain. 'I'd set the book somewhere different and change parts of what happened, too. If I do that, maybe people in Bramblethorpe won't mind?'

'Maybe they will, maybe they won't – who knows? I'm not sure I'd tell anyone about it yet, though. Murdering Alexa, even in fiction, won't win you any village brownie points,' Katherine comments.

'That's my worry – will everyone hate me if I copy what's happened? People complain when someone writes a bad review of the pub, never mind a book that brings up a potential crime in the village,' Natalya says, then she looks at me through her hair. 'What do you think, Janine? Would you write about it?'

It feels as if my body splits in two as I look at Natalya, coming to me for advice, all the while knowing that if Alexa Clarke is dead, something inside me will die with her.

Urging myself to be present, I sit forward. 'Natalya, you are not the first person to write about a missing woman, and, sadly, Alexa Clarke is not the first woman to go missing. Otis is not the first husband to be suspected of hurting his wife, and this village is not the first place where bad things have happened. These are facts of life. They are building blocks of stories. Most fiction is inspired by real events. Yours just happens to be a little closer to home, that's all. If people have an issue with you writing this, maybe they should think twice about spreading the fiction they do when they gossip.'

'I knew you'd both understand,' Natalya says. 'Thank you. Thank you so much.'

'Of course,' Katherine replies. 'And remember, we don't know what's happened to Alexa yet. You could be worrying for nothing.'

'I don't know. I mean, the police are back at Otis's house right now, aren't they?'

I turn to Natalya. 'They are?'

She nods. 'I saw them parked on the road on the way over here. Two visits in two days. That can't be good.'

'It could be that they've discovered a lead or even found Alexa. Remember, we don't know what's going on within those walls,' Katherine points out.

'I bet the woman Otis was seen with does. They were spotted in the village. She was driving his car.'

I clutch my drink tighter, praying no one picks up on my tension.

'Whoever she is, she'd certainly have the insider scoop,' Katherine agrees. 'Does anyone know her identity yet?'

Natalya shakes her head. 'I've not heard anything, have you, Janine?'

'I only know what you know. You're the ones who give me updates,' I lie.

'Well, either way, let's hope Alexa's found alive and well soon,' Katherine says. 'Right now, all I can say is that a lot of people would owe Otis Clarke an apology if he were found to be innocent.'

Natalya murmurs in agreement, but I can't find the strength to respond. The more I find out about the Clarkes, the less the word 'innocent' seems to apply to their situation.

We chat a little longer about Natalya's writing, but knowing that the police are with Otis again takes up too much of my brain for me to be a good source of conversation. It's a relief when we finish our drinks and Katherine suggests we head home.

When we leave the pub, my footsteps slow. A scowling Jim is leant on the wall outside, looking as intimidating as he did the other day. Bernie lounges by his feet, but when he sees us, he runs over, tail wagging. He sniffs us each in turn, and I crouch to stroke him.

'It's not like Jim to come into the village,' Natalya whispers. 'I thought he was banned from the pub.'

'He is,' Katherine mutters in response. 'That's what happens when you get into a fight over the cost of a drink.'

'Maybe he's catching up on what's happening with Alexa Clarke, too?' says Natalya.

'Or maybe he's here to cause trouble,' Katherine replies, tightening her grip on her handbag. When she looks down at Bernie, her mouth twists. 'Poor thing. It's probably riddled with fleas.'

'Bernie here is cleaner than most people in this village, yourself included,' Jim calls, looking over at us. Natalya stifles a gasp, but I'm too busy playing with Bernie to react. I tickle him under the chin, giggling as his tail wags faster.

My laughter gets Jim's attention. He watches me, his hard expression indecipherable. My hand comes to a stop near Bernie's neck. I can feel his pulse beneath his fur, the steady beat highlighting how much my heart is hammering now I'm in Jim's eyeline.

I'm about to withdraw my hand when Jim calls Bernie's name. 'Time to go, Bernie. Leave the woman alone.'

'He's no bother,' I reply, but Jim is already walking away.

Natalya exhales when Jim and Bernie are out of earshot. 'I swear, that man gets scarier every time I see him.'

'Jim is certainly a character, isn't he?' Katherine replies. 'I suppose he adds a bit of colour to the village. Although I'm not sure it's a colour I'd want in my house.'

Natalya snorts, but I don't join in. My heart is pounding too much from the chill of Jim's stare for that.

After promising to keep sharing updates on literary agents and Alexa Clarke, we say goodbye and go our separate ways. But before I reach my car, my phone vibrates with an Instagram notification.

Opening the app, I see I've received a new direct message.

Janine, it's Gabby. I didn't know how else to get in contact with you. I don't even know why I'm reaching out to you, but I've found something and I don't know what to do. If you're here to help like you say you are, please meet me. Does tomorrow at 11 work?

CHAPTER 26

Gabby and I swap numbers and arrange to meet at Coffee and Cake tomorrow, and for the rest of the day I'm restless and distracted. I'm so absent-minded I even slice my finger open when cooking dinner.

'Don't worry, I like a side of blood with my chicken,' Kamal jokes as he administers first aid to the wound, but I'm not immune to the wary way in which he watches me. He's worried, I can tell. I don't know how to tell him that, after agreeing to meet Gabby and where I've been today, he probably has every right to be. But I couldn't help saying yes. I don't know Gabby well, but I know enough to know that she would not message me unless she was rattled. Imagining what could have made her feel that way has me coiled tighter than a snake.

Sonya's numerous messages asking if I have updates about Alexa, and Natalya and Katherine's constant sharing of theories don't help to calm my nerves, either. I switch my phone off after dinner and try to unwind, but it's tough going. Even a bath doesn't calm me like it usually would. I lie in the bubbles until the water is cold, thinking of Alexa and how when I wake up tomorrow, another tally will be added to the list of days since she went into her garden and vanished.

It's a long time for a person to be missing.

It's a long time for no one to have any idea of their whereabouts.

My upset is mirrored in my appearance when I wake up the next day. Kamal notices, but he doesn't comment. Instead, he forces a smile.

'What's your word-count goal for the day?' he asks.

'One thousand, minimum,' I reply.

Guilt over all the lies I've told pushes me to make Kamal's lunch. He blinks when I hand him the Tupperware, and I swear I even see the glint of tears in his eyes.

'It's only a sandwich,' I say awkwardly, but I know that to my husband, it's so much more. Somehow, that makes me feel even worse.

When it's time for Kamal to leave for work, I wave him off at the front door.

'I love you,' he shouts through his open car window. My lips beg to say it back, but I can't. All I can think is how Kamal should be saying those words to someone else, not me. Someone who can give him all the things we talked about when we were dating. Someone whose wedding day promises haven't been stretched to the limits by bad luck.

Back inside, I sit at my desk, watching the blinking cursor on my laptop screen. Then, when the clock hits ten forty-five, I set off to meet Gabby.

She's already at Coffee and Cake when I arrive, sitting in the corner by the window. Her slender hands clasp a cup of coffee like it's a lifeline.

If you'd never met Gabby before, you would fall for the glamorous image she's trying to present. But I have met her before.

That's why I know that her hair was styled hastily and that her lips are usually lined and filled in with lipstick, not a quick slick of lip balm.

She's even tenser than I expected from her message, a truth that unnerves me as I sit opposite her.

'Thanks for meeting me,' she says. 'And for picking the most twee spot in England for our chat.'

Grinning, I make eye contact with Margie, who nods to confirm she'll bring me my usual order. 'Well, your message sounded urgent.'

'Sorry about that. I messaged you before I could talk myself out of it.'

Unease ripples through me. 'Is this something you need to talk yourself out of doing?'

'I don't know. Maybe,' Gabby admits, chewing on the side of her nail. 'Right now, I don't know what to think, but I need to talk to someone I can trust with this. Bizarrely, you're the only person who came to mind.'

'Me?' I say, blinking.

'You're the only one who knows what's going on to the same level I do. I thought I was doing the right thing by speaking with you. Am I doing the right thing?'

Gabby's gaze pins me to my seat. 'I don't know,' I reply. 'It depends what you're going to tell me.'

Gabby runs her fingers through her hair, grabbing a clump of her auburn locks. She's so tormented by what she's here to say that part of me wishes she would change her mind and speak to someone else instead.

'Gabby, what is it?' I ask.

Sighing, Gabby turns to an off-white handbag perched on the chair beside her and pulls something out of it. A notebook, I think at first, but on closer inspection I see that the year is printed in gold letters across the front.

'A diary?' I ask, taking the book from her.

'Alexa's diary,' Gabby replies in time for Margie to reach the table with my pot of tea. Margie's eyebrows dart upwards, her gaze fixed on the linen-bound book in my hands.

'Thank you,' I say, my tone sharp enough to stop Margie's staring. She nods and sets down my drink, all the while eyeing me curiously.

'If you ladies need anything, I'm only over there,' Margie says, offering us a level of kindness she has never shown me before even though I come here every week.

'Thanks,' Gabby replies. When Margie shuffles away, she groans. 'I've just mentioned Alexa's diary in front of the biggest gossip in the village, haven't I?'

'One of them, yes.'

Gabby groans again. 'Otis is going to kill me.'

'Why, does he not know you've brought the diary with you?'

'No. He doesn't even know I've got it.'

Moving my attention from the diary to Gabby, my eyebrows rise. 'You're lying to him?'

'I don't have much choice. If you knew, you'd understand.' Gabby takes a gulp of coffee. Her hands are shaking so much she nearly spills it as she places the mug back on the table. 'Otis doesn't know I'm meeting you. His mum's driven up from London to see him, so I snuck out under the pretence I was going to check on my apartment.'

My eyebrows lift even higher at this revelation.

'Don't look at me like that, Janine. I know I'm betraying his trust. I don't need your judgement on top of that.'

'I'm not judging you. I'm just surprised to hear you've not told Otis where you are. You've been nothing but firmly on his side in all of this.'

'I *am* on his side, that's why I'm here,' Gabby snaps. When I withdraw, stung at her tone, Gabby shakes her head. 'I'm sorry, I know I shouldn't be irate with you. This is all just so hard. I mean, what a situation Alexa has left us in! She's always pulling stunts like this, but this time she's really taken the biscuit. I've never seen Otis this way before.'

For a moment, I study Gabby. 'You like him, don't you?'

Gabby's head flicks upright at my question. 'Otis? He's my best friend.'

'That's not what I meant.'

An indignant pink tinge sweeps over Gabby's cheeks. She opens her mouth to protest, but then she deflates and offers me a small, sad nod.

'Does he know?' I ask.

Gabby's horror is palpable. 'God, no. I couldn't cope with the rejection, or the humiliation of him asking why I hadn't told him sooner.'

'Maybe that's not how he'd respond.'

'Maybe not, but that's the question I ask myself whenever I wonder how we ended up this way.'

As I observe Gabby's sorrow, I think of Sonya's assured confidence that something is going on between her and Otis. *She's wrong*, I realise. Gabby's sadness makes it more than obvious that nothing has ever happened between them, no matter how much she wishes it had.

My fingers itch to open Alexa's diary and scour it for clues, but I can tell Gabby needs to talk. So, I let her.

'Otis is my best friend,' Gabby says. 'He knows me better than anyone, and I know him just as well.'

'That's why you believe he didn't hurt Alexa.'

'That's why I *know* he didn't hurt her. Otis has a reputation for being hard, but he's the most generous man I know. You only have to look at the lives of those around him to see that. When Otis started making serious money, he bought his mum and his siblings a property each. His brother Nathaniel only has a writing career because Otis funded his lifestyle while he wrote his first book. He even supported me while I was at university, did you know that?'

I shake my head.

'I got the grades to go when I was younger, but I couldn't afford to study and care for my dad. He was sick. I gave up on my dreams of becoming a lawyer, but Otis never did. He made it happen for me and paid for a carer for Dad so I could do it guilt free.'

'Wow,' I say, because I can't think of how else to honour such selflessness.

'We're both from the same shithole South London estate, but when Otis got out, he didn't abandon the people he left behind. He put his hand out and helped us leave, too. He's a good man, no matter what people like Sonya West say.'

I try not to react to the mention of Sonya's name or betray the fact that we met.

'I can see why you're loyal to him,' I say, thumbing the corner of Alexa's diary. 'And why you love him.'

Gabby closes her eyes at the word *love*. 'I was going to tell him how I felt, once upon a time. I'd just got back from a trip to Greece. I was dating someone at the time. On paper, we were a perfect match, but Greece broke me. Everywhere I looked, I was surrounded by people who had found their soulmate. I looked at my boyfriend and realised he wasn't the person I wanted to be the other half of. It was Otis. It always had been.'

Gabby's forehead creases at the pain of hearing these words out loud. I suspect this is one of the few times she has ever said them openly.

'Why didn't you tell him?' I ask.

'I intended to. I had it all planned out. The day I landed, we met at this pizzeria we were obsessed with. Then, right as I was building up the courage to tell Otis how I felt, he told me he'd met someone.'

'Alexa?'

'Alexa,' Gabby confirms.

'Oh, Gabby, I'm so sorry.'

She shrugs in an 'It is what it is' way, but one look at her face says how much the past hurts her present.

'As soon as I met Alexa, I knew I didn't stand a chance,' Gabby says. 'I mean, you've seen photos of her, haven't you? She's stunning.'

'Looks aren't everything.'

'I know, but there's something about Alexa I could never compete with. She's beautiful, inside and out. Well, she is most of the time.'

'What does that mean?'

Gabby sighs and rubs her temples. 'I don't know. The last few days have confused me, then yesterday when I opened her diary and … look, it's probably nothing. I don't even know why I'm here, to be honest. I just needed to … I don't know. Sense check what I found.'

'What is it? What have you found?'

Gabby drops her hands and looks at me. There's a haunted sadness to her that I've not seen before, not even when she was recounting her own heartbreak.

'It's in Alexa's diary,' she says. 'Janine, I think she might have been cheating on Otis.'

CHAPTER 27

When I don't respond straightaway, Gabby reaches for the diary. 'Forget it, I shouldn't have said anything.'

'Wait,' I say, clutching it tight. 'I just need a second, that's all. In the space of a few days, I've gone from thinking Alexa and Otis were struggling but in love, to finding out she's been hiding money, and now this.'

Gabby deflates. 'It's a lot, isn't it?'

'More than I bargained for when I said I'd help,' I joke feebly, handing the diary back to her. 'Show me what you've found.'

Gabby hesitates, but then she starts flicking through the diary.

'As you know, Alexa never embraced technology,' she begins. 'She insisted on using a paper diary. Otis is the opposite, so they were forever double booking. It was a running joke between them, even if it was annoying to be on the other end of. I learned that whenever Otis and I made plans, I had to tell Alexa to put it in her diary, too, so she didn't sign him up for something at the same time.'

I bet she loved that, I can't help but think.

'The police came to the house again yesterday,' Gabby continues. 'They asked about Alexa's schedule. Appointments she attended, regular plans she had, people she met.'

'I'm guessing that's when Otis showed them her diary?'

'But that's the thing, Janine. Otis never mentioned Alexa's diary.'

I can't hide the fact that hearing this makes me gulp. 'Why not?'

'I don't know. I didn't dare ask,' Gabby confesses.

'Did you tell the police about it?'

Gabby squirms, and I eye the diary she's clutching to her chest.

'No, I didn't,' she replies, rushing to explain when she sees me frown. 'I know how Otis not mentioning the money Alexa withdrew makes him look. I wasn't going to drop him in it about her diary too, but Otis is the most honest person I know. There must be a reason why he didn't bring the diary up.'

'So, you lied for him.'

Gabby bristles at my statement. 'I didn't *lie.* I just didn't say anything. The two are very different things.'

I nod, understanding now more than ever why Gabby is such a good lawyer.

'Otis gave the police Alexa's phone and told them she doesn't get out much other than to attend a bereavement support group once a week,' Gabby continues. 'He wasn't hiding anything. He just didn't mention the diary. Maybe he forgot about it. That's possible, right?'

'I guess, but it's unlikely if Alexa uses the diary as much as you say she does.'

Gabby struggles. 'Alexa hasn't been going out for a while now. Maybe he thought she wasn't using it anymore, so there was no point bringing it up?' she suggests before slumping. 'To be honest, it's weird to me that he didn't mention it, but he must have his reasons.'

'But why would Otis hide something that could help find Alexa?'

'Honestly? I think he's scared of what the entries written inside it could mean,' Gabby replies, then she sighs. 'Look, I think we can agree that Otis hasn't been the most attentive husband recently. He will have to live with that forever, but this diary suggesting Alexa could be having an affair? Well, it would kill him if it were the truth.'

Remembering Otis, bleary-eyed and shrunken by distress, I'm forced to agree with this assessment. 'What does the diary say?' I ask, leaning forward in my seat.

Gabby thumbs through the pages then points to something. 'Alexa has been meeting someone every Friday for the last five months, see?'

Spinning the diary around, Gabby shows me an appointment that reads: *S – 1pm, Café Marco.*

I take the diary and flick back to the week before. Sure enough, another meeting with 'S' had been scheduled for Friday. Again, they planned to meet at one p.m. at Café Marco.

'You said her best friend is called Sonya,' I say, skipping over the part where I admit to meeting her. 'Could it be a recurring catch-up with her?'

'I thought that, but whenever Alexa and Sonya have plans, she writes Sonya's name in full.' Gabby flips through the diary until she finds an example at the start of the year. Sure enough, she's right: *8pm, call with Sonya.*

'Is there anyone else she knows whose name begins with "S"?'

'Not that I can think of. Not anyone Alexa would feel the need to write "S" instead of their name, anyway. Doing that is suspicious, don't you think?'

'It is strange,' I say, biting my lip. 'Did you ask Otis about the diary?'

'Not directly,' Gabby admits. 'But once I'd seen what the diary said, I asked Otis if he knew about any meet-ups or recurring plans Alexa had. He said no.'

'Maybe he was lying? It wouldn't be the first time in all of this.'

Again, Gabby bristles. 'Otis isn't a bad person, Janine. He might make stupid decisions every now and then, but he loves his wife and wants her home. Besides, if he'd have thought Alexa was having an affair, I'd have heard about it. He tells me all the time about the problems they have. Her meeting someone every Friday would have definitely come up in conversation.'

'Fair enough,' I say, although after all of Otis's lies and half-truths, I'm not sure I share Gabby's belief in this. 'But if these meet-ups were part of an affair, Alexa writing anything about it is risky, especially if Otis knew about her diary. What was stopping him from seeing this and finding out?'

'Why would Otis go through Alexa's diary if he didn't have to? He trusted her. If she said she was busy on a Friday, he wouldn't think to question her. He's not the jealous type.'

Once again, Sonya's words stir in my mind, her character description the opposite of the person Gabby is describing.

'Don't you think this is weird?' Gabby asks. 'Whoever "S" is, they've been secretly meeting Alexa every Friday at the same time and place for months.'

'That doesn't necessarily mean an affair.'

'Maybe not, but I wouldn't be here unless there was more to this than the Friday meetings. Remember when we found out Alexa was taking money from her account?'

I pull a face. 'How could I forget?'

'Well, when the police left, I asked Otis to show me Alexa's bank statement. I made a note of the dates she withdrew cash.

It turns out, she only started doing that after she'd been meeting "S" for a few weeks. What if they were collecting money to run away together?'

Gabby looks at me for an answer, but I don't have one. This is a whole other layer of deception, and one I was not at all prepared for.

'I don't know what to do, Janine. If I go to the police, it might help them find Alexa, but if Otis finds out Alexa was seeing someone else, it will kill him.'

'Again, we don't know she was having an affair,' I say, but Gabby looks incredulous.

'Secret weekly meetings and withdrawn money – what else could it be? I know this is a big accusation, but Otis and Alexa have been in a bad place for a while. Otis says they're still in love, and with my luck they probably are, but grief makes people do things we wouldn't expect. I mean, Alexa wouldn't be the first person to find comfort in the arms of someone else during a hard time, would she?'

I try not to react, even though Gabby's words burrow into the most insecure part of my heart. Kamal's late nights flash through my mind. A client dinner could be something else entirely, and I would never know. With the way things are between us right now, could I blame him for wanting to be with someone else? Someone less prickly, less resentful.

'Do you know who "S" could be?' I ask.

'No idea,' Gabby admits. 'I don't know Alexa enough to know the people in her life.'

'What about her phone? Did you look through her contacts for an "S"?'

'I can't. We gave the phone to the police. But I had an idea about how we could find out who they are.'

Before I can react to Gabby's use of the word *we*, her index finger points to another weekly event in Alexa's calendar: *Families United meeting – 6pm – Saddleforth Community Hall.*

'Is that the support group Alexa attends?' I ask, but when the name registers properly in my mind, it's like I've had an electric shock.

Families United is a support group for parents who have experienced child loss. Kamal suggested we attend a session together when we first moved to Bramblethorpe, and I did everything but laugh in his face.

'You want us to sit with strangers and share feelings we can't even share with each other?' I scoffed before walking out of the room. The conversation ended there, but it's in front of me in black and white: Alexa Clarke attended those sessions. If I had taken Kamal up on his suggestion, I would have met her again.

Suppressing a shiver, I face Gabby head on. 'What makes you think going there will tell us anything?'

'You've heard it yourself – Alexa lived a reclusive life. The only place she could have met someone was at this meeting. And the Friday meet-ups only started a few weeks after Alexa started going to the meetings, see?'

When Gabby pushes the diary back to me, I take my time flicking through it. The pages are heavy with insights into Alexa's life. Hospital appointments, gym classes, haircut reminders. At the start of the year, the plans are frequent, but then suddenly in April they stop. The U-turn is sudden, and stark.

She must have miscarried again around then, I think. I trace my finger over the empty days that come after, aching as if I'm looking at my own diary. Alexa Clarke and her grief, once again paralleling mine. The one difference is that Alexa attended support meetings to help navigate her grief. And after going to four of them, she began to meet the mysterious 'S'.

'We need to go to Families United,' Gabby says decisively. 'There's no point taking this to the police if it's nothing, and there's no point me going to Otis and saying I think Alexa was having an affair if she wasn't. He's crushed enough as it is. I've left him sitting in the same clothes he's been wearing for the last few days, watching the door and waiting for Alexa to walk through it. I can't bear the thought of what this will do to him. We have to investigate ourselves first.'

Discomfort makes my spine wriggle. 'But whoever "S" is, they might know what was going through Alexa's mind before she left. They might have been with her. They might even have hurt her.'

'Exactly, which is why we need to look into this.'

Kamal's words of warning about the danger I have unwittingly waded into crawl across my skin like ants. 'I don't know, Gabby,' I say, shifting awkwardly. 'This is starting to—'

'Please,' Gabby says, reaching across the table for my hand in a move that surprises us both. 'I don't know what to do or who to turn to. All I know is, the man I love looks like he's one bit of bad news away from breaking altogether. I don't want to be the one to push him over the edge. I need to know what Alexa was doing. I need to know who "S" is and if there was something going on between them and Alexa. I need … I need your help.'

Her plea does what Gabby intends it to. It tugs at my conscience, my fear, my desire to find Alexa alive and well.

'All we have to do is go to a meeting,' Gabby coaxes. 'Sit, listen, then ask around about Alexa at the end. As soon as we meet anyone with an "S" name, we dig deeper. It won't be a big deal.'

My body peels away from the table, pressing back into my chair. 'Do you really think it will be easy for me to listen to that conversation?'

Gabby has the decency to blush as what she's asked of me hits home. 'I don't think it will be easy, no, but it's the only way we can find out the truth. I need you with me, Janine. If I go alone and find out Otis was being cheated on, I'll never be able to control myself. Besides, how can I convincingly talk about a grief I've never felt? I don't have that life experience. You do.'

I try not to flinch as Gabby so casually outs the worst moments of my life.

Reading my face, Gabby softens. 'The meeting isn't until tonight,' she says. 'Take some time to think about it. Please, Janine. I can't do this alone.' Standing, Gabby nods at the diary. 'I'm going to the bathroom. Look through the diary while I'm gone. Look and tell me I don't need to be worried about Otis, or Alexa.'

Gabby leaves me, but her heavy departing words linger. In her absence, I leaf through Alexa's diary once more, the sadness of the empty pages aching inside me. My eyes linger on her only lifeline: Families United. Six p.m., without fail, every Thursday.

A gulp gets trapped in my throat. Would it be such a stretch to imagine that Alexa met someone there? Someone she cared for, someone she could trust? Someone who listened in a way everyone says Otis no longer did?

Someone who, perhaps, could have hurt her?

I trace Alexa's writing, the letters curved and cut deeply into the page. A mark of permanence, of someone who was most definitely *here*, once upon a time. I fight a sigh, knowing that as much as I want to withdraw from this, I won't.

I'm busy resigning myself to my fate when the front door to Coffee and Cake bursts open.

'Margie, have you heard?' calls Renee, the cashier from the village store, as she bustles inside. 'The police are back at Otis Clarke's. They're searching the house and its surrounds.'

My body lurches with panic. As Gabby exits the bathroom, she takes one look at the scene and freezes. 'What's going on?' she asks.

'The police are finally searching the area for Alexa Clarke, that's what,' Margie says, reaching for her coat. 'Renee, we should see if they want any help.'

'Franny Henderson has already organised a team of volunteers. They're on their way there now,' Renee replies, but Gabby has heard enough. Springing into action, she dashes to my side and grabs the diary.

'Think about it, okay?' she says. Without saying goodbye, she rushes out of the café.

'Anyone would think she was up to something, rushing off like that,' Margie grumbles. She leaves the counter, pulling on her coat as she does. 'I'm closing early, Janine. Sorry, neighbourly duty calls.'

It's clear from the excited flush to Margie's cheeks that there is more to her offer of assistance than simply being generous, but I don't have time to concern myself with that. There are other, more important things I need to do with my time.

Things like finding out who the hell 'S' is.

CHAPTER 28

Alexa

Five days gone

Alexa couldn't tell which hurt more – the pain in her head from where she was hit, the pain in her abdomen from trying not to go to the bathroom again or the pain in her throat from all the screaming she had done when the door to her room opened the previous night.

Never in all her life had Alexa Clarke been more terrified.

Haloed by light and dressed in all black, a figure had stood in the doorway. Alexa had tried to make out their features, but it was impossible. They didn't come close. Instead, they stood, soaking in her terror. At one point, Alexa swore she even heard them laugh. Her entire body had locked with tension, fearing that this was the end, but the blackened figure hadn't stepped into the room.

They listened to her screams, then left.

Alexa supposed, really, it was a blessing. Who knew what they would do to her once they were in the room? All night, her mind had run wild with those visions. All night, fear had held her close.

Now, in the cold light of day, it was still holding on.

Another cramp tore through Alexa's abdomen. She pressed her legs together as if doing so could save her from the inevitable, but she knew she was powerless to stop it.

She hadn't cried when it happened the first time. Nor had she cried when the urine soaked into the mattress and started to smell. Alexa simply gritted her teeth and told herself she had done what was necessary because she'd been offered no bathroom.

But reassuring herself back then had been easier. She'd had more faith that things would be okay when she hadn't yet listened to endless hours of silence or seen the white walls of the room repeatedly darken and then illuminate to show a day had passed.

A day in which she was still not saved.

Alexa's chin wobbled as the pressure in her stomach peaked. Knowing she could hold it no more, Alexa let the warmth spread between her legs and began to sob.

Whoever was holding her prisoner was doing it in the cruellest way. Attacking her like she was the enemy. Binding her like a prisoner. Confining her like an animal. Ignoring her like she was invisible.

Breaking her spirit, bit by bit.

As the spasming in her stomach subsided, Alexa sniffed back her tears. *No more crying*, she commanded. She didn't know if it was a command she could obey, but having something to follow other than fear felt good. Calming, despite everything.

When Alexa was calm, she could convince herself that this was all a terrible mistake. That she would be scooped out of this room and rushed to hospital. There, her injuries would be tended to. There, she would be reunited with her husband. There, the horrors of her time in captivity could start to be put behind her.

But ever since hearing her captor laugh, Alexa Clarke had started to suspect the most horrifying thought of all. That her captor might have left her alone that time, but they would be back.

The worst was still to come.

CHAPTER 29

Desperate to stop the buzzing of my thoughts, I call Beth on the walk back to my car. She picks up on the second ring.

'Is everything okay? Has something happened?'

'Can everyone stop asking me that as soon as we start speaking?' I reply huffily, my mood darkening further when I hear my youngest niece, Mila, wailing in the background.

'I'm going to take that snarky response as your way of saying everything is fine, thanks for asking, dear sister. To what do I owe the pleasure of this call, anyway?'

Mila's cries get louder, a sign that she is now in Beth's arms. I close my eyes and imagine her weight against my chest, her tiny arms wrapped around my neck. Needing me, loving me.

Climbing into my car before the crack in my heart grows any bigger, I clip my phone into the phone holder. 'I need a favour. If Kamal asks, I need you to say I'm with you tonight.'

There's a pause in which the only sound is Mila crying.

'You want me to lie to your husband?' Beth asks eventually.

'Yes. No. Only if he asks where I am.' I wince at how bad the request sounds when said out loud.

'Janine, what's going on? Do I need to be worried?'

'It's nothing bad. Nothing like what you're thinking.'

'You've no idea what I'm thinking.'

'I can guess, and I promise you it's not that.'

'So, it's not you shacking up with a hot farmer behind your adoring husband's back?'

'Beth, no! How could you even think that?'

'I don't know, Janine. Maybe because you're asking me to lie to Kamal about your whereabouts?'

I sigh. 'It sounds weirder than it is, I promise. This isn't an affair. Come on, Beth. I was lucky enough to find one person who could put up with my messiness. I'm not lucky enough to find two.'

No matter how much I hoped a little silliness would distract from the strangeness of my request, Beth tutting tells me it didn't work. 'Janine, be real with me. Is everything okay with you and Kamal? I know things have been tough recently, but sneaking around behind his back isn't like you.'

'Things are fine, don't worry.'

'Then why are you lying to him?'

'I . . . I've got involved in something.'

Beth's groan comes out loud through the phone. 'Nothing good has ever started with those words.'

'It's not how it sounds, I swear. A woman's gone missing in my village. I'm helping to look for her.'

'And Kamal can't know about that because . . . ?'

'Because he's already asked me to stop getting involved,' I say with a wince.

'Why?'

'Because he's worried.'

'Should he be?'

'No,' I reply, but even I detect the uncertainty in my voice. 'A woman is missing, Beth. If this was you, I'd want the entire world to be looking for you.'

'Janine,' Beth says, a sigh attached to each syllable of my name. 'Stop emotionally blackmailing me. It's not fair.'

'I'm not trying to blackmail you. I'm trying to make you understand.'

Again, Beth sighs. 'I'm not comfortable lying to Kamal about this. He's a reasonable guy. I doubt he'd ask you to stop getting involved for no reason, which leads me to think one thing: you know what you're doing isn't right. But, in classic stubborn Janine style, you're doing it anyway.'

I grimace, the character assessment brutal but fair. 'Please, Beth,' I plead. 'You know I wouldn't ask you to do this if it wasn't important. I'm not meeting anyone behind Kamal's back, I'm not doing anything stupid or dangerous. But I need you to cover for me tonight.'

Once again, my words are met with a silence that's only punctuated by Mila's distress. The sound of her tears seems to heighten my sister's worried judgement.

'Beth, I need you to do this. Sister to sister, please.'

'Fine,' she huffs, 'but this better not backfire. And you owe me, okay? You owe me big.'

'Thank you! Whatever you want, whenever you want it, it's yours.'

'I want a day with my sister,' Beth says, her voice cracking. 'I want a day where we talk and laugh like we used to. Is that too much to ask for?'

I bite the inside of my cheek to stop myself from crying. 'That can be arranged,' I say, ending the call quickly before I burst into tears. Turning on the ignition, I drive away, leaving the village and my sisterly guilt behind.

At the house, I text Gabby to confirm I'll go to the meeting. She takes an hour to reply, the search of the Clarkes' house obviously commanding her attention, but she confirms that we will meet outside Saddleforth Community Hall at five forty-five.

With the plan in place, I call Kamal. Panic is evident in his tone when he answers.

'Is everything okay?'

'It's fine,' I reply. 'I just wanted to let you know that I won't be in tonight when you come home. I'm going out with Beth.'

'Oh,' Kamal replies, but I can practically hear a smile taking over his face. 'That's great! Where are you going?'

I concoct a lie about dinner, digging my nails into my palms as Kamal becomes even happier. It's clear he thinks I'm coming back to myself after a rocky few months. If only he knew the truth.

Hanging up, I rattle around the house, doing all I can to avoid my guilt – and my workload. Tiff calls, no doubt for an update on my writing, but I let it ring out. I can't face lying again today.

CHAPTER 30

I put effort into my appearance before I set off to Families United. Maybe it's because I haven't dressed up in a long time and I miss the thrill of it. Or maybe it's because being in a room full of strangers without something like my books to hide behind is terrifying.

You can do this, I think as I stare myself down in the mirror. The motivation is enough to push me to leave my bedroom and head downstairs.

On the drive to Saddleforth, I blast the radio. A pop song I've never heard before fills my car, the autotuned voice and electronic beat the opposite of anything I usually listen to, but it's loud enough to drown out the voices in my head. Even the sneakiest ones that ask if I've stopped to think what it will feel like to be surrounded by people talking openly about their loss.

Twenty-five minutes later, I pull into the car park beside Saddleforth Community Hall. The squat one-storey building is a prime example of the ugliest version of sixties architecture. I don't need to go inside to know that the venue will be draughty and poorly insulated.

From the safety of my car, I watch a couple in their mid-twenties head towards the building, hand in hand.

They must be going to Families United too, I realise. Suddenly, all confidence that I can go through with this fades. Tonight, there will be no hiding from the truth. There will be no pretending that I am okay. No acting as if my story follows a different path.

Tonight, I will have no choice but to stare into the face of what has happened.

That thought is almost enough to make me back out of my parking space and zoom in the opposite direction, but then I remember that I'm not here for myself. I'm here for Alexa. So, I sit and wait for Gabby to arrive.

When she calls fifteen minutes later, I pounce on my phone.

'Janine,' she whispers like she's trying not to be overheard. 'I'm really sorry, but I can't get to the meeting.'

Inside my chest, my heart stops. 'What?'

'It's the police,' Gabby says, talking while walking. I hear a door close behind her. 'The search went on for longer than I thought, and now they're asking Otis all kinds of questions. As a friend and a lawyer, I can't leave him to face this alone.'

'But I'm at the meeting. I'm in my car, waiting for you.'

'I know, I feel awful, but you're going to have to go in on your own.'

My mouth gapes. 'What?'

'Please. I wouldn't ask if it wasn't important.'

'Gabby,' I snap, my cheeks burning with indignation. 'You can't be serious. You can't do this to me.'

'I didn't do it on purpose, I promise! If I could be there, I would.'

I can't help but snort at this. 'There is no way on this earth I am going into that meeting alone. I'm going home.'

'Janine, please,' Gabby pleads. 'You've seen Alexa's diary. You know there's something going on. The meeting could be the core of it all. We have to find out if it is.'

My eyes dart to the open door of the community hall. The warm, inviting light tells me that Gabby is right: Alexa's secrets could be traced back to there. If we want to know what's happened to her, I need to go inside. But the thought of entering that room on my own and hearing those people talk about grief . . .

'Gabby, I can't. I—'

'Please,' Gabby cuts in. 'I wouldn't ask if I wasn't desperate, and I'm as desperate as they come. If you won't do it for me, do it for Alexa. Things here . . . they're not good, Janine. I'm worried. We need to find her. Fast.'

It's those words that push me to swallow my apprehension, unclip my seatbelt and leave my car.

CHAPTER 31

As predicted, the community hall is as cold on the inside as the world is outside. Chipped cream walls and a faded carpet in the entrance hallway lead to a set of wooden double doors with glass panels. As I walk towards them, I hear a hubbub of commotion on the other side. It sounds like a lot of people are in there. Far more than I assumed also carry the pain that's underpinned my life for so long now.

When a ripple of laughter rings out, I freeze. My abrupt stop catches a person behind me off guard. They collide into the back of my rigid body, saying 'Shit!' as they do.

'I am so sorry!' the dark-haired woman cries, grabbing the top of my shoulder to prevent me from toppling over. 'Are you okay?'

I turn around to reply but find that, as when faced with my laptop, I have lost my words.

The woman tilts her head. 'First time here?'

Failed by language yet again, I nod.

She gives my elbow a kind squeeze. 'Come on, we can walk in together.'

On shaking legs, I follow the stranger through the doors. A large room with a wooden floor and a stage at one end greets me.

A handmade backdrop is pinned to the wall behind the stage, bearing a night-time scene I assume will be used for an upcoming nativity performance. The air is filled with the scent of cheap floor polish and coffee. A refreshments table stands in the corner of the room, providing an array of biscuits that would impress anyone's sweet tooth. In the centre of the room lies a circle of roughly thirty plastic chairs.

The volume in the hallway was an accurate indicator of how many attendees there are, but I'm still surprised by the number. Men and women of all ages have congregated on this chilly Thursday night. Couples, people standing alone, groups in tight-knit huddles. Some are laughing. Some are drinking from plastic cups. Some look so normal that I want to ask how they maintain such an excellent façade when they have experienced the thing that has brought us all here.

'Welcome to Families United,' the dark-haired woman says. 'Come on, I'll introduce you to some of the others.'

She leads me to a group of people standing near the refreshments table, homing in on a pale, pretty redhead.

'Annalise, hi,' the woman says, hugging her friend before gesturing to me. 'I met this lovely lady outside. Well, I say met, but I actually walked straight into her.'

'Typical,' Annalise says, not unkindly. 'I'd say Lola's accident prone, but I don't think that does her justice.'

The brunette I now know to be called Lola laughs. 'I usually go with "walking disaster". I broke my ankle last year just walking across my kitchen, can you believe it? Anyway, enough of my silliness. Here I am, introducing you without even knowing your name.'

As the two women look at me, I panic. Being here suddenly feels too real, too wrong, too … personal. I want more than anything to distance myself from my need to attend this meeting. To be someone, anyone, but myself.

'It's Beth,' I say, doing all I can not to flinch as I use my sister's name as my own.

'Lovely to meet you, Beth,' Annalise says, shaking my hand. 'I'm Annalise, and this is my husband, Simon.'

My blood freezes as a tall, trim man with sandy hair turns around. 'Did somebody say my name or am I daydreaming I'm popular again?'

'Behave,' Annalise giggles, nudging him. 'Meet Beth. She's new.'

'Welcome,' Simon says as he shakes my hand. He smiles, and two deep dimples pierce his cheeks. 'Don't be nervous. Everyone here is friendly enough.'

'Friendly enough? Simon, we're more than that,' Lola protests. 'We're delightful!'

As the group laughs, I can't take my eyes off Simon. Could this be who Alexa is having an affair with? With those arms and that smile, I wouldn't be surprised if so.

'Are you here alone?' Annalise asks, looking over my shoulder.

'My … my husband couldn't make it.'

Sympathy floods Annalise, but she doesn't look surprised. 'Well, don't worry about that. Some people are ready to join meetings before others. I came alone for three months before Simon felt able to attend too.'

'Then when I realised there were biscuits, I couldn't keep away,' Simon adds. Annalise suppresses an eye roll, but the way her face lights up when she looks at him tells me he could make terrible jokes forever and she would still adore him.

'My partner doesn't come either,' Lola says. 'She tells me it's good we have separate outlets for our grief. Hers is knitting, of all things.'

'My husband knits, too,' I say, but the reminder of Kamal punches me in the chest. I picture him at home, eating dinner alone, while I'm here, lying yet again.

Annalise reaches for my hand. 'Why don't you sit between me and Lola tonight? We can help you settle in.'

'Is that okay?' I ask, surprised at the emotion in my voice.

'Beth, it's more than okay! Come on, we'll find a seat before everyone rushes to nab a good spot.'

Throwing her arm over my shoulder, Annalise steers me towards the circle of chairs. As we leave Simon, I eye him suspiciously. If he's who Alexa was meeting, then I almost don't want to know. Barely five minutes into meeting Annalise, I am already furious at the idea of him cheating on her.

But as I watch Simon interact with the people around him, it's more than clear how Alexa could be drawn to him. Simon emits a warmth that every person in the room seems to gravitate towards. With Alexa alone all day and Otis so distant, it's not hard to imagine her wanting to be around someone with such an illuminating presence.

When I take a seat beside Annalise, she squeezes my hand, and I pray for her sake that Simon is not the person I'm looking for.

'Is everybody ready?' the grey-haired woman leading the meeting calls out.

Her question prompts a flurry of activity throughout the room as everyone rushes to find a seat, then the meeting begins.

It's not long before I realise it will be harder to uncover the identity of 'S' than I thought.

'There are three newcomers tonight,' the leader begins the meeting by saying. 'Let's start by going around the circle and introducing ourselves. Say your name, your profession and a fun fact about yourself.' She goes on to tell everyone that her name is Sharon Hollinger, she's a psychologist, and she enjoys running marathons.

I learn that as well as Sharon and Simon, two other people attending tonight's Families United meeting have a name beginning with 'S'. That's four people Alexa could have been meeting on Fridays. Four people I need to speak to before the night is over, but not before I've sat through the session and introduced myself.

'I'm Beth. I'm a teacher, and I enjoy open-water swimming,' I say, and with those words I fully adopt my sister's identity.

Despite every intention I had before arriving, I find myself being drawn into the meeting. Sharon speaks first, sharing that earlier this week was the fifteen-year anniversary of her son Timothy's stillbirth.

'The strange thing about grief is that people expect it to fade,' she says, 'but I feel the pain of losing Timothy as if it happened this morning. It's fresh. I think it always will be. So no, I don't think grief goes anywhere. I think you just learn to live around it. For me, this week was a reminder of that.'

From there, everyone gets the opportunity to speak, but only if they wish to.

I find myself listening with a keenness I haven't felt in a long time. At one point, I'm on the verge of tears when a woman called Rhoda describes crying in the supermarket because she accidentally walked down the baby aisle. I feel the memory so painfully, so personally, because I have been there myself. Confronted by the gummy, grinning photos on the packaging of nappies and breaking because all that I thought would be mine is not.

Then, when Rhoda finishes, Annalise raises her hand.

'This is hard to say out loud, but saying it helps make it real. Simon and I, we've … well, we've decided to try again.' Annalise takes Simon's hand, grasping it tightly.

I try to ignore the fact that Simon doesn't grip hers back with quite the same ferocity.

'It's been a long discussion, with a few arguments along the way, as I'm sure you can imagine.' A few people chuckle knowingly. 'But we're at a point where we're ready to give becoming pregnant another go. For the last few weeks, we've been meeting with another IVF consultant. Truthfully, I'm terrified, but we're not done with the dream of being parents yet. Besides, you never know if you never try, right?'

While Annalise speaks, I watch Simon. His eyes are on his wife and those dimples dent his cheeks, but I feel like I'm watching a man whose mind isn't really in this moment with us. Somewhere inside me, a warning bell rings.

'Thank you for sharing your news, Annalise. I'm sure I speak for everyone when I say we are wishing you and Simon all the best with your journey,' Sharon says, then someone on the other side of the circle raises their hand and our attention goes to them.

My focus ping-pongs around the room for the next twenty minutes until there's a gap in the conversation. I only realise I have raised my hand to speak when everyone's gaze lands on me.

'Beth, welcome,' Sharon says. 'Whenever you're ready, say what is on your mind.'

Every sense I have prickles as I take in the faces of the strangers staring at me with gentle encouragement. People young and old, rich and poor, from all kinds of backgrounds and with differing beliefs, all here because of one uniting thing: grief.

'My husband doesn't know I'm here tonight,' I begin. 'Ironic, really, because he was the one who told me about these meetings. I didn't mean to lie to him about coming. I didn't mean to tell any of the lies I've told recently, but … well, it's hard to tell him the truth. I'm scared that if I start, then I'll have to say how badly this hurts.'

Looking around the room, I see my words have struck a chord.

'Even now, after everything that's happened, I almost can't believe I'm here,' I continue. 'I mean, I spent my twenties terrified I'd fall pregnant and doing everything I could to stop that from happening, then I met my husband and all I wanted was to make a family with him. But no matter how hard we try or how close we get, it's not happening for us.'

Tears catch at the back of my throat. I go to sniff them away but then I stop myself. If there's one place I don't need to hide my emotions, it's here.

'My husband and I were happy, once upon a time,' I say. 'Sometimes I think those days are gone. It's hard not to wonder if I've changed too much to be the person he fell in love with. I keep trying to find a way back to him, back to us, but sometimes I feel so lost it's like there's no way back at all.'

There's so much more I could say, like how I cry in the shower because it's the only place I can do so in peace. Like how I get angry when I see a pregnancy announcement, even though I know I should be happy for other people. Like how every day I wake up and wonder, *What if motherhood never happens for me?* and don't know how to answer that question.

But I can't say any of that. If I start admitting the darkest truths of this experience, I'm scared I'll never stop.

When I dip my head to indicate I have finished, Annalise takes my hand in hers. The comforting gesture brings tears to my eyes.

Sharon responds to what I said, but I'm too busy holding myself together to take it in. The conversation moves on, then before I know it, the session comes to an end.

I blink, looking around the once again bustling room. 'Is that it?'

'Time flies here, doesn't it?' Annalise replies. 'Don't worry if it's a bit disorienting. Your first session is always a bit of a shock. If you're anything like me, this is the first place you'll have heard people talk about loss so openly.'

I nod because that's exactly how I feel.

'Come on, let's get a biscuit. You look like you could do with the sugar,' Annalise says, rising to her feet.

'Snack time, the best part of the night,' Simon cheers, rubbing his hands together and setting off towards the refreshments table.

'Honestly, he's such a child.' Annalise giggles and I try to join in, but her affection for her husband is something I can't smile about. We make a move to follow Simon, but an older woman intercepts us.

'Annalise, darling, how wonderful to see you,' she says, air kissing Annalise's cheeks before pulling her close and lowering her voice. 'Have you seen what's happening in the hallway?'

Annalise looks over the woman's shoulder to the double doors. I follow her gaze. The back of Sharon's head is visible through the glass, as is the flash of a neon jacket.

'Is that the police?' Annalise asks, taking the words out of my mouth.

'It is. I wonder if they're here to talk about Alexa.'

Annalise's eyebrows dip. 'Is she okay?'

'Haven't you heard? Apparently, she's missing.'

As Annalise gasps, the double doors to the hall open. A solemn Sharon leads five uniformed officers into the room alongside an equally sombre DS Mullins. Gripped by panic, I make my body small and duck behind Annalise.

'What's going on?' Simon asks, approaching our huddle carrying more biscuits than one person should possibly consume in one sitting.

'It's Alexa,' Annalise whispers. 'She's missing.'

Annalise is too focused on the police to look at her husband, but my eyes are glued to him. That's why I'm on hand to see the colour drain from Simon's face at the mention of Alexa's disappearance.

CHAPTER 32

As Sharon leads the police to the front of the hall, I stare at Simon's pale face, until Sharon clears her throat, pulling my focus.

'Can I have everyone's attention please?' she calls.

The room falls silent, all eyes on Sharon and her new acquaintances. DS Mullins scans his audience coolly, his expression blank. As his attention slides across the room to where I'm standing, I move further behind Annalise, accidentally nudging Lola as I do.

'Sorry,' I whisper. She flashes me a smile before looking back to Sharon.

'The police are here to speak to us about Alexa. As some of you might know, she has been reported missing.'

I can't be the only one who feels nervous electricity surge through the crowd, because a man in front of me rests his hand on his partner's shoulder to comfort her.

'Anyone who joined Families United for the first time tonight and doesn't know Alexa is free to go. Everyone else, I urge you to stay behind and assist the police with their enquiries. Alexa is our friend, and right now she needs our help.'

A low rumble of conversation spreads out, then everyone looks around the room to watch those who are leaving. Terror takes hold as I realise that means me. The newcomer who stupidly used a fake name, a move so odd that any police officer worth their salt would find it suspicious.

My eyes dart to DS Mullins. I know he finds my presence in Otis's life strange enough without finding me here, too. Gulping, I follow his gaze. He's still surveying the crowd, but thankfully he's looking towards the other side of the room.

'See you next time,' I say to Annalise, slipping away before she can respond.

With my head low, I weave through the watchful huddles. I imagine DS Mullins's sharp eyes following me. It feels like his stare is penetrating my back, but I keep my focus fixed on the exit, never once turning around to see if he's noticed me.

The door looms closer, freedom in sight, but right as I'm about to reach for the handle, someone on the other side swings it open.

Terrified, I stumble backwards. For one awful moment, I picture DS Rani looking back at me, but relief engulfs me when I come face to face with a uniformed officer instead.

'Sorry,' the officer says, holding the door open. Muttering 'Thank you', I scurry through it and dash to my car, setting off before there's another surprise to throw me off.

The entire drive home, my attention is only fifty percent on the road. Another bad slip of judgement considering it's a rainy night, but all I can focus on is the events of the night. Namely, meeting Simon.

There's no denying his expression was one of guilt, but guilt over what? A secret friendship? A passionate affair? Being involved in Alexa's disappearance?

My body convulses at that final thought, my unease made even more sinister when I imagine Annalise's devastation at learning Simon might be cheating on her.

Pushing my foot on the accelerator, I fight to reach the comfort of home as quickly as I can, but my drive is interrupted when the radio cuts out. Glancing at the dashboard, I see that Gabby is calling.

'So?' she asks as soon as I answer. 'How did it go?'

'The police were there, Gabby,' I croak. 'I thought they were going to see me. I thought they were going to ask what I was doing.'

'If they did, you could've said you just started attending the group. You've gone through the same thing Alexa has. It wouldn't be weird for you to be there.'

'I guess,' I reply, choosing to omit the part where I didn't use my real name.

'Did you find out who "S" is?' Gabby asks, drawing me back into the conversation.

'I think so.'

On the other end of the line, I hear Gabby inhale sharply. 'Who is it?'

'I can't be certain, but there was a man called Simon. When Alexa's name was mentioned, he acted strangely.'

Gabby's groan rings out over the car speakers. 'I knew it. This is going to kill Otis.'

'Gabby, we don't know they were having an affair.'

'Of course we do! We don't need to see photos of them kissing as proof. The only place Alexa went regularly was that meeting. That's got to have been where she met "S".'

My mouth twists. 'You need more proof than that before going to Otis with this. Simon is married. His wife was at the meeting.

She's really nice, Gabby. You can't throw an accusation like this out there with no proof.'

'Fine,' Gabby says. 'Tomorrow, Alexa and "S" usually meet. We'll go to their little café, and we'll see if Simon walks through the door.'

I blink. 'You want to confront him?'

'I want answers, Janine, and right now talking to Simon feels like the only way I'm going to get them. Are you free? Will you come with me?'

My grip tightens around the steering wheel. 'I don't know, Gabby. I didn't even want to go tonight.'

'But you did, and look how much you've learned! Besides, you talked to Simon. He knows you now. If I go to the café, I can't just start talking to him. Hell, I don't even know what he looks like! But you do.'

I squirm, unable to ignore Gabby's logic. 'Fine,' I say wearily. 'But this is the last thing I do for you, okay? I'm serious. This is getting out of control.'

'Last spy mission, I promise,' Gabby jokes tightly, but I can't even muster a smile.

After making plans to meet Gabby tomorrow at Café Marco, I hang up. It's only when the call ends that I realise Gabby hasn't told me a single thing about how the police search went.

When I pull into my driveway, I check my phone to see if she's messaged with an update, but there's no such message waiting. There are a bunch of notifications about the search from my writing group, though. Katherine and Natalya don't know much about the results of it, but Katherine knows enough detail to have me chilled.

The police were there for over three hours. Franny Henderson said she saw Otis standing in the garden with them. She said he looked guilty as sin. And apparently, people who helped with the search got asked if Alexa had ever mentioned moving back to Denmark. I wonder what that could mean?

And then the most startling message of all, sent from Natalya.

Random question, Janine, but were you with Otis's friend today? Margie said she saw you but I said that can't be right, Janine doesn't know Otis or Alexa? x

My teeth rake over my lower lip, wondering how I could even begin to explain what I was doing with Gabby without admitting to the last few days of secrecy and lies. Sighing, I close the message thread without saying a word and head into the house.

'I'm home,' I call out while removing my shoes.

'In here,' comes Kamal's reply. I wander through to the living room, where I find him watching TV while continuing his latest knitting project. A scarf for my Christmas present, although judging by the current length of it, most of my neck will be chilly.

'*Friends* again?' I ask, flopping onto the sofa opposite him. 'Surely by now you can quote it backwards?'

'So? *Friends* is comfort food, only it's comfort food for the soul,' Kamal replies, pausing the episode. 'How was your night?'

'Wilder than yours, by the looks of things.'

'Knitting is wild, okay? You've not experienced the stress of dropping a stitch to say otherwise,' Kamal jokes. 'Everything okay with Beth and the girls?'

'Everything's great,' I reply, reaching for a book to shut down any further questions.

Kamal hovers, wondering if he should try engaging me in conversation again, but then he decides better of it. As I watch him reach for the remote, I think back to Sharon's words about grief and how you learn to live around it. Suddenly, Kamal's actions are performed in a new light. Watching repeats of shows he loves because the brain power it would take to absorb something new is being used to process what's happened to us. Staying late at work because that's the only place in his life with certainty and routine. Leaving me alone rather than pressuring me to see family because he knows I need space.

'Kamal?'

My husband looks at me, his expression clueless.

'I love you.' The ferocity of my words scares me, but I don't take them back.

From across the room, Kamal's face breaks into a grin. 'I love you, too,' he replies, putting his knitting to one side. He leans forward, debating whether or not to cross the room and come to me. I make the decision for him. Standing, I walk to my husband and slot under his arm. Curled together, we watch Ross and Rachel argue about whether they were on a break until our yawns tell us it's time for bed.

Before we sleep, I check my phone one last time for a message from Gabby. I don't find one, but my group chat has been a hive of activity since I last saw it. My eyes widen when I open it and a list of links to articles from various media outlets fills my screen.

I scroll back to the first message, sent by Katherine.

Have you seen that the press has caught wind of what's happened with Alexa? It's a small article on a regional news site, but an article, nonetheless.

Attached is a link, one I click so fast my thumb moves in a blur. *Woman Missing – Have you seen Alexa Clarke?* the headline screams.

Beneath it are two images. One is a photo of Alexa, mid-laugh, seemingly carefree and full of life. The other is a photo of Alexa and Otis at what looks to be some kind of formal event, judging by their attire. The image would be lovely if not for the way Otis looks. Tense, with his hand clamped around Alexa's waist. Despite her height, Alexa looks tiny beside his bulk, and Otis's stance borders on possessive. It could be nothing, a fleeting awkward moment, or it could indicate something sinister.

Biting my lip, I read the article.

Police are appealing to the public for information on the whereabouts of a woman who went missing from her home in the village of Bramblethorpe on Saturday 20 November.

Friends and family are growing increasingly concerned after almost a week without contact from 35-year-old Alexa Clarke. It's reported that Ms Clarke's husband believed she had gone away for a few days but contacted police when he was unable to get in touch with his wife.

Well respected in the tech industry, Otis Clarke hasn't been available for comment, but sources close to the couple say he is frantic with worry.

Alexa's friend Sonya West described Ms Clarke as, 'The best person you could ever meet. She sparkles. She would never disappear like this.' She also hinted that there were problems in the couple's marriage, although police are yet to verify this claim.

'What's wrong?' Kamal asks as he climbs into bed.

I lower my phone before I can finish the article or process the fact that Sonya's quote is made of the same words she used when talking to me. The rehearsed nature of her concern makes me ill at ease, and I clam up.

Kamal glances at my screen and frowns. 'I thought you weren't involved with the Clarkes anymore?'

'I'm not, but my writing group sent a link to an article about it.'

'Well, it's good that Alexa Clarke's in the press now. Hopefully if more people know she's disappeared, then more people can help find her.'

'I know, but seeing it in the news makes it official. Alexa Clarke is missing.'

When my body slumps, Kamal takes my phone and locks it. 'It should have been official the day she wasn't at home. Otis Clarke is going to have to answer a lot of questions about how he could have handled this better, especially now the media is involved.'

'Do you think so?'

'Of course. You know how one clickbait headline can whip up a frenzy of online intrigue.' Kamal studies my drawn features then kisses my hand. 'Let's not talk about this now. It's late, we should sleep.'

'You're right,' I reply, but even when I close my eyes, I can't rest. All I can think of is Otis and the questions the world will ask when they discover how long it took him to reach out for help.

I can't help but wonder what questions they would ask if they knew he purposely avoided mentioning his wife's diary to the police, too. How long would it take for them to label him as guilty after hearing that?

Scarier still, is 'guilty' a label Otis Clarke should have been wearing all along?

CHAPTER 33

Alexa

Five days gone

As soon as night fell and she heard thudding footsteps on the stairs, Alexa knew that the captor was coming. This time, she knew that they would not stop at the door.

Immobilised by the chains, with no way to run free, Alexa started to scream. But when light from the hallway filled the white room, Alexa's scream died in her mouth.

Time slowed as her captor was unveiled. Their appearance was more petrifying than Alexa's worst nightmares could ever have imagined.

Dressed in all black, the captor looked like the kind of criminal who could seamlessly blend into the night. The absence of colour was foreboding, their thick gloves and chunky hoodie concealing any hints at their identity. But the mask they wore was the scariest part of the ensemble.

The person who clubbed Alexa Clarke over the head had chosen to hide their identity with a generic white mask, the kind sold at craft stores for people to decorate. The blankness of the mask made an already terrifying situation ten times worse. Anyone could have bought that mask. Scarier still, anyone could be behind it.

The slow, rhythmical thud of booted feet echoed out as the captor walked towards Alexa. Her brain screamed, but no sound left her lips. She was simply too scared.

By their third step, the captor was at the foot of the bed.

Alexa pressed her body into the mattress, causing a riot of pain to erupt in her skull, but anything that increased the distance between her and the encroaching threat was worth it.

By the captor's fourth step, they had passed the end of the bed.

As fear thudded in Alexa's ears, she ordered herself to focus on details. Distinctive features, unusual movements – anything that could identify the captor – but their clothing bore no brand labels to suggest they were rich or poor, fashionable or not. The only thing to note was that their clothes looked new, almost as if they were bought for this purpose.

Another footstep brought the figure even closer.

Tucked under their arm was a polaroid camera. What it was to be used for, Alexa didn't know. She didn't want to find out.

The next step came. Smaller, this time, as if the captor was enjoying the anticipation of their arrival.

Laid flat, it was impossible for Alexa to pinpoint their height. They looked tall, but most people would from that angle. They looked broad, but that impression could have been from their oversized clothing rather than their frame.

Alexa's chin trembled as she realised there was nothing unusual to note about them. They were just a body.

A body that had come to a stop beside her chest.

At first, the pair simply stared at each other. Alexa, trying to figure out the colour of the captor's eyes even though they were shadowed by their mask. Her captor, taking in the result of the injuries they had inflicted. For the brief moment in which their curiosity levels were matched, the pair were united. But the captor broke the union by raising their right forearm.

'Please don't,' Alexa whimpered.

The captor stopped, frozen as if they couldn't understand the words or their meaning.

'Please,' Alexa whispered again, her hoarse voice making her desperation sound even more pathetic.

As Alexa's tearful eyes bore through the slits in her captor's mask, she hunted for a sign to reassure her that she would be okay, but Alexa saw nothing of the sort. She tried to blame it on the mask's concealment or her impaired vision, but Alexa Clarke knew the truth: she saw no humanity there because there was none to be found.

And, as her captor moved once more, Alexa realised just how true that statement was.

The captor's gloved hand gripped her jaw, then forced Alexa's head to turn. Now she was facing the wall, the wound at the back of Alexa's head was exposed. It was deep. Even deeper than the captor thought, they were delighted to discover. The blood caked around the site was rancid. Infection would set in soon, if it hadn't already.

But before then, the captor had work to do. Curling their fingers, all but one, the captor moved towards the wound peeping from behind Alexa's blood-crusted hair.

'Please,' she begged, but the request only fuelled the captor's desire to plunge their finger into the gash obliterating the back of Alexa Clarke's head. Instinctively, a shrill scream flew from her mouth. Even with her raw throat, the sound erupting from Alexa was impressive, but it was nothing compared to the pain she felt.

The deliciousness of her scream awakened something within the captor. An energy they reserved solely for times like this. They pressed harder and deeper into the wound until Alexa Clarke's world went blank as she passed out from the pain.

CHAPTER 34

Friday should be my favourite day of the week. It's the day Kamal works from home, a post-Covid gift from his office, aimed to provide the impression of a work–life balance. For Kamal, the opportunity for a lie-in eases him into the weekend. For me, having him in the house makes keeping up the pretence that I am hard at work near impossible.

In a rare act of thoughtfulness, I've brought Kamal a coffee in bed. That's when the doorbell rings.

'Who is it?' he asks as I move towards the window.

My lips part to reply, but I'm too busy trying not to gasp.

Kamal notices my stiffness. 'Janine?' he questions. When I don't reply, he leaves the bed and stands behind me. 'Do you know those people?'

'It's . . . it's the police.'

I sense Kamal frown. 'Why would the police be here?'

'I think it might be to do with Alexa Clarke.'

I don't need to say more. Kamal springs into action, throwing his dressing-gown on. 'I'll let them in,' he says. 'Get dressed and come downstairs whenever you're ready.'

With that, he leaves the room.

Before I do anything, I message Gabby.

The police are at my house. I don't know if they saw me at Families United. Do they know about the diary yet?

When the message sends, I wait for Gabby to reply. My anxious fingers drum the back of my phone, only stopping when a notification lights up the screen. The problem is, it's from Katherine, not Gabby.

Apparently, the police found something when they were searching yesterday! No one knows what, but there are officers in Bramblethorpe chatting to people. It must be serious …

I stare at the screen, trying to digest her words long enough for a response from Natalya to appear.

Serious and more than likely that Otis has something to do with it! x

Dropping my phone on the bed, I force myself to get dressed, all the while straining to hear the muffled chatter coming from the floor below. I can't hear what is being said, but judging by the bubbling kettle, I know Kamal is making the detectives tea. Ever the dutiful host. Ever the perfect husband.

But what am I? A wife who lied when she said she would stop getting involved. A woman scurrying around behind people's backs. A keeper of secrets, not all of them hers.

Biting my lip, I run through the inevitable outcomes of the police visiting me. The neighbours will see them at my house. They will gossip, and then Natalya and Katherine will definitively find out that I have been part of the Alexa Clarke mystery after all.

Worse than that, Kamal will learn that I went to see Otis after promising I wouldn't. Maybe he'll even find out the truth about last night. Either way, he will discover my lies.

But then there's another worry. A darker, scarier worry.

If this were a book, I'd be a suspicious character. Maybe I already am. Maybe that's why the police are here. I mean, the stranger who randomly shows up to help, then pops up again when she's been advised to stay away? It's questionable, at best.

If I was writing this, I would heighten my role as the story developed, hinting that I wasn't as new to Alexa and Otis's story as I made out. A conversation with Alexa in the village store, perhaps, or a history of working with Otis. With my presence odd enough to create suspicion, I would transform into one thing: a suspect.

Terrified, I want to stay in my bedroom and avoid the consequences of inserting myself into a stranger's life, but I can't. With my nails embedded into my palms, I push myself downstairs.

The detectives are waiting for me in the living room, studying the neutral decor as if the colour of the walls can provide an insight into my psyche. They turn when I enter.

'Janine,' DS Rani says with a smile. 'Thanks for seeing us so early. We'll try to be quick so we don't take up too much of your day.'

'I appreciate that,' I reply, sitting on the sofa at the same time as Kamal enters with a tray of drinks. Without looking at him, I know he's nervous and confused.

'I made one for you, too,' he says, lowering the tray for me to grab a cup of tea.

'Thanks,' I reply, offering my husband what I hope comes across as a reassuring smile.

When the drinks are dispensed, Kamal hovers beside the coffee table. 'Should I stay?'

'No,' I reply, a little too forcefully, before turning to the detectives to explain. 'Kamal doesn't know Alexa or Otis. He's not involved.'

I'm not immune to the way my husband's eyebrows arch, especially at the word 'involved', but Kamal cannot be in this room. If he hears how I have insisted on remaining part of Alexa's story, he will be so disappointed.

'I'll be in the kitchen if you need me,' he says, turning to leave. Before he goes, he catches my eye. My features remain impassive, because no smile or 'It will be okay' gesture could make anyone feel better about the unannounced arrival of two detectives.

Moments after Kamal exits the room, we hear him rattle about in the kitchen, making as much noise as he can to prove he isn't listening to our conversation.

'Have you found Alexa? Is that why you're here?' I ask, smoothing my hands down my thighs to release some of my tension.

'Not yet. Right now, we're still piecing the situation together,' DS Rani replies.

'As I'm sure you can tell, it's not the most straightforward case,' DS Mullins adds. 'The delay in reporting and what we've uncovered since we last spoke have thrown up a few questions. We're hoping you might be able to help answer them.'

'Sure, but I don't know how much more I can tell you,' I reply awkwardly.

'Well, let's chat and see, shall we?' DS Rani replies. 'Since we last saw you, we've made good headway with learning about Alexa's life. Otis informed us she was attending a bereavement support group. We're conducting interviews with her associates there as we speak. And, since we last spoke, we have learned that Alexa's card was indeed being used fraudulently. A student claims to have found it on the street near Manchester University.'

My eyebrows furrow. 'And they used it?'

'Apparently, a life-hack TikTok inspired a trend of people using lost bank cards until they're cancelled,' DS Mullins replies. 'Anything to help the cost-of-living crisis, it seems, even if it is fraud.'

As I smile tightly, DS Rani continues. 'CCTV shows the student picking up the card.'

'And Alexa?' I press. 'Does it show her dropping it?'

DS Rani hesitates. 'No,' she admits. 'But the location the card was found is interesting. It was found near a café called The Grounds. Have you ever heard of it?'

I shake my head.

'It's close to the university campus. It's also two streets away from Otis Clarke's office.'

'Oh,' I reply, my voice small.

'Oh indeed. Janine, when you were with Otis in Manchester, how did he seem?'

I think back to that afternoon. It's only a few days ago, but with everything that's happened, it could have been another lifetime. 'He was tense,' I say.

'Is there anything else you can add to that description?'

I pause to think. 'All I remember is that we waited for a long time and Alexa didn't show. Otis was worried. That's why he called you.'

'And did you believe his upset to be genuine?'

'Yes,' I reply, shrinking at my former naivety. 'I think that was the moment it hit Otis that Alexa really was gone. He seemed furious with himself for not doing more sooner. I believed him on that. Before you arrived, we were out walking. Searching the fields at the back of the house for Alexa.'

DS Mullins leans forward. 'A field behind his house, you say?'

I nod, but when I notice the detectives' eagerness, it dawns on me. 'You found something there, didn't you?'

When DS Mullins and DS Rani share a glance, my heart stops.

'What was it? What did you find?'

I know my questions cross a line, but DS Rani must suspect that telling me will make me open up to them more.

'We found a tennis ball,' she says eventually. 'We think it was probably left behind by a dog walker, but it was stained with something. It's been sent off for testing, but we're under the assumption that the stain could be blood.'

DS Rani's first sentence is booming in my mind so much that I barely hear the rest. 'Did you ... did you say a tennis ball?'

DS Rani scours my stunned reaction. 'Is there something we should know?'

I go to swallow, but my throat is too tight. 'The day you first came to the house, Otis spotted a tennis ball in the field. He – he picked it up and threw it.'

Both detectives cannot hide their surprise.

'Otis Clarke found what appears to be a blood-spattered object moments before we arrived to ask about his missing wife, and he threw it?' DS Mullins asks.

'He did, but it all happened so fast. Maybe Otis didn't see the stain.'

Dubiousness is written all over the detectives' faces, but they don't push me. They don't need to. My confirmation that Otis had seen the tennis ball is more than enough.

DS Rani sets her sights on me once more. 'Has Otis ever mentioned Denmark to you?'

The sudden swerve in conversation is disorientating, but as DS Rani studies my reaction, I realise that was intentional.

'He told me Alexa was from there, if that's what you mean,' I say.

'Has Otis ever mentioned a desire to travel there with Alexa? Maybe even move there?'

I blink. 'No. He's not mentioned it in any context other than being Alexa's birthplace.'

The detectives nod and the conversation moves on. I try not to be alarmed by questions like, 'How did Otis seem when you first met him?' or 'Did Otis share with you what he and Alexa argued about?', but I can't help it. Each time a question that casts doubt on Otis is fired my way, that man and his wife shapeshift before me.

But then DS Mullins speaks and it's like a torch is being shone directly into my eyes. 'If I'm honest, Mrs Rai, the thing I still struggle to explain is how you came to be involved in this to the level that you are. Helping a stranger I can understand, but your role here goes beyond that of a concerned citizen.'

'I . . . don't understand,' I reply, even though I know exactly what he's hinting at.

'Okay, Mrs Rai. Why did you meet Alexa Clarke's best friend and share theories with her?' DS Mullins's words drill me to the sofa. 'Sonya West was very distressed when we spoke to her. She's adamant Otis has something to do with whatever's happened to Alexa. She says you share that belief.'

'That's not true,' I protest. 'It's Sonya who thinks that.'

'And what do you think?'

'I . . . I don't know,' I reply with a bite of my lip. 'Does Otis know I met Sonya?'

'Why does it matter if he does?'

I don't know how to answer the question.

When the silence stretches to an uncomfortable level, DS Mullins flips through his notepad. 'There are other elements of your involvement here that raise questions. For example, we know you've spoken to Mrs Clarke's neighbour, Dorrit Holbeck. And Otis said that the day he met you, he returned home to find you trespassing on his property. Is that true?'

I answer with a shamed nod, waiting for DS Mullins to mention seeing me at Families United, but he doesn't.

'Perhaps now you can see my concern. As someone who claims to be an innocent helper, some of your actions don't match that description. You could even say they are sneaky. We thought, if you didn't have anything to hide, you would be open to providing us with an answer as to why that is.'

As I baulk at DS Mullins's interrogation, DS Rani leans closer. 'What we're trying to ascertain, Janine, is if there's anything you're not telling us. If there is, now is the time to share it.'

Gabby handing me Alexa's diary flashes in my mind, as does Simon's face at the end of the Families United meeting.

So much guilt.

So many secrets.

But as I'm on the verge of telling the police about the diary and my suspicions about Simon, I remember Gabby and Annalise. Gabby, who isn't quite as tough as she pretends she is, whose broken heart makes her as blind and reckless as me. Kind-hearted Annalise, who doesn't need the upset of having the police knock on her door if there's no reason for them to.

'Like I said, I heard Alexa was missing and wanted to help,' I reply. 'I approached the situation like I'd approach a book. That's why I looked closely at Alexa's bank trail and why I went to see Sonya. I was trying to piece together the jigsaw of what happened.'

'Something we have in common,' DS Rani says. 'I'm sure you're aware that we can only build a jigsaw when we have all the pieces.'

'If I had more pieces, I'd share them with you.'

'I'd like you to think about that statement carefully, Mrs Rai,' DS Mullins replies. 'I think you know more than you let on. I think there's something else here. Something you're not telling us.'

It's DS Mullins's suspicion that breaks me.

'Alexa Clarke suffered four miscarriages,' I blurt.

'Yes, we know about them,' he replies somewhat dismissively, but I shake my head.

'No, you don't understand. Alexa suffered miscarriages like … like me.' I swallow the lump that appears in my throat. 'I want to find her. I want to help. I want … I want …'

Even through the blur of my tears, I see the change in the room. DS Mullins sits rigid while DS Rani oozes sympathy, an emotion I find almost as unbearable as DS Mullins's discomfort.

'My involvement might not make sense to you, but that's why I wanted to help,' I whisper.

DS Mullins opens his mouth, but DS Rani shoots him a look that says, 'Leave it.'

'In that case,' she says, 'it's time we left you to enjoy the rest of your day.'

My movements are stiff as I lead the detectives to the door. They make a point of thanking Kamal for the tea and wishing us both a good day, but their words wash over me.

As soon as the front door closes behind them, I exhale. I lean my forehead against the door, my skull rattling with a million thoughts, most of them centring around Alexa's diary.

A diary the police know nothing about.

A diary I didn't tell them about, but how could I? DS Mullins already looks at me suspiciously. Imagine how it would sound if I told them I secretly went to Families United and foolishly used my sister's identity?

The police are already interviewing people from Families United. They will find Simon there and figure it out, I tell myself. *You did nothing wrong.*

I lift my forehead from the door and tap it onto the wood two, three times, as if to hammer the reassurance into my skull.

'Janine?'

Turning, I find Kamal standing a few feet behind me, gnarled with worry.

'What did the police want?' he asks.

'They … they found a bloodied tennis ball at the back of Otis's house. They're testing it to see if it's Alexa's blood.' The words don't seem real even when I say them out loud.

'Fuck,' Kamal whispers. 'So they think he's hurt her?'

'It sounds that way, but I don't know, Kamal. Otis seems so …'

I trail off as Kamal's eyes flash with fear. 'I thought you weren't seeing him anymore?'

'I'm not,' I reply quickly. 'The police were here to go over my statement in case I'd missed something.'

'Did you tell them you wouldn't know of any developments? That you've not been around Otis Clarke for days now?'

My smile strangles itself. 'Of course. I've got nothing to hide.'

Upon hearing those words, Kamal comes to me and wraps me in a hug. 'Let's leave this to the police to sort now, hey? This has been scary enough.'

'Definitely,' I reply, but as I hold my husband close, I can't help thinking one thing: how can the police sort out anything when they have only been told a fraction of what's going on?

CHAPTER 35

Having the police at the house was stressful, but knowing the news would quickly spread through the village was somehow worse. Barely fifteen minutes after they leave, Natalya messages me.

Franny Henderson is saying that the police are at your house. Is it true?

The question makes me so anxious that I want to stay home all day, but I can't give my nerves their usual power. Not when I promised Gabby I'd go with her to confront 'S'.

In the safety of my office, I google 'Café Marco'. My intestines knot when I read that there are three cafés with that name in the UK. Two are over three hours away. One is in Saddleforth. My mouth dries as I read the address, the likelihood of Simon being 'S' growing with every second.

Grabbing my phone, I message Beth.

I need you to cover for me with Kamal again. I promise I'll make it up to you x

Beth calls seconds after reading the message, but I ignore her and get ready to go out.

'Beth's asked if we can meet again,' I shout from the bottom of the stairs, stuffing my feet into a pair of boots so I can leave as soon as I've dropped the excuse. 'She needs to chat about Mila.'

Kamal appears on the landing. 'Again? Is everything okay?'

'Beth was saying how difficult Mila's behaviour is,' I say, reaching for the doorhandle. 'I think she just needs someone to reassure her that she's a great mum and Mila won't grow to be a teenage delinquent.'

'Anything I can help with?' Kamal calls as I open the door. Guilt bites at me.

'It's a sister talk kind of thing. Don't worry, it will all be fine,' I reply before scurrying outside. I know I've left my husband wearing an expression that looks a lot like worry, but I can't care about that when one p.m. is creeping up on me.

It's only when I'm behind the wheel that I remember Families United isn't the only time I've heard Saddleforth referenced in relation to Alexa Clarke. Days ago, in the village store, Mary confessed that Franny Henderson saw Alexa there with another man. The memory does little to dissuade me that Annalise isn't going to have her heart broken in all this.

Beth calls when I'm at the end of my road. I let the call ring out, but when she rings again, I answer.

'Are you in the car?' she asks, her tone sharp. 'Where are you going?'

'Nowhere important. I'm heading out for some writing snacks.'

'Writing snacks, really? Come on, Janine. Are you going to tell me the truth, or do I have to wait until the police show up to be told that you got yourself into a dodgy situation hunting for this missing woman?'

My stomach lurches. 'How do you know about that?'

'You're not the only one who talks to Kamal, you know.'

'Kamal told you what's been going on?' I ask, the sense of betrayal I feel cutting deep.

'Don't act so shocked. You've been all over the place recently, and this morning, the police showed up on your doorstep. Kamal's worried. By the sound of it, rightfully so.'

'I wish you'd all stop worrying about me,' I grumble.

'Well, we wish you'd stop giving us reason to worry. You should be focusing on yourself and healing after what you've gone through, not this.'

'All I do is think of what I've gone through,' I can't help snapping. 'I don't need you all to do that for me, too, and I definitely don't need the constant reminders of what happened.'

'Janine—'

'No,' I cut in. 'You don't get to tell me what to do, Beth, okay? For once, just leave me alone.'

I hear my sister protest, but I hang up before she can finish her sentence. Immediately, guilt engulfs me. I shouldn't have spoken to Beth like that. I shouldn't have hung up. I shouldn't have done any of the things I've been doing recently, but here I am, still doing them.

I wish I could say why in a way that makes sense. I wish ignoring my deadline and pushing away the people whose only crime is loving me was something I could explain, but I can't. All I can do is keep my foot on the accelerator as if the answer can be found in Saddleforth.

It should be a relief when I arrive, but if anything, it's a marker of how far I have slipped from reality.

As soon as I step inside Café Marco, my suspicions that Alexa might have been having an affair intensify. With its traditional decor and intimate atmosphere, Café Marco strikes me as the perfect casual date spot. I can almost picture Alexa and Simon flirting over steaming cappuccinos and flaky pastries before sharing a sugary kiss.

I spot Gabby sitting by the window, beckoning me over.

'I was worried you wouldn't show,' she says, inviting me to take a seat next to her.

'Part of me wishes I hadn't,' I reply, removing my coat.

'It feels real now we're here, doesn't it?' Gabby says, biting her lip.

I don't reply. Instead, I take note of my surroundings. Although it's around lunchtime, the café is blessedly quiet. Other than an elderly couple and a group of new mums and their babies, we are alone. There's no Simon – or Alexa – in sight.

When I'm settled, a waitress comes over with a bottle of water for the table and takes our order. After she returns with my croissant and hot chocolate, and a coffee for Gabby, all there is to do is wait.

'I've brought my laptop,' Gabby says, turning it to face me. 'Alexa wasn't very discreet. I've found Simon on her Facebook friends list.'

'Maybe she didn't need to be discreet. Maybe it's not an affair.'

Gabby grunts dubiously in response. Reaching for her laptop, I flick through Simon's 'About Me' section.

'Simon Brooks, thirty-six, born in Newcastle,' I mutter.

Flicking through the rest of Simon's profile, I tense at every photo of him with Annalise. Family parties, gushing posts on significant dates, mini-break snapshots – they share so much of their relationship with the world it's verging on too much. Each moment looks happy, but I know if they're attending Families United, then beneath the surface there has been more sadness in their lives than a person should ever feel.

'He's very attractive,' Gabby says. 'It's not hard to see why Alexa would be tempted.'

'I guess,' I reply, knowing all too well that the truthful answer to that is 'I know'. My eyes linger on a photo of Simon that showcases his good looks and natural charisma, wondering if he really is the man Annalise believes him to be. I'm so engrossed in that question that I almost don't notice him walking through the door.

CHAPTER 36

The world screeches to a halt when I finally register Simon's presence. I blink twice, waiting for his features to rearrange and become the face of a stranger, but they never do.

'That's him, isn't it?' Gabby hisses. Disappointment crushes my chest, but it soon transforms into white-hot fury when I think of Annalise embarking on the scariest time of her life under the impression that she has a loving husband by her side.

'Yes,' I whisper.

The bastard, my lips fight to add, but I hold it together enough to watch Simon make his way through the café. He's dressed in a pale blue shirt with the top two buttons undone. His sandy hair is styled – not obsessively but enough to let you know he takes care of himself.

But it's not Simon's outfit or looks that capture my attention – it's the energy he buzzes with. There's a desperation to him that jars with the chilled vibe of Café Marco. He scans the room, his hope dimming with each second that passes, until he spots me.

Simon takes a step backwards, unable to hide his surprise. The desire to flee or pretend he hasn't seen me flashes in him, but as I raise my hand to wave, Simon realises it's too late.

'Beth, is that you?' he says as he approaches our table.

I blink, momentarily forgetting I'd used my sister's name as my own. I feel Gabby's gaze on me, hot and confused, but I catch myself before my confusion shows.

'It is,' I reply. 'How lovely to see you again!' Snapping Gabby's laptop shut so Simon doesn't see his Facebook profile on the screen, I gesture to a seat opposite. 'Join us, if you'd like. We could use a break.'

'Oh, I don't want to interrupt,' Simon says, backing away.

'Please,' Gabby says, her tone borderline desperate. 'You're more than welcome.'

Simon takes another quick glance around the café before sinking into the chair.

'So,' I say after introducing Gabby and Simon. 'What brings you to Café Marco?'

Simon's squirming fluster reinforces my worst fears. 'Just grabbing a coffee.'

'Is this your usual midday break spot?'

'Me? No, I – I don't come here often,' Simon stammers.

Gabby pounces on this. 'Really?' she says, her tone so confrontational that I almost kick her under the table.

'I don't usually get out to coffee shops, either,' I say, smiling to gloss over Gabby's intensity. 'But a break was needed today!'

Simon nods, then his eyebrows furrow. 'Wait, I thought you were a teacher? Shouldn't you be at school right now?'

Ignoring my internal screaming, I widen my smile. 'Gabby and I both are. This is our planning time. We thought we'd go to a café so we didn't get roped into clearing out the PE cupboard,' I joke. 'How about you? No work today?'

My phone interrupts the flow of conversation by ringing. As Simon jumps, Sonya's name lights up the screen. My heart skips a beat.

Snatching my phone before he reads who's calling, I decline the call and switch my setting to Do Not Disturb. I don't know if Alexa ever mentioned a friend called Sonya West to Simon, but him confronting me about how I know her isn't the way I want to find out.

'Sorry about that,' I say. 'You were telling us about your job?'

'Right,' Simon says, his Adam's apple bobbing as he gulps. 'I work in sales. Fittings and fixtures for construction jobs, mostly.'

'Sounds interesting,' I reply, which might be the most outrageous lie I've ever told. 'Do you not work on Fridays?'

'They're my half-days. The afternoon is time for myself.'

Beside me, Gabby snorts. Again, the temptation to kick her is strong, but just then a waitress sidles up to the table to take Simon's order.

'Good to see you, Simon,' she enthuses as she stops beside us. 'Alexa couldn't make it this week?'

As my eyes bulge, Simon turns an almost inhuman shade of crimson. 'She's – she's busy,' he says before ordering a latte.

'No panini? I'm shocked,' the waitress jokes, but Simon's curt response soon wipes the friendliness from her. She leaves with a swiftness that's almost as abrupt as his ending of the conversation.

When the waitress is out of earshot, I turn to Simon. 'Alexa? The missing woman they mentioned at the meeting?'

Simon struggles to contain the lies on the tip of his tongue, but instead of saying any of them, he settles on a one-word response.

'Yes.'

As soon as Simon says it, Gabby slaps her palm on the table. 'I fucking knew it,' she snaps, her face twisting in rageful disgust.

I want to react as boldly as Gabby, but the news hasn't filled me with anger. It's made me numb. Suddenly, being here seems like the most ridiculous thing I could be doing when I have a deadline looming and a marriage I don't want to ruin. I shake my head, furious with myself for once again wading in deeper than I wanted to. I mean, why am I involving myself in Alexa's life like this? Why do I care so much about a woman I don't know? This attachment has caused me nothing but grief. It's resulted in me sitting opposite the man she has been having an affair with, all the while knowing that his wife is out there, planning for the family she is desperate to start.

Why put myself through this?

Why fight for someone who is willingly compounding someone else's pain?

'What's going on?' Simon asks, looking from Gabby to me and back again.

'How can you seriously ask that?' Gabby snarls, grabbing her laptop and stuffing it in her bag. 'I knew Alexa was up to no good! I mean, who the fuck takes off like this if they're not having an affair?'

'Alexa?' Simon echoes, his forehead creased. 'Do you know where she is?'

'I should be asking you that, seeing as you're shagging her!'

Simon's head jerks back as if he's been slapped.

'You disgust me,' Gabby hisses, shuffling out of her seat. When she's stood, she faces me. 'I need to go. I can't be here. I can't look at him.'

'Gabby,' I say, trying to stop her from walking away, but it's too late. She's already storming out of the café. Torn, I make a move to follow her, but Simon grabs my wrist.

'Please, you don't understand,' he begins, but I pull my hand from his.

'Simon, I met you at Families United. Of course I understand! I wake up every day knowing how losing a child tears your life apart, just like you. Unlike you, I don't use it as a justification for breaking my vows.'

Without listening to another of Simon's feeble excuses, I leave the table and head for the door.

'Gabby!' I call as I step out into the chilly air, but she rushes down the cobbled street, heading towards her car.

'Beth, stop!'

Simon's pathetic pleas follow me down the road. I increase my pace to avoid them, but inches away from my car, a hand grabs my arm.

'Please listen to me,' Simon begs, spinning me to face him. 'You've got it all wrong! I'm not having an affair with Alexa Clarke. We talk and we get on, but Alexa – well, she's giving me and Annalise the money to fund another round of IVF.'

CHAPTER 37

I would be mortified about having to walk back into a café I'd just stormed out of if I weren't so numb from the shock of Simon's revelation. Ignoring the curious glances of everyone in Café Marco, Simon leads me and Gabby back to our table and tells Gabby to take a drink of water when she collapses into her seat.

'Do you want me to get you something to eat? You're really pale,' he says, peering into her face.

Gabby shakes her head and gulps her water. The glass clatters against her teeth, her hands unsteady. Simon watches her closely.

'Who are you?' he asks.

'This is Gabby,' I reply when she doesn't. 'Otis's best friend.'

A look of recognition sweeps over Simon's face. 'I see,' he says. 'And you are?'

'Janine,' I say, grimacing when Simon reacts to my real name. 'I'm ... a friend of Alexa's,' I add.

'And you're here because ... ?'

'We found Alexa's diary. We know the two of you have been meeting. We thought you were having an affair.'

'Are you?' Gabby asks, her voice croaky and raw.

'No,' Simon replies, shaking his head. 'No, we're not.'

Gabby hangs her head behind a curtain of her hair. She looks so devastated that for a split second, I can't help thinking she *wanted* Alexa to be having an affair.

'Do you know where Alexa is?' I ask, redirecting my focus to Simon.

'No.' Devastation tints Simon's voice. 'That's why I came here. I hoped ... I thought I might walk in and find her here.'

I nod, understanding that wish exactly. 'You meet Alexa once a week?'

'We do. As friends, though, I swear,' Simon rushes to correct. 'Although I know how it looks. Alexa and I both do, that's why we meet in secret. Two people who met at a child loss support group, leaning on each other? It's a rumour waiting to happen.'

My lips twitch, knowing that was exactly what Gabby and I had believed.

'How did the meetings start?' I ask.

With a sigh, Simon looks off into the distance. 'It's hard to explain, really. Alexa started attending Families United meetings earlier in the year. From the get-go, she and I clicked. At her first meeting, we were both at the snack table, eating our body weight in biscuits. We cracked a few jokes, but we got chatting properly at her second meeting. I think I said more about how I felt to Alexa in those few minutes than I had to anyone in months.'

'Even Annalise?'

Simon flushes but nods. 'You know how it is. Sometimes talking to your partner about loss is hard. I don't want to upset Annalise by bringing it up, but that doesn't mean I don't need to talk about what's happened. Trust me when I say I love my wife. You've met Annalise, you know how amazing she is. I would never risk what we have, ever.'

'I believe you,' I say, a response that makes Simon exhale. Gabby, meanwhile, says nothing.

'Alexa and I meet once a week for a coffee,' Simon continues. 'It helps to have a space separate from meetings where we can talk freely. We meet for a couple of hours. Other than Families United, I think it's pretty much the only time Alexa sees anyone.'

My heart aches as the loneliness of Alexa Clarke's life is reinforced yet again. 'That's so sad.'

'It is. I worry about her. It's not good to be alone when you're grieving.'

'You think Alexa's alone?'

Simon's forehead scrunches. 'Janine, Alexa Clarke is the loneliest person I've ever met.'

Across the table, Gabby flinches. I wipe a drop of water from the side of my glass to distract myself from the hollowness I feel at Simon's statement.

'You said Alexa was paying for your IVF?' I ask.

'Not all of it, but most of it,' Simon admits. 'After the pandemic, I lost my job. Annalise and I managed to keep the house, but our savings took a big hit. I've got another job now and we're slowly getting back on track, but my new place doesn't pay anywhere near as much as the last.'

'That's why you need the money from Alexa?'

Simon nods. 'Annalise found a clinic with high success rates. It's a fancy private one, the kind that charges you for breathing in the waiting room. Even with sinking every penny we had into it, we couldn't make the numbers work. I told Annalise I'd ask my parents, but she wouldn't let me. She said, "We're not a charity case."' Simon sighs and rubs his temples. 'Annalise never used to be sensitive about money, but when you're struggling with fertility, people are exhaustingly sympathetic. I know they're only trying to be nice, but it's painful, and we've had years of it. Annalise is sick of people looking at her like she needs saving.'

'I know that feeling,' I reply.

Simon smiles sadly. 'What a club to be in, huh? Losing a child … well, it changes how people see you. It changes you as a person, too. Over the years, parts of Annalise have hardened. She refuses to be seen as weak or dependent, and that includes accepting financial help. I respect her position, I really do, but I know how much a baby means to her. I'd rob a bank if I had to, if it meant we could try.'

'Annalise probably wouldn't like that.'

Simon laughs. 'Probably not. Luckily, thanks to Alexa, I didn't have to turn to crime to fund the treatment. A few months ago, I admitted that Annalise and I were struggling with the IVF fees. She stepped in to help. Annalise would have refused it, but I couldn't. It was too generous an offer to miss out on. I never asked for the money, mind you. And I told Alexa I'd pay her back every penny.'

The walls of my throat thicken as I imagine Alexa pushing her own grief to the side to help Simon and Annalise. Deep inside, the ache that begs for her to be okay grows.

'Does Annalise know you're getting money for the treatment from Alexa?' I ask.

Simon hesitates, then shakes his head. 'I've told Annalise I've taken on extra work,' he admits. 'Sometimes I say it's overtime, but mostly I say I'm helping my cousin at his construction company. I tell her he gives me cash so we can avoid paying tax and put all the money into IVF.'

My right eyebrow raises. 'Alexa pays you in cash?'

'Always. That way Annalise won't find a trail from her bank to mine.'

As Alexa's cash withdrawals are cast in a new light, all I can think of is how this news changes everything.

'Is Annalise suspicious about the money?' Gabby asks.

'I don't think so,' Simon says, but the words weigh heavily on him. 'I don't want to lie, but this is the only way I can afford to make Annalise's dreams of being a mum come true.'

'Why don't you just take the money?' Gabby asks hotly. 'Why do you have to meet Alexa, too? Surely you see how suspicious it looks.'

Simon's squirm is back. 'I do, but in many ways Alexa's the best friend I've ever had. I don't find talking easy, and some things are too personal to share with an audience at Families United. There are things I can't say to Annalise, either. I mean, how am I meant to tell her that I'm terrified of what another round of IVF will do to us? Last time things didn't work, it nearly killed me. I don't know if I can go through that again.'

As Simon hangs his head, I reach out and squeeze his hand. 'I'm glad you have Alexa to talk to.'

'Yeah, but now she's missing, and I don't know what to do to help her,' Simon replies tearfully. 'I came to Café Marco today on the off-chance she'd be here. Silly, right?'

'That's not silly at all,' I soothe, but Simon is struggling to contain his emotions and barely hears me.

'You really have no idea where she is?' Gabby asks.

Simon shakes his head. 'Alexa messaged me the day she went missing to say *I'll get more biscuits next week*. That was our code. It meant she would have another instalment of cash for me. Innocuous enough to anyone who saw it, but we'd know what it meant. I was so busy, I didn't see the message until Saturday afternoon.

Apparently by that point, she was gone.' Simon presses his head into his hands. 'I keep going over it, thinking if I'd have replied sooner, would it have made a difference? Would she have told me if something was wrong?'

All too familiar prickles of dread pierce my skin. 'Do you think something was wrong?'

'That's the million-dollar question, isn't it? There's no way to answer that. Alexa is grieving like me, like you, so of course there's something wrong, but maybe there was more? Maybe Alexa was unhappy in a deeper way?'

'Do you mean unhappy in her marriage or something?' I ask, trying to keep my tone neutral despite the heavy question I'm asking.

'I don't know what I mean. All I know is, a few weeks ago Alexa said she no longer recognises the man she married, and now she's missing.'

Beside me, Gabby stiffens, but I remain composed. 'Alexa said that?' I ask.

Simon nods, firing a cautious glance Gabby's way. 'That's why when I first heard the news, I thought she'd left him, but now almost a week has passed and Alexa's not let anyone know where she is or if she's okay. That's not like her. She wouldn't worry people like this.'

Even though it makes my skin prickle with goosebumps, I push myself to ask the question despite fearing the answer. 'What do you think has happened?'

Simon's features twist. 'I don't know. I don't want to think it's anything bad, but Alexa being missing for so long only points to one thing.'

When Simon meets my gaze, he doesn't have to say what that one thing is. The fear that Alexa might be dead is written all over his face.

'Otis would never,' Gabby says vehemently, but I don't share her confidence.

'What else did Alexa say about Otis?' I ask.

'She said – she said her husband has a big personality,' Simon says, avoiding looking at Gabby while he speaks. 'While she's shrunk because of what's happened, he's grown. He's taken on more work, made more money and been away from home for longer. But from what Alexa's said, all that success comes at a price.'

'That's a big accusation to make,' Gabby says hotly.

'I'm not accusing anyone of anything,' Simon corrects. 'But Alexa said Families United was the only place she laughed anymore. That's sad, now that I think about it. And worrying, don't you think?'

'A little,' I reply, though the tightening in my chest says it's more worrying than that.

'Every marriage has problems,' Gabby says, pink splodges colouring her cheeks. 'Otis works hard; he's a high achiever. Since when was that a crime?'

'It's not,' I begin, but my response irritates Gabby further.

'So why are you both acting as if Otis has done something wrong?'

'We're not, but this is the closest we've been in days to hearing Alexa's perspective on things,' I try to reason, but Gabby's defensiveness won't hear it.

'Otis is worried sick, Janine. You've seen him. How could someone who is that worried have been such a bad husband?'

'Because sometimes, we only see things when it's too late,' Simon says, silencing the table in one fell swoop. We all take a moment to breathe, the introspection only broken by Gabby pushing back her chair.

'I only came here to see if Alexa was having an affair. I've got all the answers I need,' she says, grabbing her handbag once more. 'Are you coming, Janine?'

I know Gabby wants me to leave with her, but one glance at Simon and I know there's more he wants to say.

'I'll stay and finish my drink,' I reply, even though my hot chocolate is stone cold now. Gabby knows this as well as I do. The corners of her eyes pinch, but I don't shy away from her scrutiny.

'Fine,' Gabby huffs, throwing her bag over her shoulder. 'I guess I'll call you later.'

I watch her leave, her auburn hair billowing behind her. Then, when she is gone, I turn back to Simon, waiting to hear what he could not share before.

CHAPTER 38

With Gabby gone, Simon's shoulders relax, but only slightly. Every part of him radiates concern, and I know from one glance what he is thinking.

'You think Otis has something to do with Alexa's disappearance, don't you?' I ask.

'He's the only person I can think of that would,' Simon replies, swallowing hard. 'And statistically speaking, whenever anything bad happens to someone, the perpetrator is usually someone they know. Someone they're close to. Alexa doesn't have many people in her life that she's close to.'

'Only you and Otis, by the sound of things.'

Worry creases Simon's forehead. 'You can't seriously think I have anything to do with her disappearing, do you?'

'I don't know,' I reply truthfully. 'I came here to find out who Alexa was meeting and what they knew. As for other judgements, I'm not sure it's my place to make them.'

'I swear to you, Janine, I didn't hurt Alexa. I never would, but I can't say the same about her husband. You should know that according to Alexa, Otis is strong-willed, impulsive and under a lot of pressure. Those aren't ideal traits at the best of times, but after what they've both gone through, I can only imagine how those characteristics manifest. Pushed far enough, who knows what he could do?'

I grip my mug, trying not to let my fear show as once again Otis transforms from loving husband to suspect.

'The first time I met him, I thought he was an arsehole,' Simon adds.

I blink. 'You've met Otis?'

'Sure, at Families United. He came with Alexa.'

I can't hide my surprise at this. 'Otis attends Families United, too?'

'God, no,' Simon says, pulling a face. 'He came to one meeting, left partway through and refused to entertain the idea of going back. He left Alexa to grieve on her own.'

'He said as much himself,' I reply, an answer that surprises Simon.

'Wow,' he replies. 'Alexa was trying for weeks to get him to admit that. Funny how it takes her to disappear for him to see what a shit husband he's been.'

'I don't know if he meant to be shit,' I say, struggling to find my words. 'There's a lot about Otis Clarke that I don't know, but I saw him a couple of days ago and he was a shell.'

'Yeah? Well, Alexa said he's been a shell of her husband for a long time now. She's been a shell of herself, too.'

My mouth twists in sympathy. 'I met Alexa once,' I say. 'At a fertility appointment. I didn't know who she was. It was only when I saw a photo of her that I realised who had gone missing. But what she said to me that day helped. There's a bond between people like us, I think. People who can look at someone and see that they share a connection through something so awful.'

'Is that why you want to help find her?'

'It is,' I admit before locking my eyes on Simon. 'Simon, you have to go to the police with this.'

Shutters slam down over his face. 'I can't. They'll find out about the money.'

'I know, but you won't be able to hide this forever. The police are going to find out you were meeting Alexa. I mean, all I did was look through her diary. You're in there as a recurring Friday meet-up.'

Simon's concern spikes.

'You saw the police last night,' I continue. 'They're looking for a missing woman. They need all the help they can get. They need to hear exactly what you've said to me today.'

All life gets sucked out of Simon at my words. He flops back against his chair, his expression glazed. 'They can't find out about us meeting. It will ruin everything.'

'Simon, you and Alexa weren't doing anything wrong.'

'Anything wrong? I've been secretly meeting another woman every week for months. I've been taking her money to fund fertility treatment for my wife, then lying and saying I've earned it. What part of that isn't wrong?'

'But you said there was nothing going on between you and Alexa.'

'There *is* nothing going on, but that's not the point. The point is that every day, I lie to my wife. When I say I'm working extra hours, when I say the money is ours, it's all lies! Annalise has been through enough without adding this to the mix.'

'But you've lied for her benefit,' I argue.

'So? A lie is still a betrayal of trust, no matter how good your intentions are.' Simon lets out a pained groan. 'How could I be so stupid? How did I not guess this would come back to haunt me?'

As Simon presses his knuckles into his eyes to stop himself from crying, I think of all the lies Kamal has digested over the last few months. I've told many, but none have tortured me as much as Simon's lies torture him.

What does that say about me as a person?

What does that say about my marriage?

Swallowing those acidic thoughts, I lean forward. 'Simon, the police have Alexa's phone. They will find out about you through your contact history. When they do, it will look bad if you haven't come to them first.'

'Alexa and I delete our messages, though,' Simon says.

'They're the police, Simon. They have ways of knowing who someone has been in touch with and how often they are.'

Simon rests his head in his hands, the epitome of a man with the weight of the world on his shoulders. 'This is such a mess.'

'I know, but a woman you call a friend is missing. You might be able to help find her. You can either go to the police yourself, or they can show up at your house one day when you least expect it.'

Simon flinches at the image of Annalise opening the door to the police. 'But I don't know anything about Alexa's disappearance. I don't know where she is.'

'So? Your friendship with Alexa can help build a bigger picture of her life before she disappeared. Besides, the police are under the impression that Alexa was syphoning money to leave Otis. You need to tell them what that money was really for.'

Simon groans, his head dropping once more. 'But what if Annalise doesn't understand? What if she can't forgive me?'

'If you explain the situation like you did to me, I'm sure she'll see why you did this.'

Simon pales as he lifts his head to meet my gaze. 'What if she doesn't?'

I don't have it in me to explain the alternative ending. 'The truth is going to come out one way or another. Right now, you have the luxury of deciding which way that is. Either get ahead of it and control the narrative, or let the police show up and tell Annalise a version where secret meet-ups are as dodgy as they sound.'

'Secret meet-ups.' Simon groans. 'It sounds so bad when you say it like that.'

'You needed a friend, Simon. Alexa was that person for you. There's no crime in that.'

'I just hope Annalise sees it that way,' he replies, sniffing back tears. 'You know, I knew Alexa wouldn't be here today, but I came anyway. I hoped I'd walk in and see her sitting at our usual table, waiting for me.'

'I kind of hoped that, too,' I admit. But the more time that passes, the more my hope of ever seeing Alexa again dims. Now, the light is so dull, it's almost extinguished.

CHAPTER 39

Alexa

Six days gone

Bloodied, dazed and confused, Alexa stared into the lens above her. Her eyes rolled, willing themselves to disappear into the back of her skull so she didn't have to witness another moment in the white room, but the captor gripped her chin, keeping her alert.

The click came first, then the blinding flash, followed by the whir of a polaroid being printed.

Alexa didn't know what, or whom, the polaroids were for, but the captor had been taking them ever since they first came into the room. They'd homed in on Alexa's face as it scrunched when her skin was sliced. They'd taken a snapshot of how her blood trickled down her skin. Print after print, the worst events of Alexa's life had been documented.

Alexa wondered if the photos were being sent to her husband to extort him for money in exchange for her return. She wondered if he would pay the ransom or not, then shook her head. That shouldn't even be a question. Things between them had been bad, but they loved each other underneath it all.

If the images were being sent to him, then Alexa knew that she could cling to hope. There was no way anyone could see photos of a person reduced to a shell and not do everything in their power to save them. Especially if it was someone they loved.

But the darkest side of Alexa's brain warned her that there were other uses for such images. Perhaps the captor never intended to share them. Perhaps they were for them and them alone. Kept like sick trophies to mark their cruellest days. A scrapbook that they could flick through on cold nights and relive their most horrific actions.

And if that was the case? Well, Alexa knew that there was no way she was getting out of here alive.

'Please,' she rasped, moving even though the chains weighed her down.

The captor reached out and grabbed Alexa's hand. She knew what was coming before it happened. But still, Alexa Clarke roared in pain as her index finger was snapped clean in two. Punishment for her thinking she had even the slightest bit of autonomy in this situation.

Again, the camera framed up the injury.

Again, a light flashed and a polaroid was printed.

Again, Alexa Clarke found herself wishing for the welcoming embrace of death.

CHAPTER 40

I listen to the radio on the drive back to Bramblethorpe, but it's not enough to stop my conversation with Simon from infiltrating my mind.

It's clearer than ever how shut off from everyone Alexa was, especially Otis. A man who has lied to me, to Gabby, to the police. A man both Simon and Sonya describe in unflattering terms.

I bite my lip, thinking of how, by this time tomorrow, no one will have seen or heard from Alexa in a week. Seven days is a long time. Long enough to change a life, for better or for worse. You can fall in love in seven days. Have an affair that destroys your marriage. Find out you're pregnant, then learn that you no longer are.

I'm so focused on untangling my thoughts that I barely notice I'm back in Bramblethorpe, driving too fast for this village and its winding roads. The first time my surroundings register with me is when Bernie races across the road ahead, chasing a rabbit.

'Fuck!' I screech, slamming on my brakes and waiting for the sickening thud of impact.

Thankfully, it never comes.

Releasing the tension from my face, I open my eyes to see Jim in the centre of the road, scooping Bernie into his arms. He holds him to his chest as if Bernie were a baby, then locks his furious gaze on me. My spine pins me to my seat as Jim storms towards my car.

'Why the hell were you driving so fast?' he bellows. 'It's a thirty zone around here!'

My hands are shaking so much it takes me three attempts to wind my window down. 'I'm so sorry. Is Bernie okay?'

'I don't want your apology. I want to know why you were speeding.'

I glance at my hands, white-knuckling my steering wheel, but when Jim follows my eyeline, he thinks I'm looking at my phone clipped into its holder.

'I hope whatever's on your phone is more important than a life,' he spits, then kicks the side of my car. A terrified yelp escapes me at the menace behind the impact.

Jim doesn't give my fright a second thought, though. He stomps away, still cradling Bernie. Remorseful tears blind me as I watch him go, but I can't blame Jim for being so angry.

Slumping forward, I rest my forehead on my steering wheel, breathing deeply to fight my tears. I'm losing my grip on everyday life, I can feel it – but the more I tangle myself in Alexa's story, the harder it is for me to walk away. A tear trickles down my cheek and lands on my jeans. I watch it soak into the material, staining the denim darker.

'I don't know what to do,' I whisper, but my upset is interrupted by the sound of a horn beeping. Jerking upright, I glance in my rear-view mirror. Of course it would be when I'm crying in the middle of the road that there's traffic in Bramblethorpe.

Trembling from the aftershock of my almost-collision, I set off driving, slower this time. The sting of my tears grows as I pass Jim and Bernie further along the road, peaking when I notice Jim glaring in my direction.

The sight of my house has never been more welcome, but as I draw nearer, I notice something odd. There are two cars in the driveway.

One belongs to Kamal.

The other belongs to my sister.

The questions surrounding her unexpected appearance are screaming at me by the time I pull into the driveway. I take a second to build my courage before leaving my car. When I do, my legs are trembling even more than they were when I nearly hit Bernie.

I find Kamal and Beth in the living room, standing sombre and silent.

'What are you doing here?' I ask, dropping my handbag on the sofa.

'I'm asking the questions here, Janine, not you,' Beth snaps. 'Namely, where the hell have you been?' Kamal dips his head at my sister's icy tone, but he doesn't tell her to be nicer.

'Jesus, Beth. There's no need to bite my head off.'

'You'd know all about biting people's heads off, wouldn't you?'

Ignoring her, I turn to my husband. 'Shouldn't you be working?'

'Shouldn't you be, too? Or in all your obsessing over Alexa Clarke have you forgotten you have a job?' Beth cuts in frostily.

I step backwards at my sister's hostility. 'Why are you so angry with me?'

'Angry? Janine, I'm way past angry. I'm furious. When are you going to stop playing with people's emotions? When are you going to stop acting like how they feel doesn't matter?'

'What are you talking about?'

'Look around you, Janine. Everyone is sick with worry. Mum can barely speak about you without crying. When's the last time you called her? Called any of us, for that matter. No, the only time we hear from you is when everything's falling apart.'

My body clenches, wounded. 'That's not fair.'

'None of this is fair, Janine. Most of all on everyone around you. I mean, have you noticed that I've had to leave my children, again, to run to your aid? Have you noticed anyone else's struggles, or are you still ignoring what's staring you in the face?'

Squaring my shoulders, I hold Beth's gaze and refuse to acknowledge what she is saying. I'd have thought my petulance would increase my sister's anger, but the crack in her voice when she next speaks tells me it did the opposite.

'You know how much we love you, so why do you treat us with such contempt? It's as if we're your enemies, not the people who care for you most. I know we can't begin to understand how you feel, but we want to be here for you. Please, let us. Stop shutting us out.'

As her words do their best to chip at me, I shield myself from the attack. 'I don't shut you out.'

Beth sighs. 'If you can't admit doing it when you dodge my calls and refuse to meet, at least acknowledge doing it to Kamal. You practically ran out of here earlier, using me as your sordid little alibi. No one had any idea where you were, yet again.'

I glance at my husband, so compressed by worry he can barely lift his head. 'I told you I was going out.'

'Yes, with me, which was a lie,' Beth snaps. 'You didn't say where you were going or what you were doing. You just left, hours after the police came to visit. Was Kamal meant to be reassured that all was well? He called me, panicked that you'd disappeared for another wander until three a.m.'

Shamefaced, I lower my gaze, but Beth isn't done with me yet.

'Once again, I left my children with our mother to help look for you. We thought you'd been in an accident. We drove all around Bramblethorpe. We even stopped for a chat with your new friend Otis.'

My stomach drops. 'You saw Otis today?'

'Yes, but he hadn't seen you. No one had. And better still, you thought it was a good idea to not pick up your phone.'

'I didn't get any missed calls,' I argue, but then I remember putting my phone on Do Not Disturb in Café Marco. Cringing, I pull my phone from my bag and change the setting. Straightaway, the screen fills with missed calls and voicemails, some from Sonya, but most from Kamal and Beth.

I go to apologise, but Beth continues before I can.

'Twice in two days you've told Kamal you've been with me when you haven't. Twice you've asked me to lie for you, and now you're home, acting shocked that we're worried, so guess what? After months of living with the constant dread that I'm going to get a phone call saying something terrible has happened, I've finally had enough.'

'I didn't ask you to check up on me,' I protest.

'No, you didn't, but that's what you do for people you love. You keep an eye on them when they're having a hard time. You are patient and you help, but the way we're helping needs to change. Playing nice and waiting for you to come around in your own time doesn't work with you, Janine. It never has, even when we were kids. So it's time for me to step up and be the sister you've always been to me. It's time for me to say enough. You need help. You need to go to therapy and learn that as horrible as this time is, you will get through it.'

Everything in me bristles at my sister's words. 'I'm fine.'

'No, you're not fine and you're not doing as good a job at pretending you are as you think. Kamal knows you've been lying. He knows you're not writing or taking your meds.'

The bottom of my world falls away with that revelation. I look from my sister to my husband, his wearied stance striking me harder than any punch ever could. 'You know?'

Kamal nods. 'Tiff reached out a couple of weeks ago,' he croaks. 'I knew your deadline had been extended, but I thought you'd been given six months. Tiff told me it was only three.'

Again, guilt engulfs me.

'Tiff told me that you'd not handed in any pages,' Kamal continues. 'I've known for a while about the pills, too.'

I have never heard my husband sound so defeated. I almost want to cover my ears at how heartbreaking his empty voice is. 'Why didn't you say anything?'

'I wanted to give you space to come to me when you were ready. I kept talking about writing, hoping it would give you the chance to open up. I tried to make taking your medication as easy as possible. I thought if I did all that, then it wouldn't come to this.'

As Kamal's voice splinters, so does my ribcage. The bones pierce my lungs, stealing my breath. 'Kamal,' I say, stepping towards him, but when he looks up, his potent sadness stops me in my tracks.

'I'm losing you, Janine. I've no idea how to stop it from happening, but I can't pick up the slack anymore. I've tried taking you to a doctor. I've tried letting you work through this how you see fit. I've let you lie, let you sneak around, let you forget work and plans and relationships, but I'm tired of coming home and not knowing where you are. I'm tired of thinking you've hurt yourself. I'm tired of waking up worried and going to sleep worried. I'm tired, Janine. I'm so tired.'

'We all are,' Beth adds. 'We're right here, saying we want to help. Don't push us away.'

As I study the faces of the people I love most, everything that's happened over the last few years ploughs into me. The cramps, the tears, the shame. Loss in all its unfiltered, unedited rawness.

'I don't like lying to you,' I reply, my throat thick with emotion. 'In fact, I hate myself for it, but I can't seem to stop. I know I should be writing. I know I should take the pills and go to counselling.'

'So why don't you?' Beth pushes.

'Because I'm scared.'

'Of what?'

My brain screams at me to lie. To shout, storm off, do anything but share the deepest, darkest part of my soul, but as I absorb my sister's concern, I realise that the time for lying has come to an end.

'I'm scared that if I take the medication, I'll stop feeling the pain,' I whisper. 'It's the only thing I have that reminds me that they were once here. There's no baby in my arms, no nursery filled with love. The pain is all I have. I'm scared that if I start feeling better, it means I'll forget them.'

'Janine,' Kamal says, reaching for me, but I hold my hand up to stop him.

'Please, I need to say this. I need to explain. I watch you all trying to make things right for me, but nothing will ever make me feel better about what I've lost or the way I've changed. The person I am now – she isn't me. I can barely leave the house, never mind see friends or go dancing or do any of the things I used to love. I don't want to be this person anymore. I want to be who I thought I was going to be. I want to be a mum.'

With those words, I dissolve into tears.

This time when Kamal reaches for me, I don't protest. As he wraps me in his arms, he speaks into my hair. 'I know I can't fix this, but please let me be there for you while you try to. You are everything to me.'

'I shouldn't be,' I sob. 'Not anymore.'

Kamal takes my head in his hands and brushes my hair from my cheeks. 'How can you not see what's staring you in the face? I will always, always love you, Janine.'

Crumbling, I hold my husband properly for the first time in a long time. We cling to each other, weighted by the perpetual crush of sadness, but reminded that we're not the only person feeling it. And, more importantly, that we don't need to carry it alone.

CHAPTER 41

For the first time in a long time, I feel some form of peace. Beth calls Mum and tells her she's staying the night. While Kamal cooks dinner, my sister and I sit with a bottle of wine. We talk about loss. We talk about our childhood. We talk about my nieces, work and how the hell I'm going to get back on track with my writing. And, at the end of the day, I climb into bed with my husband and don't pull away.

'I've missed you,' I whisper into the crook of Kamal's neck.

'I'm right here,' he murmurs back. 'I'll always be right here.'

My sleep is broken and accompanied by sadness, but still, I sleep. When I wake up, it's to my husband handing me a freshly made coffee.

'I debated whether to show you this,' he says, his phone in his other hand. 'But I think you'll want to see it.'

Sitting upright, I look at what's loaded on the screen. A well-groomed Sonya stares out from the home page of a national news site. In her manicured hands, she holds a picture of Alexa.

Grim-faced, I skim the article. Sonya has made Alexa headline news, and Otis the perfect villain.

Otis Clarke might seem like a nice guy, but I know the truth. Darkness lies within him. Soon, the whole country will find out what he's really like and what he has done to my best friend.

'This is . . .' I breathe.

'Brutal,' Kamal finishes my sentence for me, then takes my hand in his. 'Are you okay?'

Biting the side of my cheek, I nod.

'This is why I was worried, Janine,' Kamal says gently. 'Neither of us know who Otis Clarke is.'

'I know, it's just . . .' I trail off, staring deep into Kamal's concerned eyes. 'I've sat with Otis Clarke, Kamal. I've seen him lie, seen him get angry, seen him break down. There are sides to him and stories about him that unnerve me but . . . I don't know. There's a difference between someone being emotionally stunted and pig-headed and them being a murderer.'

'Perhaps, but you don't need to worry yourself with that. That's a job for the police.'

'But this article . . . imagine if someone wrote it about you. Imagine how your life would change. You know what the world is like. These day, things are shared online and never forgotten. Anytime anyone googles Otis's name, this will come up. Does he deserve that if he's not guilty? Does anyone?'

Slowly, Kamal nods. 'I guess we're all quicker to assume the worst than we are to seek the truth.'

'That's all I've wanted to do here. Seek the truth. Help Alexa.' Filling my lungs, I squeeze my husband's hand. 'I'm going to ask something big of you, but if you understand me half as much as you've said you do, then you'll support me on this.'

'What is it?'

'I need you to be okay with me going to see Otis today.'

Kamal's eyebrows rise, but I continue before he can say anything.

'Otis will be feeling vulnerable now. Hurting. You've seen the article, Kamal. We both know what people are saying. I want to check that he's okay. And, honestly, if there's going to be a time when Otis might be fully honest about his marriage, this is it. I need to see him.'

'You don't need my permission to do that,' Kamal says.

'I don't want your permission. I want your blessing.'

After a moment's hesitation, Kamal tucks me under his arm and presses a kiss to my hairline. 'One of the things I most love about you is how relentlessly you care. Listening to you talk about Alexa last night made me realise how my worry has clouded the way I've seen things recently. If you think helping her is how you need to spend your time, who am I to say otherwise? You are more than capable of looking after yourself. So if you can't rest until you find Alexa Clarke, then don't. I'll be here whenever you're ready to call it a day and come home.'

Burrowing into Kamal, I fill my lungs with his scent. 'What did I do to deserve you?'

'Funny, I ask myself that every day. Now come on, let's get dressed and go downstairs. We need breakfast.' Kamal hops out of bed and stretches his hand out to me. For the first time in a long time, I take it with no ulterior motive.

Beth's nursing a mug of coffee at the table when we enter the kitchen. She holds her hand up when she sees us. 'Don't be loud. I'm too fragile to take it.'

'You only had two glasses of wine,' I cry.

'Two too many. I lost all my tolerance after giving birth. One whiff of alcohol and I've a hangover these days.'

Laughing, I join my sister at the table while Kamal cooks up a feast. We eat and swap stories, the lighthearted bantering lifting the darkness of the last few days. But when the final scrap of food is eaten, I turn to my husband.

'I'd better go to Otis,' I say.

'Otis Clarke?' Beth's eyes widen, bigger than the now empty plate in front of her. 'Is it wise to see him again? He's all over the internet, marked as a killer.'

'I think we can allow Janine to decide if it's wise or not. Besides, at least we'll know where she is this time,' Kamal says with a wink. His joke cuts the tension, and once again I am reminded why I love him.

When breakfast is tidied away, Beth walks me to the front door. 'I'll probably be gone by the time you get back,' she says. 'Have a good day, okay? No going missing again.'

'I'll try not to. Say hi to the girls for me.'

'You can say it yourself when we see you tomorrow.'

I watch hope grow in Beth as she wonders if I'm going to say yes. I can't help but smile. 'I guess I'll see you tomorrow, then.'

We cling to each other, then I command myself to leave the house. A second longer in that embrace and I know I would have refused to let my sister go.

Apprehension fills the air as I drive towards Maple Crescent. All the contradictory stories I've heard about the Clarkes over the last few days fill my mind, loud with warning. The sight of Jim and Bernie approaching Maple Crescent sends me spiralling further, the memories of Jim kicking my car making me shrink into my seat.

But the biggest hit of dread comes when I turn onto Maple Crescent and a dramatic scene comes into view.

CHAPTER 42

Two police cars are parked at the entrance of the Clarkes' driveway, and uniformed officers have been stationed out the front. This is shocking enough, but the crowd assembled at the taped-off cordon is what makes me gasp. It's almost as if the entire village has congregated on the street.

I've seen many of the faces around Bramblethorpe. They always seemed friendly. I never imagined they would be the kind of people to take photos of the police outside someone's home and swap gossipy theories, but many of them are doing exactly that.

Villagers aren't the only people trying to sneak an exclusive. As I park my car and squeeze through the crowd to get to the police tape, I clock a camera crew and reporter setting up. My body jolts. I hadn't prepared myself to see journalists here. It only makes me worry more. Maybe something else has been uncovered – something I've yet to hear about. Clenching my jaw, I pray it's not bad news about Alexa.

But my horror peaks when my eyes lock on Sonya, looking more vengeful than ever. Her smug smirk makes my breath catch, then she nods her head towards the driveway, indicating for me to look.

Following her gaze, I see a hubbub of activity playing out. Central to it all is a hunched Otis. Standing beside DS Rani and DS Mullins, he's staring at the ground in a daze. He looks so small and broken, it's hard not to feel sorry for him, but beyond Otis is an even sorrier sight. The front door of his impressive house is wide open, inviting figures in white all-in-one suits to enter it.

Forensics.

Suddenly, another figure steps out of the house and crosses the driveway. Gabby, looking quietly furious but ever the professional. She addresses the police, then turns to Otis. Lifting his down-turned head, she speaks to him, then to DS Rani and DS Mullins. Being so far away, I can't hear what they're saying, but I lean closer instinctively.

'Excuse me,' an officer says, stepping forward and blocking my view. 'You can't pass.'

'But—'

'Unless you're with Mr Clarke's legal team, I'm going to have to ask you to move on,' he says firmly.

I open my mouth to object, but DS Rani notices what's going on and breaks from Otis's side.

'It's all right,' she calls as she walks towards me. When she reaches the police tape, she offers me a tight smile. 'Janine, how are you?'

'I'm okay. Is Otis under arrest?'

DS Rani glances at the cluster of eavesdropping press then lifts the police tape for me to duck under. She leads me partway up the driveway and turns us away from prying ears.

'We have a warrant to search the house,' she says. 'It seems Otis hasn't been as honest with us as we'd hoped. We have you to thank for helping uncover that.' When my eyebrows dip in confusion, she leans closer. 'Simon Brooks came to speak to us about his relationship with Alexa. He said you told him to come forward to help us find her.'

My head lifts. 'You've found Alexa?'

When she sees my hope, DS Rani's face creases with sympathy. 'No, but I'm sure once we speak to Otis again, that may change. We'll be bringing cadaver dogs to the house later today, too.'

'Cadaver dogs?' I gulp as a white-suited figure emerges from the front door behind DS Rani's shoulder. 'Does that mean you think Otis killed her?'

'Janine, I'm going to speak candidly here, not as a police officer but as someone who knows how much finding Alexa means to you. I know you've been hoping that she would be found alive and well. We all have – but truthfully, from the moment we were made aware of Alexa's disappearance, we suspected foul play.'

I close my eyes as the statement cracks my heart.

'No one goes into their garden and vanishes. No one. Our job here was to determine if something had happened to Alexa, or if she orchestrated her disappearance so she could escape her marriage.'

'Do you really think she'd do that?'

DS Rani bites her lip, weighing up how much to tell me. 'Things have happened within the walls of that house that Otis has not shared with you. I can't say much more than that, but we have reason to believe that Alexa was a very unhappy woman.'

'But – but Otis said Alexa loved him,' I stumble. 'He said they were happy.'

'What someone in denial says and the truth are very different things. Alexa's internet history shows searches for divorce lawyers and properties in Denmark, suggesting an intent to leave. We have statements from Simon Brooks and Sonya West saying that she wanted out of the marriage. We have evidence, Janine. Evidence that proves Otis's assertion that things were okay is wrong. And last night, we got confirmation that the stain on the tennis ball we found was blood. It matches Alexa Clarke's DNA.' I recoil, but DS Rani reaches for me. 'I'm not telling you this to upset you, but to help you walk away. We'll be taking Otis to the station soon for questioning as a formal suspect. We expect him to be charged within the next twenty-four hours.'

A gust of wind howls through the trees at those words. Shivering, I let it pass over me.

DS Rani rests her hand on my arm. 'I know you feel a connection to Alexa Clarke, but you and she are not the same. What happened in her marriage is not a blueprint of what will happen in yours. Loss might be universal, but how it shapes us is personal. Leave what has happened here behind. Focus on yourself and your future.'

'I just . . . I just wanted Alexa to be okay,' I croak.

'We all did, Janine. We all did.'

Sniffing back tears, I look up to the sky. Thick white clouds hang overhead, blocking out any sign of sunlight, a sure sign that winter is coming. A new season, bringing the old one to an end.

A new beginning, but only for those ready to see it that way.

'I'd like to leave now,' I say. 'I don't want to be here when you take Otis away.'

'Of course. We'll need to speak to you again at some point, but for now I think it's time you went home to write your next bestseller.'

DS Rani and I share a smile. Then, without looking back, I leave Otis's police-infested driveway behind, feeling both heavier and lighter at the same time.

CHAPTER 43

Alexa

Seven days gone

Fading. If Alexa Clarke had to describe herself in one word, that would be it. But if fading felt like this, then Alexa didn't mind. Fading was far better than facing another second of the torture she had endured during her time in the white room.

Never again would Alexa Clarke look at common household items in the same naive way. Not when her time with the captor had taught her an array of different purposes they could have.

A pair of tweezers, for example, could scour skin as effectively as a blade if plunged into it hard enough. It was all about the force and depth of the cut. That ratio was something the captor had been working hard to perfect. Alexa's smooth skin had been optimal for their experiments.

The belt of a dressing-gown might help keep the cold at bay, but it was also an excellent tool to choke someone with. Twice the captor had wrapped a flannelette cord around Alexa's neck. Twice they had strangled her to the point she passed out.

In fact, every time the captor entered the white room, they brought a new object with them. They would hold it in the air to show Alexa what it usually does. Then, once the innocent function was demonstrated, the captor would show Alexa their version of how best to use it. Each time, a polaroid was taken to document the occasion.

Everyday innocent items, taking on the role of something else entirely when in the captor's hands.

Alexa Clarke, waiting for the moment her body finally surrendered completely.

A moment that was creeping closer.

A moment she hoped would hurry up.

As someone shuffled about downstairs, Alexa wondered if that meant the captor was preparing to come into the room again. She wanted to care about what they were going to do next time, but she couldn't. There was nothing left inside her to give to those worries. No spirit, no fight, no hope. The captor had taken it all.

Fading. Yes, Alexa Clarke was fading. Fading into the darkness of sleep, where no pain and sadness could ever touch her again.

CHAPTER 44

I keep my head low as I duck under the police tape and head towards my car, but I should know better than to think that would stop me from being recognised.

'Janine, wait!'

Sonya's shouting hurries me along Maple Crescent, but she jogs to catch up with me.

'What did the police say?' she says, intercepting me. 'How screwed is Otis?'

Her unashamed glee snaps something inside me. Everything becomes too much. Otis and his shapeshifting personality, Gabby and her refusal to accept that he might not be a saint, Sonya and her strange, self-absorbed ways. And in the centre of it all, Alexa Clarke, still missing.

I come to a stop with my hands balled into fists. 'Do you even care about Alexa, Sonya? Or do you just care about getting one over on Otis?'

Stunned, Sonya blinks. 'Of course I care about Alexa. She's my best friend.'

'A best friend you never visited! A best friend whose story you couldn't wait to cash in on.'

Sonya's cheeks colour. 'What the hell, Janine? You're supposed to be on my side.'

'There are no sides in this! A woman is missing. All I wanted to do was find her. No secret motive, no using this story for my own gain. When you look back at everything you've done, can you honestly say that?'

'You know nothing about how I've spent my last few days.'

'You're right, I don't, but I'm sure I'll read about it in tomorrow's newspaper. Now if you'll excuse me, I'm going home.'

I make a move to walk away but Sonya grabs me by the arm. 'Aligning yourself with a killer, huh? There I was, thinking you had more of a brain than that. Clearly, you're not as clever as your books suggest.' I flinch, a reaction Sonya smirks at. 'Did I hurt you? Good. We could have found Lex days ago if it weren't for you thinking you could play detective.'

'Leave me alone,' I say, pushing past Sonya before I say something I'll regret.

'You should leave solving crimes to your characters,' she calls after me. 'They're the only ones who know what they're doing.'

Even though I tell myself not to let Sonya get to me, her cattiness is hard to ignore. Tears blind me as I continue down Maple Crescent, but I refuse to break down with Sonya and the band of local gossips behind me.

Taking my phone from my pocket, I go to call Kamal, but as I unlock it, I spot several messages from Natalya in our group chat. My stomach drops.

The police are at Otis's again and guess what? So is Janine! Looks like Margie was right … She's been hanging around to scoop the story after all. How could we be so stupid to trust her?! x

Then the others, sent a few minutes later.

This is awkward. I obviously didn't mean to send that in the group chat, but now a private conversation between me and Katherine is out in the open, I guess I can speak the truth.

Janine, it's hurtful that you convinced me to write about Alexa Clarke while mining the story for a plot of your own. Worst of all, you pretended to know nothing about what was going on. If you'd been honest about your involvement, I would have backed off, but you lied to me and Katherine. That's not what we signed up for when we started this writing group.

I'm not sure I feel comfortable sharing my work with someone so dishonest. I don't want to speak for Katherine, but I think maybe it's best you don't come to writing group anymore.

My lips part as I come to a stunned standstill. At first, I think my upset is indignation over Natalya accusing me of something I didn't do, but when my chin wobbles, I admit the truth. My writing group is my lifeline, but as with everything else, I have found a way to fuck it up.

Tears well up in my eyes as I type then delete different responses.

Don't come back? Fine! I don't know why I went to meetings in the first place.

Don't abandon me. Please. I need you and Katherine.

But whatever I type, it doesn't make this situation hurt less. I feel like a teenager again, all awkwardness and insecurity, trying to keep up with ever-changing social rules I don't understand.

'Janine?'

I jump, startled to see Dorrit standing at the edge of her garden. Blushing, I wipe my eyes with my sleeve.

'Are you okay?' Dorrit presses.

Are you okay? – famously the worst question you can ask someone who is in tears.

As my face crumbles, Dorrit reaches her hand out. 'Come on. This is nothing a cup of tea and a biscuit can't make better.'

Even though I suspect she's wrong about that, I slip my phone to Do Not Disturb and follow Dorrit towards her home.

The house is even more picture perfect close up than it is from the kerb, all old bricks and rural charm. We enter through the back door, stepping into a kitchen that looks like something from an 'Ideal Farmhouse Kitchen' article from the nineties. From a tartan dog bed in the corner, Magnus looks up as we enter the room.

'It's all right, Magnus. Janine is a friend,' Dorrit says. Magnus lowers his head in relief. 'I don't know why he bothers. The last time he acted like a guard dog, my husband was still alive, and he's been dead for six years.'

Before I can say how sorry I am to hear that, Dorrit indicates for me to sit at the rickety table in the centre of the room while she makes our drinks.

'You have a lovely home,' I say as I succumb to her orders.

'Thank you. It's too big for me to manage on my own these days, but I won't sell it. No, the only time I'll leave this house is in a body bag.' As soon as the words leave her mouth, Dorrit glances over her shoulder at me. 'I didn't mean to be insensitive. Not with everything that's going on with Alexa.'

I duck behind my hair and study the grain of the wooden table.

'You don't want to believe death is what's happened here? It is. They don't send that many police cars for a woman they think has gone to pick up a loaf of bread and got lost on the way home.'

'You don't hold back, do you?'

Dorrit chuckles. 'When you get to my age, you tend to become a little blunt. I'm sorry if my words are hard to hear, though. The good thing is, the end is coming, I can tell. I'm sure we'll get answers soon.'

I look up as Dorrit approaches the table with an assortment of biscuits arranged neatly on a patterned plate. 'Do you really think so?'

'I do, dear. The dark cloud that's been hanging over Bramblethorpe will soon pass.' Dorrit selects a cookie and hands the plate to me. 'Eat. You look drawn.'

The bubbling kettle announces it has finished boiling as I accept the biscuit. Taking an obligatory bite, I watch Dorrit shuffle back to the counter.

'Do you mind if I ask you about Alexa?' I ask.

'Be my guest, but I wasn't lying when I said I don't know her well.'

'I know, but you never know what might come up in conversation.'

Dorrit laughs as she carries two mugs of tea to the table. 'That sounds like a line from a detective show,' she says, lowering herself onto the seat beside me. 'Go on then, what would you like to know?'

'Everything, I guess.'

'Then I'm afraid I'm the wrong person to ask. I told you, Alexa Clarke might be my neighbour, but I don't know her. Not really.'

'Well, would you say Alexa was happy?'

'What a question! Are any of us happy? We're all good at pretending we are, but are we? Alexa Clarke is my neighbour. I see her put the bins out or sit in her garden. I can't tell if she's happy. She certainly doesn't seem it. But I can tell you one thing: she's lonely.'

'How do you know that?'

'Because lonely people know how to spot other lonely people,' Dorrit replies, and I find myself looking at her with new eyes. Dorrit's home is big enough for a large family, but now it's reserved for only her and Magnus. There's an air of decay about the place, as if no matter how hard she cleans, the job is still too big for her to do alone. In fact, now when I look around, I see that loneliness is such a way of life here, it's practically ingrained in the walls.

'Either way, happy or sad, Alexa changed during the time she lived here,' Dorrit continues. 'I've been thinking a lot recently about how reclusive she became. I never saw anyone go into that house and rarely saw Alexa leave. Other than for her walks, of course.'

My ears perk up. 'Her walks?'

Dorrit nods. 'Like I told the police, walking was the one thing Alexa did every day. It was pretty much the only time she left the house.'

'Do you know where she went?'

'Oh, here, there and everywhere, I imagine. You don't have a figure like hers without working to maintain it. Even those genetically blessed reach a point where they must exercise,' Dorrit jokes, patting her stomach.

'Did she go out at the same time every day?'

'She usually went in the morning. Mid to late morning, perhaps.'

'How long did she stay away from the house for?'

Dorrit studies me sadly. 'You have so many questions, dear. I wish I could give you answers, but I can't. Sometimes I'd see Alexa walking down Maple Crescent, other times through the fields opposite. I suspect she went into the fields at the back of the house, too. There was never a pattern. I think she just forced herself to go outside once a day.'

'Dorrit, I need you to think carefully,' I say, trying to keep composed despite the pounding in my chest telling me we are getting close to something significant. 'In all the times you saw Alexa go for a walk, did you ever see her with anyone?'

'No. I told you, Alexa Clarke is as lonely as they come.'

'Did you ever spot anything unusual about Alexa's walks?'

'Unusual about a walk? I don't understand.'

'It sounds silly, I know, but was there anything you can think of that struck you as odd? Anything at all?'

Dorrit's wrinkled skin creases more than ever as she concentrates. 'There is one thing that was a bit odd, now you come to mention it. Once or twice, I saw Alexa walking with a tennis ball. She'd throw it in the air and catch it as she went.'

My breath catches in the back of my throat. 'Did you say a tennis ball?'

Dorrit laughs. 'Is that not strange enough for you? I've never known anyone take a tennis ball for a walk. Not anyone who doesn't have a dog, anyway.'

My focus darts to Magnus. He lifts his head to stare back at me, the light catching his brown eyes.

'But what do I know? Maybe a tennis ball isn't odd after all,' Dorrit says, offering me a biscuit, but my mind is racing too much for me to take one.

It hits me like a bolt of lightning: the tennis ball the police found wasn't left behind by a dog walker or group of children. Alexa had it with her the day she went missing. She had it with her because she *was* meeting someone that day.

And I think I might know who.

CHAPTER 45

My chair scrapes across the floor tiles as I launch myself to my feet.

'Is everything okay?' Dorrit asks, but I'm so busy scrambling to leave that I only answer her with a quick nod.

Rushing out of the house, I leap into the world outside. It's as chilly as it was earlier, but after Dorrit's revelation the air feels icier than ever. I leave her garden behind, cutting down the gravel path and heading back to Maple Crescent.

My shoes slap the pavement as I race down the road, passing the Clarkes' house, the police and the nosey bystanders. They watch me with an even keener curiosity than before.

'Running to Otis? You've just missed him,' Sonya shouts after me, but I don't care what she has to say. I'm too preoccupied by looking for the sign that points out the public footpath running down the side of Otis's house.

I sprint down the dirt track, sending dead leaves scattering behind me in all directions, until the bare branches of trees overhead knot into an eerie canopy of winter woodland. The woods at the back of the Clarke house, otherworldly but most importantly, narrow.

As the road behind me disappears, Bramblethorpe is swallowed by nature. I keep my gaze fixed ahead, looking through the trees to the fields that I know are coming. Twigs break underfoot, the only sound that can be heard in this silent slice of countryside.

Breaking through the final wall of trees, I reach the first field.

The blessing of a clear day means I can see what Alexa meant when she described this view as fields that go on forever. Long grass stretches ahead of me as far as the eye can see. But it's not what's beyond the field that I want to find – it's who I suspect is in it.

I push forward into the grass, my head turning this way and that, searching for a figure in the distance, but all I can see is the serenity of nature. I walk deeper into the field, straining to see far ahead, but no one comes into view.

'Hello?' I call out, waiting for a reply that never comes.

Dejection overcomes me as I realise the only thing keeping me company is the panting of my own breath. Folding at the waist, I rest my hands on my knees and fight to catch my breath as well as steady my wavering emotions.

I was so sure I was onto something. So sure this was it.

Straightening up and turning around, I stumble back towards the trees. Their trunks are dense, a barrier blocking me from the rest of the world. My gaze focuses on their hostility until a movement in the shadows makes my heart stop.

Slowing, I edge forward until the woodland draws closer. That's when I see the shape that's hidden in the trees.

The shape that's moving closer to me.

A person.

When they finally emerge from the dense line of woodland, I lose the ability to breathe.

'You,' I whisper.

CHAPTER 46

As Jim stands before me, Dorrit's words about lonely people knowing how to spot other lonely people echo in my mind, and all of a sudden, everything makes sense. The tennis ball, the daily walks on the edges of Bramblethorpe: Alexa Clarke was lonely, but she wasn't alone. Not since she had made contact with someone who was as lonely as she was. A person so on the edges of society, no one would know she was meeting them out here.

A person who had the power to hurt her with no one ever finding out.

A scream bubbles in my throat, but it gets trapped there as Jim steps forward.

'You're not going to run over my dog today, are you?' he asks, but his downturned features harden when he sees my alarmed expression. 'So, you've figured out about me and Alexa then?'

I force myself to nod.

'Are you going to tell the police?'

The question dries my mouth. 'Do I need to?'

'That depends. Is it suspicious to you that someone might want to befriend me?' When I don't reply, Jim's eyes narrow. 'You're looking at me in a way I don't like. What, do you think I'm going to hurt you?'

Jim's ominous words and the isolation of the field heighten my paranoia. 'I—I don't know,' I stutter.

'In that case, maybe it's time to end this conversation,' Jim replies, then he reaches for something in his coat pocket.

Finally, a scream escapes me, ragged and terrified.

Jim tilts his head before delving deeper into his pocket and pulling out a bright red ball. He holds it in the air for me to see then hurls it across the field. Bernie dashes after the ball, parting the tall grass with ease. I watch him go, aware of Jim's stare burning into me as I do.

'You said Alexa befriended you?' I manage to ask.

'She did.'

The swish of the grass stops momentarily as Bernie picks up the ball, then begins again as he zooms back to us. Jim strides forward to meet him. The problem is, by walking forward, he moves closer to me.

'Talking to me isn't a crime, you know,' he says. 'People around here might act like it is, but it's not.'

I flinch at his sharp tone, but Jim is too busy accepting the ball from an overexcited Bernie to care about my discomfort. He holds the sphere in the air, toying with Bernie before propelling the ball into the distance once more. It soars as if thrown by a professional cricketer, and it takes all my willpower not to dissolve over the sheer strength of Jim's body.

We watch Bernie disappear into the overgrown grass, the sound of his excited barks contrasting with the mounting tension.

'The police have taken Otis,' Jim says. 'They're clearing out of the house as we speak.'

If my heart was pounding before, it's nothing compared to the rate it's beating now. I picture DS Rani and DS Mullins driving away under the impression that they have the culprit. The house abandoned and empty. Me hollering for help, and no one there to provide it.

'They've got the wrong person, if you ask me,' Jim continues. 'Useless with grief and not there when he should have been, but I don't think Otis hurt Alexa.' Jim's eyes lock on mine. 'Seems like you share my belief.'

All my senses are on high alert, begging me to run, but as Jim continues to approach, the only thing I seem to be able to do is remain frozen. Terrified, my eyes scour his oversized coat and its pockets. Pockets containing dog toys and treats, and who knows what else.

That thought sends me stumbling backwards, and the darkness in Jim cements. 'Is there something you want to ask me?' he says.

When I don't reply, Jim moves forward again, closing the space between us until he could touch me if he stretched his arm out. Bernie chooses that moment to rejoin us. The ball sits in his mouth, but the sight of his wagging tail can't calm my erratic heartbeat.

'Good boy,' Jim says, accepting the ball before glancing at me. 'Go on. I know you want to ask something. Spit it out.'

The grass swallows my trembling legs as I step backwards. 'Why haven't you gone to the police to say you were friends with Alexa?'

'What good would that have done?'

'You could have told them what Alexa was like. How she was struggling. How she felt about Otis.'

'What Alexa told me was private. Personal. Not to be shared.' Jim tosses the ball in the air and catches it. Bernie barks at the teasing, the sound jarring my already fraught nerves.

'Well, you could have at least helped the police figure out what she did every day.'

Jim shakes his head. 'That's not my job.'

'Alexa's missing. If you had nothing to hide, you would have gone to them.'

Jim throws and catches the ball once more. The sound of it hitting his coarse skin rings out like a slap. 'Like I said, it's not my job.'

'Some friend you are,' I retort, then immediately know it was the wrong thing to say. Jim's face clouds over.

'You think if I'd gone to the police, they'd have listened? Someone like Alexa talking to someone like me? Tut tut, they'd say. Look at the size of him, listen to the rumours. It's got to be him.'

'But if you're innocent—'

'Since when do people care about innocent and guilty, right and wrong? They only care about what makes a good story. You only have to listen to what everyone around here says about me to know that. What, you struggle with your marriage ending and get angry once after too many drinks, and that's it, you're a bad guy forever? How is that fair?'

I flinch as Jim hisses that last question at me, but he isn't finished with his rant yet.

'My family have lived in Bramblethorpe for four generations. When I was younger, I helped half these people tend to their land, but a few bad decisions made at the worst time of my life and now I'm an outcast! You'd think your wife leaving you would earn you a bit of sympathy, but not around here. Not with these folks. Alexa was the only person who bothered to look beyond that, and now she's gone.'

'Gone?' I echo.

As Jim looks me dead in the eye, my blood turns to ice.

'Gone,' he repeats, and all hope that I will leave this field alive deserts me.

CHAPTER 47

'Alexa didn't care about stupid rumours and mindless gossip,' Jim continues, taking another step towards me. 'She was my friend. She loved Bernie, too. We talked. There's nothing wrong with that.'

'I never said there was.'

'No, but you're acting as if there is. Standing there looking at me as if I'm evil personified. What about the woman she walked with, huh? The nosey neighbour. You don't have a problem with her. But me? Me you do.'

'I don't have a problem with you,' I squeak, but the terrified pitch of my voice makes Jim scoff.

'Sure you don't. You're acting as if I'm what they say I am, and I don't like it.' Jim brushes aside strands of grass that are only inches away from me. 'What, do I scare you? Do you think I'm a monster, too?'

My brain roars at me to move, but fear has me paralysed.

'Do you? Do you think I'm a monster?'

Jim's so close to me now that I can see a smattering of scars on his left cheek from teenage acne. I see a kink to his nose, telling me that it was once broken. Probably when he was a boxer.

My breathing rasps with fear, making Jim come to a sudden stop.

'I'm not, you know. A monster, that is,' he says, then the corners of his eyes squint. 'Not unless I'm pushed to become one.'

Something inside me kicks into life at those words. I don't think, I don't rationalise, I just move. Launching myself forward, I shove Jim in the centre of his chest.

The level of my aggression is so unexpected, he stumbles and topples over a clump of grass. Bernie barks in outrage, but I don't waste a second of the head start I just bought myself. Leaping past Jim, I sprint towards the treeline ahead, heading for the safety I pray is on the other side.

'Stop!' Jim calls, scrambling to his feet to chase after me, but his shout only makes me move quicker.

'Help!' I holler as I fight my way through the grass.

A growl behind me shoots terror down my spine, but fear makes me flee faster. I race onward, clawing through the grass until I reach the narrow patch of woodland. Before tearing through it, I peer over my shoulder. Jim is lurching after me, still in the field, his movements slower as he reels from shock. I know it won't last long, though. Jim is a big man. I know he has the ability to close the distance between us should I dare slow down.

So I don't. I propel my body forward until the blanket of trees envelops me, concealing me in their darkened embrace.

'Help!' I screech, praying that the shout is loud enough to carry through the woodland.

The sound of grass swishing behind me warns that something, or someone, is in hot pursuit. The barks tell me it's Bernie, but Bernie is always by Jim's side. Who knows if they're together now? I don't dare stop to confirm if that's the case.

Jim shouts again. 'Stop!'

The proximity of his voice terrifies me. Twigs snap as my feet pummel the ground. Raggedly, I scream for help. I think I hear someone shout out from further ahead, and use it as fuel to keep going.

Another bark cuts through the air, echoing between the trees. Through the gaps in the tree trunks ahead, I see a flash of the back of the Clarkes' house. The familiar sight makes me cry out, but it also distracts me from plotting my route. My foot catches on a thick root sprawling across the ground, sending me flying.

Shrieking, I soar through the air until I land in a crumpled heap. My body skids across the ground, the shock of the impact rattling through my ribcage. For a split second, I lie with my face in the dirt, winded and disbelieving, but then something knocks into my foot.

I spin onto my back, the perfect position for Bernie to throw himself on top of me. As his paws dig into my stomach and chest, I cry out. Bernie seems to relish the sound, barking in response before launching himself at my face.

Panic oozes from me as I feel something wet on my forehead. *Blood*, I think, but then I realise it's Bernie licking me. His happiness is so unexpected, it almost makes me laugh.

'Bernie, no,' I say, trying to push him off, but then I hear a man shout.

'She's over here!'

Scrambling backwards, I do my best to rid myself of Bernie before Jim catches up, but as more shouts echo around me, I realise they're not coming from Jim. Twisting my [illegible] find DS Rani leading four uniformed officers towards me.

Relief strips me bare. Flopping against [illegible]nd, I burst into tears. As Bernie makes it his mission to l[illegible] away, I let [illegible] I'm too wiped to fight him off anyway.

'Janine, are you okay?' DS Rani says, kneeling beside me and doing her best to control Bernie so I can sit up.

'It's Jim,' I sob. 'He's coming for me.'

DS Rani pulls me into a sitting position. 'Who's Jim?'

'He lives on the edge of Bramblethorpe,' I sniff, wiping my cheeks with my dirt-crusted hands. 'Alexa met him for walks.'

Then there, appearing through the trees, is Jim. This tall, imposing man who looks like he could crush you with one flex of his arm muscles.

DS Rani doesn't need to know more. She shouts a series of orders to the officers, who rush towards Jim. Panicked, Jim turns, stumbling back towards the field, but it doesn't matter. The police are onto him. A delighted Bernie chases after them, oblivious to the fact that this isn't a game but a manhunt.

I watch them go, not yet trusting that this nightmarish moment is over.

'I thought you'd left,' I croak. 'I thought Jim was going to hurt me.'

'You're okay, Janine. Everything is okay,' DS Rani reassures me.

With her steady hand on the centre of my back, I slowly find myself coming to my senses.

'I'm jus[illegible]ad I hadn't set off after Mullins and Otis yet,' DS Rani says. 'A mi[illegible] later and I wouldn't have been here to hear your calls for help.'

The 'wh[illegible] attached to those words bristles every hair on my body, then [illegible]s of shouts from the fields make us both jump.

'You can[illegible] Otis until you've spoken to Jim,' I say, grabbing DS Rani's a[illegible]u need to ask him about Alexa. Dorrit Holbeck saw Alexa le[illegible] for a walk every day. She said Alexa sometimes had a tennis [illegible] her.'

A shout ri[illegible] the distance, followed by a bark from Bernie.

'The tennis ball you found wasn't random,' I continue. 'It was Alexa's. She was carrying it the day she went missing, because she was going to meet Jim, yet he never came forward to tell you that. Why would he keep that secret? What is he hiding?'

DS Rani pauses, listening to the bark-spiked commotion in the field. When it echoes louder, she turns to me and whistles.

'Two suspects in one day, huh? Let's hope you make as good a real-life detective as you do a fictional one, S. K. Atherton.'

With those words, DS Rani pulls me to my feet. I wince as a jolt of pain shoots up my ankle from my fall, but the hurt doesn't matter. Standing signals that maybe, finally, this might actually be over.

CHAPTER 48

DS Rani supports my limping frame back to Maple Crescent. With Otis no longer here, the crowd has dispersed and the reporters have gone.

'Peace at last,' DS Rani comments as I ease myself from her grip. When I grimace at bearing my body weight, her features cloud with concern. 'Do you need to go to hospital?'

'No, I need to go home.'

Her sceptical gaze lingers on my injured ankle. 'Are you sure?'

'If I'm still in pain later, I'll ask Kamal to take me there. I promise.'

Even though she doesn't look reassured, DS Rani nods. 'Take care of yourself, okay?'

She gives me a smile. It's one that I've seen on DS Rani's face before. It says that she understands me and my pain. I wonder how many women I've met in my life who share that same smile. People who hide their hurt behind important careers, day trips and nights with friends. People who show that life goes on after loss, but that doesn't mean you forget.

The sound of voices coming from the public footpath makes us turn. Seconds later, Jim appears, cuffed and escorted by two officers.

My body locks as our eyes meet, the anger I expected to see in Jim nowhere to be found. Instead, all I see is hurt.

'Get home safely,' DS Rani says over her shoulder as she goes to Jim. I'm too numb to reply.

I watch as Jim is bundled into a police car. All the while, he keeps his head low. All the while, I tell myself that he intimidated me. Chased me. Hid the truth from the police. But still, the look in his eyes when he saw me clings on.

When Jim is driven away, DS Rani follows in her car. She waves to me as she passes and I wave back, then I am alone once more.

Wrapping my arms around my waist, I set off towards my car, doing all I can to push the shooting pain in my ankle from my mind. I tell myself to enjoy the stillness after the chaos, but there's something about the silence that isn't reassuring after all.

Lifting my head, I look down the street, my gaze hovering on Dorrit's house. Then it shifts, travelling back up the road until it stops on the Gothic dream home to the side of me.

Out of nowhere, I hear Jim's words like he's beside me, whispering in my ear.

'What about the woman she went for walks with, huh? The nosey neighbour.'

My mouth dries. In all my panic, I'd heard him, but I hadn't really *heard* him. Not in the way I should have.

My body moves without being told to, taking me up the long, curved driveway. A variety of plants, shrivelled by autumnal frost, line the route, adding to the mysterious splendour of the place. At the door, I stop. I raise my hand and push the doorbell.

My nerves sizzle as it rings out into the house, but I tell myself to remain calm. Being Alexa Clarke's next-door neighbour doesn't mean this is the person Jim was talking about. There are plenty of other people on this street he could've meant.

Be calm, I reason.

Inside, I hear the slap of footsteps drawing closer.

I hear the click of a latch being unlocked.

Then, as the door is thrown open, I come face to face with the last person I expected to be on the other side of it.

CHAPTER 49

Katherine blinks when she sees me standing here.

'Janine,' she says. 'This is a lovely surprise!'

My mind shouts, telling me to react like I'm not in shock, but I doubt I pull it off. 'You … you didn't tell me you were Alexa's neighbour,' I hear myself say.

Something flashes in Katherine's eyes, too fast for me to put a name to it, but then her forehead rumples in confusion. 'I'm sure I did.'

I shake my head. 'No, never.'

Katherine's smile widens as if this omission is of little consequence, but all I can think about are the times we have spoken about Alexa. Not once did Katherine let on that she lived next door.

'Are you here about Natalya's message?' Katherine asks, her eyebrows dipping. 'I hope you know that I didn't approve of it being sent. I still very much want you to be a part of the group. I feel like we're really forming a friendship, Janine. I'd hate for it to end now.'

As Katherine reaches for my arm, I tell myself to smile. Relax. I don't know if her living next door to the Clarkes is suspicious. Truthfully, I can't even be certain that she didn't already tell me she was their neighbour. My mind has hardly been steady recently. It's possible I've forgotten. Besides, I've already accused one person today, I can't accuse another. Not without proof.

'Can we talk about the message?' I say, pushing myself to remain calm. 'I feel like I should explain what's been going on, if you've time?'

Again, a flicker of emotion travels over Katherine's face, but she masks it. 'Sure,' she says brightly, stepping back into the house. 'Let me grab my coat and we can go for a walk.'

'I'd rather sit, if that's okay,' I say. 'I've hurt my ankle.'

I'm not immune to the way Katherine's shoulders freeze. 'But it's a lovely brisk day. Perfect for a walk.'

'I know, but I don't think I'll make it very far without having to ask you to carry me.'

Hearing the jokey tone I inject into my voice, Katherine smiles. 'Of course. Come in.'

As I take a pained step into the hallway, it strikes me how the moody, atmospheric style outside carries through to the decor inside. The next thing to hit me is the smell. Overpoweringly floral, it's as if someone has littered a million bowls of potpourri around the place.

'Sorry about the smell,' Katherine says as if reading my mind. 'I make scent bags to keep my clothes fresh. I've started selling them online. Anything to earn a bit of money with writing not quite panning out yet.'

'At least you're writing in a home as beautiful as this.'

'I'm glad you like it. To be honest, the house is more Eddie's taste than mine, but I haven't gotten around to redecorating since he passed. It's a big job when there are this many rooms. Plus keeping things as they were reminds me of him. I can almost pretend he's still here. Silly, really.'

'It's not silly at all,' I reply.

'Go through to the dining room and get comfortable. I'll make us a drink,' Katherine says as she heads to the kitchen.

After hanging my coat on the banister, I hobble down the hallway and peep into the rooms I pass, marvelling at the uniqueness of Katherine's home. Decorative vases and brass antiques litter every available surface, casting shadows on luxurious patterned wallpapers. Peeping into the living room, I hunt for signs that Alexa Clarke could have been here. Two mugs, two books on the coffee table, anything that hints at the presence of a second person, but there are none.

As much as I would love to explore the rest of the house, my ankle begs me to rest. When I reach the dining room, I slot into a seat at the head of the table. There, I study an impressive artwork depicting a bleak mid-winter day that's hung over the fireplace until Katherine returns carrying two full-to-the-brim teacups.

'Let's hope they live up to the drinks at Coffee and Cake,' she quips, setting them down.

'This is much better. We've no Margie listening to what we're saying.'

Katherine titters at my joke. 'She is a character, isn't she? I've tried to add someone like her to a book before, but alas, Margie is stranger than fiction.'

'Imagine if you did create a character in her honour. She'd probably give you free cakes for life!'

Once again, Katherine laughs. The move relaxes her, and in turn, me. This is Katherine, who I have tea with once a week. Katherine, who shares her writing with me. So what if I didn't know where her house was? That doesn't mean there's anything for me to fear.

'Speaking of books, I should explain my side of Natalya's message,' I say, resting my forearms on the table. 'I need you to know that I was only talking to Otis to help find Alexa. I wasn't copying anyone's work.'

Katherine waves her hand to dismiss my comment. 'It's fine. Natalya doesn't own this story.'

'But I'm not writing about Alexa. I'm not writing about a missing woman at all. If you could see my manuscript, you would know how true that statement is.'

'I believe you. Although I must say, your time with Otis will have provided valuable insights should you ever decide to write about that topic again.'

When I sip my tea, the liquid is so hot it scalds my tongue. 'What do you mean?'

'Well, you must have seen something that could be useful for your writing. Maybe an interaction with the police or a mannerism you could use to bring to life a guilty character. Something Otis said, perhaps?'

Katherine's question catches me off guard. I sip my tea again, if only to give me a moment to wonder how to answer it.

'I'm not fishing for gossip,' Katherine assures me. 'I just enjoy realism in writing, as you know. I've never seen that level of devastation up close. I wondered if you had any pearls of wisdom to describe what it was like?'

'Terrible,' I reply bluntly. 'I watched a man realise his wife might be dead.'

'Yes,' Katherine says softly, lowering her head. 'Yes, that must have been awful.'

The atmosphere swells, an unexpected level of sadness filling the air. The way my body shifts tells me I'm not comfortable describing the worst time of Otis's life like this.

'Do you mind if I use the bathroom?' I ask.

Katherine startles at my sudden derailing of the conversation. 'I don't have one on the ground floor, and I'm not sure using the stairs with that ankle is wise,' she replies.

'My only other option is to go here, and I don't think either of us want that,' I joke.

'Still,' Katherine says, reaching for my arm. 'I'm not sure using stairs when you're injured is a good idea. You don't want to hurt yourself more.'

Even though the words were said with care, something about them makes me shiver. Pulling myself from Katherine so she can't feel the thrum of panic in my pulse, I use the table to haul myself upright.

'You seem to be in a lot of pain,' Katherine says, but when I manage to stand, she falls silent.

'I'll be in more pain if I don't go to the toilet,' I reply, trying to keep the hitch of fear out of my voice. 'Do you not want me to go upstairs or something?'

Weakly, Katherine smiles. 'Of course not. The bathroom is the second door on the landing.'

'Thanks,' I reply, tensing at the throbbing in my ankle as I walk.

'Come straight back down,' Katherine calls after me. 'You don't want to stand for too long. And remember, it's the second door!'

Using the wall to support myself, I limp to the foot of the stairs. Beads of sweat prickle my brow as I climb the stairs – but halfway up, I notice the strangest thing. The smell has changed. The pungent florals are there, but something else is mingled with them. A sour undertone that makes my eyes water. With each step, it gets stronger.

Slowing my ascent, I look around for the source of the odour, but all I see are floral carpets and ornately framed paintings.

'Did you find the bathroom okay?' Katherine calls after me.

Her voice nudges me back to life. I set off again, shouting over my shoulder, 'Almost there.'

The summit is near when I spot the second door, ajar to unveil a porcelain sink and intricate tiling. Heaving myself over the final step, I pause to catch my breath, but the odd smell distracts me. My nerves sizzle, but I order myself to be calm. I'm at Katherine's house. There is nothing to fear here.

Suddenly, I hear her moving on the floor below me. The sound is so unexpected, I take a step backwards and almost tumble down the stairs. Gripping the banister to stop myself, I fight to steady my breath.

'This bathroom is gorgeous,' I shout.

I hear Katherine laugh, but the closeness of the sound is a shock. It sounds as though she is directly underneath me, not in the dining room where I left her.

'Glad you made it,' she calls. 'I was worried you were stuck on the stairs.'

Katherine's footsteps ring out as she heads back to the dining room. A prickly panic ignites my skin. It warns me to go back down the stairs, but as putrid air fills my lungs, I can't fight my curiosity.

Turning away from the bathroom, I shuffle down the landing and hunt for the source of the smell. Gently, I push open the first door to unveil an impressive master bedroom next to the bathroom, complete with a four-poster bed. The door after that opens to another bedroom, this time one that clearly belonged to a teenage boy. After that is an office, with dark oak furniture and shelves crammed with books.

My lips part in wonder at its old-fashioned beauty. Everything about it is opulent and antique, as if each piece of furniture has its own story to tell. The engraved wood desk is commanding and authoritative, and there is a burgundy leather chair perched behind it. Part of me wants to comment on how beautiful the room is, but Katherine cannot know I'm snooping.

Although it feels akin to reading her diary, I step inside, flinching as the floorboard creaks beneath my foot. I freeze, waiting for Katherine to call out to me, but the house is silent.

When I'm sure she's not coming, I step deeper into the room and study the books filling the shelves. I catch sight of a spine that reads, *Kick Writer's Block . . . For Good!*

You'll have to borrow that, I think before coming to a stop beside Katherine's desk. A framed handwritten note is perched beside her laptop. Picking it up, I read the treasured words.

The world needs to hear your voice, my love. One day I will see your name in print. Never give up x

My chin dimples at Eddie's message. The rejections Katherine's received seem all the crueller when cast in this light. I set the note down with an unsteady hand, wondering how Katherine would react if she saw me prying like this. The thought has my heart pounding. Moving my focus away from the note, I scan the rest of the desk. A stack of papers sits in the centre, with an expectant fountain pen perched beside them.

Glancing at the door, I look for a sign of Katherine, but all I hear is silence. Relieved, I focus back on the papers. Before I can stress about how terrible it is to read someone's work before they're ready to share it, I pluck the first page from the pile and begin to read.

Alexa Clarke didn't feel her skull splinter at first.

Even the shudder-inducing crack of the initial impact took a few seconds to register with her.

Alexa's momentary ignorance could suggest how unexpected an act of violence was in her life. Maybe the hostile beauty of the late November morning had captured her attention. Maybe she suddenly remembered something – an appointment she had to attend or that she hadn't turned the iron off.

I inhale sharply. For as long as I've known her, Katherine has been a romance writer. I've read samples of her work many times, but it's never been like this. This is dark and unnerving.

My skin tingles as I wonder what made Katherine write such a twisted tale. Biting my lip, I glance at the door again, half expecting to see her standing there, alarmed at my intrusion, but I'm still alone.

I know I should put the manuscript down and leave, but a rush of adrenaline goads me to read on. Only a little. I skim to the end of the chapter, my hand rising to my mouth as it concludes with Alexa Clarke being struck over the head in a field behind her home.

A sinking feeling floods my limbs. Katherine's fictional retelling echoes reality uncomfortably closely. The writing is so vivid, so realistic, it's like I was there with Alexa when she was attacked.

Shuddering, I thumb the rest of the manuscript and skim read sections describing the horrific torture of Alexa Clarke, chained to a bed in a white room, and the heroic actions of a plucky young detective trying to find her. The time stamp at the top of each chapter makes my hands shake.

Forcing myself to breathe slowly, I drop the manuscript. I've been up here too long. Limping out of the room, my throat constricts at the rancid odour – it's so much stronger out here. Whatever is causing the stench must be behind one of the remaining three doors. As my gag reflex kicks into life, so does my brain.

You've smelt something like this before, it says.

That's when it hits me.

While researching for my last book, I sat in on an autopsy. While I was interviewing the pathologist afterwards, a body arrived that had been found three weeks after the person died.

'Do you want to know what death smells like?' he asked.

'What kind of thriller author would I be if I said no to that?' I replied.

The answer was a far less nauseated one. The repulsive smell stayed in my nostrils for days, despite me only popping my head in the room where the body lay for a moment. Acrid and pungent, like rotting meat only ten times worse. I would never forget the smell of a decomposing corpse.

And somehow, Katherine's house smells exactly like that.

It only registers with me why that could be a split second before something crashes into the side of my skull.

CHAPTER 50

I can't move.

That's my first thought when my head finally stops spinning enough for me to register that I am still alive.

Open your eyes is the second, but try as I might, they cling to the blackness of denial.

Behind me, Katherine grumbles. 'Why did she insist on coming upstairs? I'm barely halfway through the book.'

I'm about to ask her what she means by that when I feel her hands wrap around my ankles. The injured one smarts, but Katherine doesn't give me a second to protest before she starts dragging me across the carpet.

'What are you doing?' I cry.

Or at least, that's what I try to cry. In reality, the only sound coming out of my mouth is a garbled moan.

'You're awake,' Katherine says, yanking me harder. 'Great. That will make this even more difficult.'

'What are you—' I croak, but I never get to finish my sentence because Katherine's hands move to my waist and flip me over.

The wound on my head roars as it presses against the carpet. The pain is so fierce, the shock of it forces my eyes to open.

A sombre Katherine looms above me, the door to the room at the end of the landing right behind her. How did I get to this side of the landing? Gulping, I realise Katherine must have dragged me.

'Why did you have to come up here, Janine?' she complains. 'I was going to ask you for a quote for my book cover. Now I have to kill you instead. All that wasted PR potential.'

As Katherine sets her hands on me again, I order my body to fight back, but it's too dazed to obey. She pins my hands to my chest with her knee. Then, from the back pocket of her jeans, she pulls out a length of rope and a kitchen knife.

I recoil at the sharp blade, but Katherine shakes her head.

'I'm not going to stab you here, silly. It will ruin the carpet.'

Resting the knife on the floor, Katherine begins coiling the rope around my wrists. Desperately, I try to pull my hands free, but she swats my attempts away.

'I've got to restrain you. You might try to escape otherwise, and I'm too tired for that. I was up all night perfecting a torture scene.' Katherine pulls the rope tighter, crushing my wrists together. 'Writing coaches always say how important the start of a book is. They rarely talk about the build-up or the end, but you've got to make sure readers don't see the big reveal coming, haven't you?'

My brain strains to make sense of what Katherine is saying. Everything about this feels surreal and wrong.

With my binds securely in place, Katherine stands by the door. 'Brace yourself. She's not smelling great these days.'

Then, Katherine presses down on the handle.

If I wasn't already on the floor, the stench that escapes the room would have me on my knees. Bile rises up and burns my throat.

My body jerks to the side to vomit, but Katherine stops me by pushing me onto my back. As I choke on vomit, her hands make themselves at home on my ankles once more.

When the grip of her bony fingers tightens, something primal in me comes to life. I thrash my limbs, convulsing, desperate not to be dragged into the room.

'Janine, stop!' Katherine shouts, but I refuse to listen.

Jerking my body in all directions, I expect Katherine to become more aggressive, but instead she drops my legs. They land with a thud that clatters through my skull. I let out a pained groan, but the sound is cut short when Katherine kneels beside me and grasps my jaw.

'What's so special about you?' she hisses. 'You don't know literary theory. You're not well-read. You've never even taken a creative writing course. Yet there you are, in the window of every bookshop I see. You don't deserve it. Not as much as I do.'

I stare at Katherine through a fog of confusion. 'This … this is about a book?'

'Oh, don't dismiss the thing that's earned you thousands just because you're going to die for it. That's so hypocritical.' Katherine lets go of my head with such venom, it flops to the side. 'You know what it's like to have a story inside you, but do you know what it's like to have every publisher in the world say you're not good enough to tell it? To have spent your entire life picking up your children's socks and cooking dinner, then when you finally get time to do something for yourself, being told you shouldn't have bothered?'

Katherine tips her head back to stare at the ceiling. I follow her eyeline, taking in the tiles above me. My head is reeling so much from the attack, the pattern seems to be moving.

'I've had a lifetime of flimsy justifications from people who wouldn't know talent if it punched them in the face, yet they control whether I make it or not. They say my writing isn't bold enough, isn't active enough, isn't realistic enough. Not realistic enough, eh? Let's see how realistic it is now I've described death more accurately than anyone ever has before.'

Gulping, my attention moves back to the woman before me. 'What have you done?' I whisper.

When Katherine fixes her stare on me, gone is any sign of the person I thought I knew. Instead, I come face to face with pure evil.

'You always say real life is inspiration for stories, Janine. Well, I just happened to make my real life all about the tragic demise of Alexa Clarke.'

The world around me stops. 'You've – you've killed Alexa?'

'All those twists, yet you couldn't figure this one out? And you call yourself a thriller author.' Katherine tuts, standing and stretching her neck, while a disbelieving sob escapes me.

'Why?' I cry.

'It was an accident,' Katherine admits. 'Alexa's death, writing a crime novel – it was never meant to happen. But they're always the best stories, aren't they? The ones that come to you through the mist.'

With a sigh, Katherine leans against the wall behind her.

'I always go for a walk a day, rain or shine. When she was alive, so would Alexa. We'd occasionally bump into each other. Over time, we got chatting. I'd tell her about my writing. She'd tell me about her life. But that day . . .'

Katherine's eyes close as a ripple of rage washes over her.

'I'd just been rejected again. This time by an agent I didn't even want to work with,' Kathrine spits the fact like it's poison. 'Do you know how demoralising that is, to be told "no" by people you don't value? I went to walk it off, then I saw Alexa. It was clear she'd been crying. God knows about what. That woman had it all.'

Otis's fight with Alexa that morning flashes in my mind. Him, asking if they should stop trying for a baby. Her, desperate to grow their family. A sinking feeling takes over me, knowing that whatever happened next changed everything for them both.

'I told Alexa about the rejection, and do you know what she did? She snapped, Janine. Right there, in the fields behind my own home! She told me that she didn't have time to listen to me complain. That some people had real problems, as if what I'm going through doesn't matter. And then she had the audacity to turn her back on me and walk away. Well, do you know what? I saw red. I saw *red*.'

Goosebumps race across my body as I understand the implications of Katherine's words.

'I never intended to write crime, but as soon as I picked up that branch? It was like the power of God was in my hands. I hit her twice on the back of the head. She crumpled like a piece of paper.' Katherine's body trembles, coming alive with each new detail she recounts. 'All those months of listening to you talk about the importance of immersive research were spot on. You were right – there's no better research than actually doing the thing! From that moment, I knew exactly what it felt like to be a killer.'

The sting of blame sits heavy on my chest. My words, innocently delivered. Never did I imagine this could be the consequence.

'Alexa died in the field?' I croak.

'Not quite, although she might as well have. I must say, it was annoying how fast she gave in. I'd hoped to find out a little more about the experience of a captive, but she barely survived the first night. I've had to imagine most of her reactions, can you believe it?'

Katherine looks to me to verify her frustration, but I'm too shocked to respond.

'I must have hit her head too hard, but at least I managed to get a few cuts in before her blood stopped pumping,' she continues. 'It's a shame I had to do the breaking of her bones later. Torturing a corpse isn't as accurate as torturing the living. Still, I've described the decay of death perfectly. Who writes realistically now?' Katherine laughs, then she pushes the door to the room at the end of the landing open wider.

I peer inside. A mottled, purpling hand hangs limply over the side of a bed, with every finger bent out of shape and a chunky metal handcuff coiled around the slender wrist.

On the fourth finger, I spot something I recognise.

Alexa Clarke's emerald ring.

A loud, guttural wail breaks free from the centre of my chest.

'Oh, be quiet. You didn't even know her,' Katherine snaps.

'You killed her!' I shout through tears. 'You killed Alexa!'

Katherine tilts her head. 'Why are you so upset? This is your writing theory coming to life! Besides, aren't real people the inspiration for all characters, all stories?' Katherine grins, triumphant when I don't have the strength to argue. 'Don't mourn Alexa Clarke, Janine. Not when she will go down in history as one of literature's greatest victims. And I will go down as one of the greatest writers because I brought her real death to life!'

I shake my head, trying to knock the truth out of my skull, but it stays lodged there, more distressing than I could ever have imagined.

'It's been hard working to such a tight deadline,' Katherine complains. 'There's not a lot of time after death before a corpse starts to smell. I don't think I could have thrown the police off my scent for much longer, pardon the pun.'

When I don't laugh, Katherine nudges the bottom of my foot with her toes.

'The scent, Janine, get it? Because Alexa smells so terrible now. Oh, you're no fun,' Katherine sighs when I don't respond. 'Luckily, I've always been good at planning my stories. I knew exactly how to buy myself time. Dropping Alexa's bank card near the university to make Otis think she was still alive was a particular stroke of genius. One thing I learned as a lecturer is to never underestimate a student's need for a night out, Janine. Never.'

A horrified sob bursts from me, making Katherine frown.

'Don't pity Alexa. She's not the innocent victim you're making her out to be. I've told you what she said to me. It was beyond cruel. She deserved it.'

'No,' I groan. 'No one deserves this.'

Katherine's nostrils flare. 'Stop. I won't be made to feel guilty for what I've done. If you think practically, not emotionally, you'll see I did Alexa a favour. Alexa and Otis were never together, and when they were, they were miserable. Alexa told me that herself. I saw it, too. The rest of the time, Alexa trailed around that ugly house or went for walks with Jim, of all people. Can you imagine a life as depressing as that? I did Alexa a favour by killing her.'

I'm already dizzy, but when Katherine grabs hold of my injured ankle I roar in pain. It's only when she's dragged me halfway through the door into the small white room that I realise I am being pulled towards Alexa Clarke's rotting corpse.

Screaming like I've never screamed before, I reach out with my bound hands to grab onto something, anything. My fingertips scratch the skirting board, then a door frame, but they slip before I get the chance to grab on.

My desperate cries grow louder. Twisting at the waist, I angle myself closer to the banister until my fingers connect with one of the wooden rails. I cling on, curling my fingers around it because I know as soon as I enter that room, I will not make it out alive.

Katherine yanks me, but I hold strong. Snarling in frustration, she drops my legs and comes to a crouch beside me.

'Why are you being so difficult?' she spits. 'Why can't you even try to understand my side of things? You have no idea what it's like to be me, Janine. No idea. I've spent my life looking after my husband and children. I pushed my dreams, passions and identity to the side for them. Now they're gone, and what do I have to show for myself? Nothing. Writing is the only thing I've ever wanted to do. The only thing that's ever been mine. I just want someone who isn't my husband to tell me I'm good enough, but it's always a no. And now infants like Natalya are getting yeses ahead of me! It's not fair. What, am I too old? Too suburban? Does my voice not matter?'

My shoulders curl inward at the shrillness in Katherine's voice.

'This book is my goal, my purpose, and no one is going to stop me from achieving it. Not even you.'

With those words, Katherine reaches for me.

'No!' I protest as her hands scrabble to pry mine from the banister.

'Let go, or I will break every finger you have.'

To prove her point, Katherine peels the little finger on my right hand back and twists it. I cry out, my howl peaking when the bone pops to announce it has broken.

Katherine gasps in delight. 'That's the noise Alexa's fingers made, too!'

She reaches for my hands once more, but her joy is cut short by a knock at the front door.

Before my lips can part to shout for help, Katherine clamps her hand over my mouth. I scream against it, a mixture of snot and tears dampening her skin. My shouts only make Katherine hold tighter.

Whoever is at the door knocks again before flipping open the letterbox.

'Hello?' they call out into the house. 'Janine, are you there?'

I would recognise that voice anywhere, even through the thickest haze of terror.

Beth.

Beth is at the door.

CHAPTER 51

Katherine feels my body lurch at the sound of my sister's voice. Her hand crushes my mouth as she lowers her face inches away from mine. 'If you scream, I will kill her. Do you understand?'

I don't have to question if Katherine is serious about her threat. I can tell by the manic glint in her eyes.

'Janine?' Beth calls again through the letterbox. 'I know you're here. We set up Find My Phone last night, remember?'

Hatred fills Katherine's features. 'Of course you did,' she mutters before grabbing the knife from the floor. She holds it to my throat, the chill of the blade icing my pulse. 'You scream, she dies, got it?'

When I nod, Katherine's hand loosens. She pauses, ready to strike should a peep come from me, but I remain silent.

'Good girl,' Katherine says as she stands. She slips the knife into her back pocket and smooths down her appearance before skipping down the stairs with a jovial trill of, 'Coming!'

Resting my forehead against the banister, I watch Katherine open the front door halfway. The angle I'm laid at means I can't see Beth, but I can see the knife sticking out of the back of Katherine's jeans.

Run, I itch to scream, but the chilling threat of the weapon warns me of the consequence of that shout.

'Is everything okay?' Katherine asks.

'I don't know, that's why I'm here. Do you know Janine Rai?' The concern in my sister's voice breaks me in a whole new way, and a single tear slides from the corner of my right eye.

'Janine? Yes, she's in my writing group. Wonderful woman. Is everything okay with her?'

'That's what her husband and I are trying to figure out. She came to speak to Otis Clarke earlier, but she's not been home since. We saw online that he's been arrested, so there's no reason for her to still be here. Her car's parked on the road, but she's nowhere to be found.'

'How odd. Have you tried calling her?'

'Countless times, but she isn't picking up. Recently, she's been a fan of putting her phone on Do Not Disturb.' At the irritation in Beth's voice, Katherine lets out an expertly acted sigh of concern.

'Well, I can see why you're worried, but I'm afraid I haven't seen Janine since our last writing group meet-up.'

I drag myself along the landing to peek at my sister, but the closer I get to the top of the stairs, it's only more of Katherine's hallway that comes into view.

'Really?' I can hear the frown in Beth's voice. 'That's so strange. The Find My Phone app says she's here.'

'Here? At my house?' Katherine laughs. 'Strange indeed! But you know what signal in rural places is like. It's patchy at best. Maybe Janine's still at Otis's?'

'There's no one there, I've already checked. Even the police have gone.'

Those words cause Katherine's hand to move to her hip. As her fingers come to rest inches away from the handle of the knife, my heart thunders.

'How odd,' Katherine replies, mirroring Beth's concern. 'I can't think of why that would be other than a signal issue. Perhaps the app is a little muddled?'

'Maybe,' Beth replies hesitantly. 'Are you sure you've not seen Janine?'

'Positive. If I hear from her, though, I'll tell her to get in touch with you.'

'That would be great, thank you,' Beth replies. 'I guess I'll leave you to your day. Thanks again for your help.'

'Anytime,' Katherine says. As she begins to close the door, I know this is the moment I should shout for help. If I want to be saved, this is my chance. My only chance.

Maybe Beth could outrun Katherine.

Maybe she could overpower her.

Or maybe she could end up dead.

Never has a thought filled me with such devastation. Beth, slain on a doorstep, all because she came looking for me.

My little sister who never gave up on me, even when I'd given up on myself.

Tears choke me as my mind casts itself back to my best childhood memories, each one centred around Beth. Sharing a bedroom meant arguing one minute, being best friends the next. It meant giggling as we pushed our beds together to sleep beside each other. It meant shouting about borrowed clothes, drawing on each other's toys, reading each other's diaries. It meant sharing secrets, sharing hopes, sharing everything that mattered.

It meant a bond forged like no other, forever.

A bond I hope my sister knows means the world to me, because once Katherine shuts that door, I know I will never see Beth again to tell her.

But if closing that door means keeping Beth alive, then I'm fine with that. Clamping my lips shut, I roll onto my back and say a silent goodbye to my sister, and to my life.

CHAPTER 52

'Wait!'

Beth's sudden shout makes my blood run cold. My eyes snap open, my neck twisting to look back to the hallway. I turn in time to see Katherine stiffen then draw the front door back.

'Yes?' she asks.

'If you've not seen Janine, then why is her coat hung up at the end of your banister?'

A petrified gasp catches in the back of my throat as everything around me stops. Even the speck of dust floating past my eyeline seems to pause, captured by this twist of fate.

'Excuse me?' Katherine says, her voice eerily calm.

'That yellow coat behind you – it's Janine's. I always tell her she looks like a duck wearing it,' Beth says, moving closer to the door. 'Why is it here if she isn't?'

Katherine is the first to move. As her shock transforms into rage, she lets out a frustrated screech before reaching behind her back for the knife.

'Beth, run!'

The words leaving my lips are so shrill, so terrified, they sound inhuman. Adrenaline takes over. My bound hands or the gash in my head don't stop me, not when Beth's life is on the line. I scramble to my feet.

I hear my sister call my name, but it's the sound of her scream that really gets me moving. Staggering along the landing, I stumble to the top of the stairs in time to see Beth force open the front door and Katherine lash out with the knife.

'Beth!'

My legs buckle as my sister ducks from the blow, just in time. The knife embeds in the doorframe, splintering the wood with a sickening sound. Had Beth been a second slower, it would have been her throat.

From her position on the floor, Beth looks for me. She screams when she sees me at the top of the stairs, bloodied and bound.

Katherine spins to face me, her features twisting in fury when we lock eyes. 'You little bitch! You couldn't stay quiet, could you?'

As Katherine clambers over Beth to reach for the knife, I bark at Beth to run. My sister follows my orders – but instead of making a break for freedom, she thunders upstairs towards me.

'Janine, you're bleeding! Why are you bleeding?'

'Beth, stop. You shouldn't be here,' I shout, but she's too busy wrestling with the rope coiled around my wrists to listen.

Her trembling hands fight against the knots. 'They won't come loose!'

'Beth, please! You need to go,' I cry, nudging her with my knee, but she stays put.

'Don't be ridiculous! I'm not going anywhere without you.'

'Please,' I plead, but as the front door slams shut, I realise it's too late.

Terror engulfs me. I look at Beth. She is too distressed to notice what's going on around her, but I'm not. I know what is coming next before I hear the words.

'You should have listened to your sister,' comes an eerily calm voice from the foot of the stairs.

As Beth's eyes meet mine, I watch fear flood them.

'Move,' I whisper.

Beth shakes her head, confusion guiding her movements, but with a watery smile, I do what needs to be done. Stepping in front of Beth, I push her back with my shoulder. In doing so, I come face to face with Katherine as she ascends the stairs.

'How sweet,' she pouts, gripping the knife tighter. 'Maybe I should include a sisterly standoff in my book. Pulling on the heart-strings always sells well, doesn't it? Especially when the heroics end in death.'

Behind me, Beth whimpers. I widen my stance to protect her. 'Let Beth go. I'm the one you have an issue with, not her.'

'What, let her go so she can run straight to the police? I don't think so. Not when I haven't finished my manuscript.'

'No story is worth this!'

Katherine's nostrils flare. 'That's easy for you to say, isn't it? You've got the books, the contract, the fans. You've met your life's purpose, yet you dare to look down on me as I chase mine.'

'Katherine, you've killed someone!'

'So? "Real life is the basis for stories", you say. If you believe that, how can you judge me for bringing a horror story to life in mine?'

Beth's fingers curl around the top of my arm. She tries to pull me away from Katherine as she advances up the stairs, the knife in her outstretched hand, but I don't move.

'Janine,' Beth whispers, 'Janine, please.'

'You couldn't stop playing detective for five minutes, could you?' Katherine hisses. 'You couldn't let me have my moment. What, are you afraid of the competition? Afraid people might prefer my books to yours? Well, you'll get what's coming to you, S. K. Atherton. Mark my words: I won't only take your life, I'll take your bestseller title, too.'

'Janine,' Beth wails.

Her fear makes Katherine's lips curl into a smirk. 'Listen to your sister's horror. Listen to her realise her life is over because of you. That's right, Janine. There will be no grand rescue, no miraculous ending like in your books. Right here, right now, you will die, and you will take your sister with you.'

Those are the words that do it. The ones that jump start my lifelong, primal instinct to do anything for the ones I love. Jerking my elbow backwards, I knock Beth to the floor before launching myself at Katherine.

Beth cries out, 'No!'

The fear in her voice is the last thing I hear before I plough into the woman intent on writing a deadly conclusion. When our bodies collide, the momentum of my leap powers us down the stairs. I can't tell where Katherine ends and I begin, whose scream is whose, which parts of my body are in pain and which aren't.

All I know is, when I reach the bottom of those stairs, I reach the end.

CHAPTER 53

Thirteen months later

When Natalya Forsyth's *A Killer Novel* was released, many were horrified, but when it catapulted to the top of the bestseller list, they weren't surprised. True crime was booming, and people couldn't get much closer to the action than by reading a book about a murder that was written by a friend of the culprit.

It was a grey, rainy day when Katherine McFarlane learned of Natalya's stratospheric success. Guards reported that her rageful screams could be heard from the other end of the prison wing.

'It's my story!' she hollered when they rushed to see what was going on. 'She's taken my story!'

But as Katherine's writing group had discussed, no one person owned a story. Truth was subjective. Fact could be fictionalised. And Natalya's talent had ensured that the book was engrossing enough to earn a slew of five-star reviews.

The only time Katherine's version of events was shared with readers was in court. Extracts of the damning manuscript were given as evidence, proof of her wicked act.

Sonya West heard the news of Natalya's success while in her home office. A camera was pointed at her, live streaming her reaction to the followers she had amassed since the truth about Alexa's death made headlines.

'My best friend deserved better,' she sobbed, all the while making sure the T-shirt she had been gifted by a fast-fashion brand was visible in the shot.

Beth Atherton learned the news after dropping her daughters off at day care. The announcement was made by a chipper radio host who had bet their co-star ten pounds it would happen. As the presenter cheered his win, Beth crumbled, unable to understand how profiting from her pain was something to celebrate.

But then again, a stranger's ability to detach from the horror and embrace the drama was not new to Beth. While she sat in therapy, other people were discussing the worst time of her life over cocktails. While she struggled to leave the house, strangers dissected her experience online, their opinions racking up thousands of views, likes and shares.

Fighting for composure, Beth carried on driving until signs for Bramblethorpe appeared at the roadside. Counting to steady her breathing, like her therapist had taught her, she sailed down the country roads.

When she made it to 147, the sign for Maple Crescent came into view.

When she made it to 153, the house she swore never to set foot in again was beside her.

Beth pushed on the accelerator, meaning that by the time she counted to 155, she had reached her destination. Braking and pulling to a stop behind two cars parked on the road, Beth twisted to look past the SOLD sign at the end of the driveway. More cars were in front of the house at the end of it. A typically well put-together Gabby was waiting beside one of them. When she saw Beth, she waved, a move that made Beth curse. It was too late to drive away now.

'You made it,' Gabby said when Beth reached her. 'Just in time, too. The others are already at the field, but I said I'd wait for you.'

'What if I hadn't shown?'

Gabby shrugged. 'I trusted you would.'

As the women headed for the garden, Beth's knees knocked. *This was the route Alexa took the day she was killed*, her brain reminded her, as if she didn't already know that. As if she didn't carry that knowledge like a second skin she could never shed.

Sensing Beth's distress, Gabby linked arms with her until they reached the fence. One after the other, the women clambered over it, with Gabby holding out a steady hand to help Beth. Once over the other side, they walked through the trees to the field where the others were waiting. A small group of people – once strangers, now friends, brought together by tragedy. Solemn despite the bright colours Otis had asked them to wear.

Kamal reached for Beth as she approached the crowd. 'Thanks for being here. I know it's the last place you'd want to be.'

They hugged, then Beth stepped back and caught the eye of the others impacted by Katherine's senseless actions. Jim, Dorrit, Simon, Annalise and more. Even one of the detectives who investigated the case was there. But everyone knew there was only one person Beth had come to see.

'How are you?' Beth asked as she reached her sister.

A habit whenever they were together now, Beth touched Janine's arm to prove she was really there. Her brain needed the reassurance. Understandable, Beth's therapist said, given that there was a point in time when Beth thought she had lost her sister. When she had flown down the stairs and pulled her broken body away from Katherine, screaming at the knife sticking out of Janine's ribcage.

Metallic-scented blood had soaked into Beth's clothes and hands as she tried to stem the worst of Janine's bleeding, but it seemed it would never stop.

'Don't leave me,' Beth had screamed, but Janine's pale face suggested that she was already slipping away.

Beside her, Katherine lay unconscious. Beth remembered looking from her sister's body to that of the woman responsible. Hatred swelled in her chest, more than any person could possibly contain.

Sometimes, in the early hours of the morning when sleep had evaded Beth for too long, she could still remember the dark thoughts that came to her mind. Thoughts of unlodging the knife from Janine's ribs and driving it into Katherine's heart.

But then Beth heard footsteps. She looked up from her position on the floor to find Kamal racing towards them, his face filled with a horror that haunted her even now. He'd heard the screams. He'd come running. Like Beth, he too thought Janine was gone.

The only reason Katherine was still alive was because of Kamal. If he hadn't appeared, Beth knew what she would have done. She would have become a murderer too, a fact that terrified her. It almost made her understand how Katherine snapped in a moment of white-hot rage. Almost made her realise how close humans are to animals.

Almost.

Nausea clogged Beth's throat as the worst of her memories threatened to pull her under, but then Janine's face broke into a smile.

'I'm good,' she said. 'Glad we're all here.'

'And you're sure you're okay?'

'I don't have a headache, if that's what you're asking.'

Janine saw how Beth tried to laugh at the joke, but she knew her sister struggled to make light of the impact of that day. Janine couldn't blame her. Beth had visited every day during Janine's weeks in hospital. She'd seen how headaches were the tip of the iceberg when it came to the trauma legacy of her injuries.

Taking her sister's hand, Janine tried to silence Beth's worry. 'Really, I'm okay.'

With that, Janine turned to witness the event they had gathered for. After a moment, Beth did the same.

Beside a hole in the ground stood a proud sapling, ready to be planted. Beside that stood a man whose face wore the pain of losing the person he loved most.

'I'm going to keep this short because public speaking was more Lex's forte than mine,' Otis began, his self-deprecation breaking the nerves jangling the air. 'Today is for Lex. A day where I choose to look at the people who are here to honour my wife and the friends I've made. Where I see Annalise and Simon and remember how something beautiful has come from the darkness.'

Everyone's attention flicked to Simon and Annalise, lingering on her well-rounded stomach. The hope of a new life, thanks to Alexa's generosity. A kindness Otis vowed to spend his life passing on through The Alexa Clarke Foundation, a charity set up to fund and support people through IVF, miscarriage and beyond.

Turning from the crowd, Otis looked to the small oak tree beside him. During their first visit to Denmark, Alexa had taken him to see *Kongeegen*, the 'King Oak', famous because it was possibly the oldest oak tree in Europe. To Otis, it seemed fitting that he would honour his wife, his queen, in such a way. May her tree stand tall for hundreds, if not thousands, of years, too.

'Lex and I came here because we wanted to build a home together, forever. One look at these fields and Lex was sold on living here. A place wasn't a home to Lex if it wasn't at one with nature. So, I stand here, promising that I shall not remember this spot as where she died, but as somewhere she lived. I might not be able to stay, but she can, forever enjoying the view she adored.'

Fighting tears, Otis grasped the trunk of the tree and manoeuvred the roots into the hole. The strain of marking such a painful moment sent tears down his cheeks, the weight of his grief heavier than any tree ever could be.

With Bernie in tow, Jim broke from the crowd to help. The sight of two important men in Alexa's life honouring her in such a way brought a lump to Janine's throat.

When Jim and Otis were released without charge, an unlikely friendship blossomed between them. Who better to understand the impact of losing Alexa than someone who cared for her, too? Who better to understand the heartache of infertility than a man whose wife left him when they discovered he couldn't have children? Jim and Alexa had bonded over the pain of not being able to start families, and now Jim and Otis had, too.

Together, the men lowered Alexa's tree into the ground, settling it in its final resting place. Then, when there were no more words to be said, the crowd headed back to the house.

Annalise and Janine were the last ones to step over the threshold. Annalise's fast-approaching due date and the stiffness in Janine's hips saw to that.

'Hurry up, you two,' Gabby joked. 'Janine, anyone would think you'd been through a horrific injury in the past, walking at that snail's pace.'

Janine giggled. Gabby's dark humour was one of the things she loved most about her, although most people couldn't understand how Janine could laugh at such a horrific turn of events. Then again, Janine always coped with life's cruellest tricks in her own weird, wonderful way.

Sometimes it was through lying.

Sometimes it was through joining the search for a missing woman.

Sometimes it was laughing in the face of the pain that would underpin the rest of her days.

When everyone was inside, Otis pulled Janine to the side. 'Can we talk?'

Janine nodded and hung back, waiting for everyone to file into the kitchen for the refreshments Gabby had prepared. When they were alone, she faced Otis. 'Is everything okay?'

'As fine as can be expected, but I wanted to speak to you about something.'

'Oh?'

'Gabby and I are packing up Lex's office tomorrow ahead of the move. I haven't touched it since she ... since she left. It's where Lex kept the things that mattered most to her. You might think this is odd considering you and Lex only met once, but I was wondering if you wanted to take something to remember her by?'

Janine's eyebrows arched. 'Is that okay?'

'Janine, it's thanks to you that we know what happened to Lex. I owe you more than I can ever repay.'

'You owe me nothing,' Janine said, squeezing his arm. 'But if you're sure, then I'd love to keep something of Alexa's. Thank you.'

Nodding, Otis held his arm out to assist Janine with the stairs.

It was hard for Otis not to wallow in guilt over the way things turned out. Had he not let pride rule him and had he gone to the police sooner, Janine may never have been in Katherine's house that day. Never have almost died. But fears his wife was cheating had driven Otis's choices. It had been foolish to hide the bank withdrawals and diary because he was scared of what they might mean. He had lost Lex anyway, and Janine was left paying the price of his mistakes.

When they reached the third door on the landing, Otis stopped. 'This is it. Lex's office.'

The crack in his voice made Janine reach for him. 'Otis, if you need more time—'

'No,' he said, shaking his head. 'No more time. No more pain. I'm ready for this.'

With those words, Otis Clarke walked away. Janine watched him go, knowing that guilt would always press down on his shoulders, no matter how much money he raised or how many families he helped.

When Otis was gone, Janine pushed open the door to Alexa's office. A laugh escaped her as a stream of sunlight illuminated the pastel walls. The pale colours were so similar to the walls of Janine's own writing space, it was uncanny.

Entering the room, tears came to Janine's eyes as she saw how much of Alexa's personality paralleled her own. A polka dot mug sat on the desk, chipped like Janine's favourite one at home. A rainbow-shaped stationery holder contained a selection of pens from the same brand that Janine liked to write with. Notebooks with patterned covers were stacked on a shelf, bought in the hope that the stunning designs would ensure the prose written inside was equally as beautiful.

Then there were objects that were uniquely Alexa. A framed print of an Anna Ancher painting. A filing cabinet Janine knew would be full of the paperwork Alexa struggled to throw away. A rose-scented hand cream perched on the white desk.

And the bookshelves – as impressive as a library's, they contained many of Janine's favourites. Her eyes drifted across the spines, scanning the names of iconic authors that popped from them. Margaret Atwood, Sally Hepworth, Toni Morrison … then Janine's gaze settled on three books she recognised.

One thing united them: the name S. K. Atherton.

The pen-name still belonged to Janine, but her next book would not be published under it. In a turn of events that surprised even her, Janine was currently working on a different kind of novel. A romance about a couple who were nearly torn apart by infertility but found their way back to each other. The tonal change felt both therapeutic and exciting.

Janine's repaired pelvis twinged as she moved towards her books. She plucked them from the shelf. Delight overcame her as she observed the creased spines and frayed corners. That they had been so well read was more beautiful to Janine than if they had been pristine.

She carried the books to the desk, but as she went to set them down, Janine noticed a piece of paper sticking out of her most recent novel. Sliding it from the book, she unfolded it to reveal a handwritten note.

My love, you have been so patient with me, so kind. You have shown me that an end is a beginning in disguise, and you have been a friend above all else. In the space of a few short months, you have brought me back to life.

Now I am ready for a fresh start, far away from here. Us, together, like we always talk about. I have found a place in Denmark. We could make it our new home.

If you are ready to leave everything behind and come with me, then I am ready for the future. Whatever it looks like, as long as it is with you.

All my love, Alexa

The ground beneath Janine's feet shifted as everything she thought she knew about Alexa Clarke crumbled. Reading the note again, she hunted for a clue as to who it was for.

A fresh start, our new home – could that mean the note was meant for Otis? Otis, who needed to know that his wife had not given up on their marriage, no matter what people said?

The space of a few short months – did that mean Simon? Simon, who insisted his time with Alexa was platonic and who was about to welcome a baby with Annalise?

A friend above all else – was that referring to Jim, whose friendship only came to light after Alexa's death?

Who had Alexa Clarke seen a future with? A future so promising it had given her hope during her darkest days?

Janine's mind only stopped racing when Kamal called her from the foot of the stairs. 'Everything okay up there?'

Her mouth opened and closed, wondering how to answer that question.

'Janine?'

Slipping the note back into the book, Janine made a decision. It wasn't a choice she made lightly, but she knew secrets were powerful things. Like writers, a secret was both the creator and the destroyer of worlds. And the person holding the pen, the one unveiling the secret? Well, they had to be prepared for the fallout, whatever that may be.

'Everything's fine. I'll be down in a minute,' she called. Tucking the book under her arm, Janine chose the object she would remember Alexa by. Someone flawed, someone human, someone who was loved.

Then, with one last look around the office, Janine left the room and walked away, vowing that Alexa Clarke's final secret would stay hidden, forever.

ACKNOWLEDGEMENTS

Usually, I start my acknowledgements with an explanation of why I wrote the book. So, here we go.

When I turned thirty, the societal narrative around me seemed to change overnight. Conversations suddenly centred on children: Do you want them? When will you have them? Is your relationship strong enough for a family? Should you freeze your eggs, just in case? Then there were the 'hurry up' comments. Time's ticking. Don't leave it too late. These conversations felt weighted in a way they never had before.

But outside of that discourse, I saw a different side of having children. Friends who suffered miscarriages or were undergoing IVF. Or people who, like me with a diagnosis of PCOS, didn't know if children would be on the cards.

Because of this, these conversations sometimes felt intrusive. Questions, even innocently asked ones, were hard to answer. Hurtful, on occasion.

From this, the idea of writing a book with this twist as well as one that touched upon the reality of fertility issues came to life. With that in mind, I must acknowledge the stories that helped me write this book. I am grateful to those who shared their experiences. I am so, so sorry for your loss and so proud of your strength.

Now onto the thank yous!

The first thank you must go to my agent, Dan of The Pilkington Agency. Dan might be the one person on the planet who loves the twist in *The Secrets of Strangers* more than I do! Thank you for pushing for TSOS to end up in readers' hands.

To Anthea and the team at Simon & Schuster for bringing TSOS to life. Your vision and care for what you do is unparalleled! A special shoutout to Anthea, Lizzie, Celia and Shannon for all your editorial work. I will learn to consistently use commas and standard English, not Northern slang, one day.

Outside of my publisher, my writing is championed by many bookstagrammers, booksellers, bloggers, bookshops and reviewers around the world . . . thank you to each and every one of you. I look forward to new releases so I can get on the road, see you and give you the biggest hugs! Thank you for all you do to support authors, books and a love of reading.

It would be impossible for me to name and thank every reviewer within my word count, but I want to shoutout members of The Official Jess Kitching Reader Group. Your help with the cover reveal, wobbly word count days and just general awesomeness gets me through.

Thank you to Daniel of Avid Readers Club, whose reviews, beta-reading and friendship started from book one. Helen, aka @fhclibrary, for meeting online and fast becoming one of my favourite real-life friends. Katy and William from Tea Leaves and Reads, whose bookshop might just be the happiest place on earth . . . I am so happy we finally met IRL! My favourites from The Word Count Pod, Jo, Fiona and Jacq . . . LEGENDS, the lot of you.

Phil and Craig, aka HappyValley BooksRead, for many things, but mostly the Girls Aloud singalongs. Alyse for being my New Zealand champion. And Madi (@faitheinbooks) and Catelyn (@itsprobablyonmytbr) for . . . well, everything. From bookstore visits to book launch afterparties and everything in between, I am SO grateful to have you in my life!

To all the authors who quoted for TSOS, THANK YOU! I know how busy you are, so thank you for taking the time to read a 300+ page book.

To my friends across the globe . . . I love you. You always make me feel like a 'cool friend', even though most of the time I'm in PJs and living in a dream world. Thank you for telling me to rest when I need to (Katie and Robyn, I'm looking at you!), and for always, always being there. PS. Beth, I tried to change the title to 'The Beth Book', but apparently *The Secrets of Strangers* is better for a thriller . . .

To M, for bringing out my dorkiest smile.

To my family, both in the UK and Australia. I wish I had the words, but I don't. Thank you. Just . . . thank you. I need to write more books so I can dedicate one to each of you. Mum and Dad, you are the best. End of.

And finally, to you – for picking up this book. Thanks for spending time with these characters, and with me. It's wonderful to see you here.

Photo credit: Jess Howell

Born in Bradford, England, Jess Kitching is an avid reader, writer and binge-watcher who splits her time between the UK and Australia. After graduating Huddersfield University with a First in English Literature, Jess worked as a primary school teacher before becoming an author. Her three previous thrillers have been internationally published and described by readers as 'thrillers with heart'. Her debut romance, *The Life Experiment*, was *Women's Weekly*'s Best Romance of 2025.

To find out more, visit jesskitchingwrites.com
or Instagram @jesskitchingwrites.